"Mom, help!"

The cry was real and coming from outside. Shaking off sleep confusion, I dashed out the door. Stones and twigs jabbed my socked feet as I sprinted through the dark.

"Celia! Honey? Where are you?"

A response came from up the hill. I ran toward the main house, where a jacked-up orange Jeep idled next to Victor's VW.

"Over here, Mom, look!" Celia and a twenty-something woman I didn't know pressed their faces to the picture window that looked into Victor's sunroom and beyond to his living room. I joined them, smooshing my nose against the already steamy glass.

"Oh no, no . . ." I grabbed my daughter and twisted her away from the view.

"God, Mom," Celia sputtered. "Be careful."

I didn't have time to deal with her manners or what might have been a whiff of alcohol on her breath. I pounded at the window, praying that Victor would get up, even as I knew he wouldn't. He was slumped in the flickering lights of the altar candles, a wreath of marigolds around his chest, a gun in his hand and blood trailing down his temple.

Bread
of the
Dead

A SANTA FE CAFÉ MYSTERY

ANN MYERS

ῶ𝓂

WILLIAM MORROW

An Imprint of HarperCollins*Publishers*

William Morrow
An Imprint of HarperCollins*Publishers*
195 Broadway
New York, New York 10007

First William Morrow mass market printing: October 2015

William Morrow® and HarperCollins® are registered trademarks of HarperCollins Publishers.

Printed in the United States of America

10 9 8 7 6 5 4 3 2 1

Acknowledgments

Many, many thanks to all those who helped and supported me in writing this book. I owe huge thanks to my awesome agent, Christina Hogrebe, and the team at the Jane Rotrosen Agency for believing in the book series and for finding it such a wonderful home at Avon/HarperCollins. To Emily Krump, my fabulous editor, I am so grateful for your enthusiasm, insight, and guidance. I'm humbled to have the HarperCollins team behind me, including publisher Liate Stehlik and marketing director Shawn Nicholls, as well as Eileen DeWald and Greg Plonowski in production. Thanks, too, to Tom Egner for the gorgeous cover design.

From start to finish I've been encouraged and inspired by many writers. My thanks to Kara for all our writing chats and to the ever-encouraging Sisters in Crime Guppies and Pikes Peak Writers.

On the home front, I owe more than I can ever express to my family, especially my husband Eric for bringing joy to my life, and my parents Jane and Barry and parents-in-law Mary and Dany for their love and support. Most of all, my grandmother, Mary Myers, still writing in her nineties, is an inspiration to us all.

Finally, a heartfelt thank you to readers and lovers of books everywhere.

Bread
of the
Dead

Chapter 1

I love holidays, especially those with food, which is pretty much any holiday worth celebrating. I adore painting pants on gingerbread men and molding chocolate into bunnies, and I'll jump at any excuse to make and eat pie. But right now, lugging a box of skulls across downtown Santa Fe, I wasn't so sure about *this* holiday. Perhaps it was the weather turning blustery and cold, or my friend Flori, who was starting to worry me. Or maybe it was all the bones. I'm not a big fan of bones, but you can't have the Day of the Dead without them.

November first was a few days away and Santa Feans had decked out their adobe city in every manner of festive death décor, from painted skulls to dancing skeletons. I paused in front of a particularly elaborate window display, hoping to distract Flori from her complaints of the past several blocks.

"Check out this storefront, Flori," I said to my elderly friend and boss. "There's an entire wedding party plus a mariachi band. Impressive!"

I peered in at a diorama populated by Barbie-doll-sized skeletons. They strummed guitars, danced, drank, and laughed, their chalky white figures adorned in colorful flowers and formal attire. A wall of disembodied skulls watched over the joyfully macabre scene. Like the skulls I was carrying, they were made of sugar, water, and powdered meringue, and decorated in rainbow swirls of icing.

Flori stopped beside me, setting down her bag and bumping her Harry Potter–style glasses against the windowpane. "Nice," she said. "I do like a mariachi band. They make any event fun."

My eyes kept returning to the bride and groom. Bony elbows linked, they raised champagne flutes, gazing at each other starry-eyed.

"This whole holiday is kind of sad," I muttered, my gaze fixed on the skeletal couple. If they'd found true love, they discovered it too late. A familiar anxiety prickled through my chest. Nearly three months ago my best friend Cass and I raised margarita glasses to celebrate my divorce from Manny Martin, Santa Fe's busiest philandering cop. I was the one to ask for the divorce, and I'm certain I did the right thing. Since then, however, I haven't worked out a new me to celebrate. I am once again Rita Lafitte. I am once again single. I am also forty-one, living on a café cook's income, and sharing a seven-hundred-square-foot cottage with a teenage daughter wrestling with her own emotions. It's not exactly the inspiring stuff of women's magazines.

Flori smiled up at me. "People will know you're not a local if you talk like that, *cariño*. Día de los Muertos is a holiday for the dead, but it's made for the living. It's a time of joy, a reminder that death comes to us all and we must enjoy our time in this world." She gave my arm a squeeze. "And I would be enjoying too, if Gloria wasn't such a sneaky cheat."

My eighty-year-old friend had relaunched her rant: her nemesis, Gloria Hendrix, and her alleged cheating at Santa Fe's Day of the Dead baking contest.

I tried to assure her, but I knew I might be fibbing. "You'll win this year," I said, shifting my box of skulls to the opposite hip. "Your *pan de muerto* is the best."

That part was true. Flori's *pan de muerto*, or bread of the dead, is utterly delicious, and I should know. I've eaten loads of it over the last several weeks, readily ditching dieting aspirations for the sake of taste testing. Imagine a French brioche, soft and golden with sinful amounts of butter and eggs. Then imagine that same pillowy bread scented with orange zest and anise seeds and shaped in the form of a toothy skull. That's Flori's *pan de muerto*. Our customers at Tres Amigas Café beg for it, and Flori has taken home blue ribbons in baking contests from Taos to Albuquerque.

The last two years, however, Flori has lost to Gloria Hendrix. That's where my fib came in. I feared that Flori might be defeated again, and I didn't like it any more than she did. I wasn't upset because Gloria was a relative newcomer like me. I didn't mind that she was from Texas, a state that native New Mexicans like Flori love to loathe. I didn't even care that she was a flashy socialite who threw around her money and influence. What bugged me was Gloria's boasting, her bragging about a bread that—if the rumors were true— she didn't make herself. Word in my culinary circles was that Gloria's housekeeper, Armida, baked the victorious loaves. So far I hadn't sifted out the truth. However, Armida flees across the street whenever she sees me or Flori coming. This, in my mind, is evidence enough of Armida's co-conspirator guilt.

Flori wasn't fooled by my words. "I might not win, Rita, and I wouldn't mind being beaten by Armida if she entered in her own name. She comes from a cooking family. Her mother did a fry bread that could make grown Navajos weep."

She picked up her bag and took off down the street. I had to jog to avoid being bested by a petite octogenarian with bad knees. Flori, how-ever, wasn't carrying around a dozen extra heads at seven thousand feet above sea level.

"It's the principle," I agreed, siphoning air through my teeth to hide my panting. "Gloria shouldn't be bragging about something she hasn't done."

"Exactly." Flori's mica eyes had a dangerous sparkle. She slowed and looked furtively over her shoulder, as if checking for Gloria and her spies. "I have a plan," she whispered. "A way for us to catch Gloria and Armida in the act."

I feared what Flori was cooking up. My elderly friend is famous around Santa Fe. She's renowned for her tasty tamales, her fabulous frijoles, and her amazing *carne adovada*. She's also a well-known snoop, with a sixth sense to boot. When I started working at Tres Amigas, just after moving to Santa Fe some three years ago, I had no chance of hiding my own sleuthing tendencies from her. But I was always a reluctant sleuth, and now I was giving it up for good. If only Flori would listen . . .

"We'll get out my new zoom lens," she was saying. "Then we wait until dark and hoist you over Gloria's garden wall. You find yourself a view of the kitchen and wait until you can catch Armida in the baking act. Photographic evidence. That's what we need. We'll get them both disqualified. Ha!"

I struggled to find a nice, polite way to say, *No way*!

Flori kept going. "I've already checked out her perimeter. No sharp pointy bits on the wall that I can see, and all those home security signs are probably fakes."

"But Flori—"

"Don't worry, Rita. I'll fix you some snacks in case you have to stay out there awhile. What would you like? *Frito* pie? That worked well last time, except for the chili con carne going cold and getting in your hair when you tangled with that cactus." She chuckled at the memory of my *frito* fiasco.

I didn't care what she said. I wasn't about to be hoisted anywhere. The last time I heaved myself over a wall on one of Flori's snooping quests, spilled chili wasn't the worst of our problems. Drug dealers were, and we hadn't gone looking for them in the first place. That was the old me, though. New me wouldn't chase after criminals or stick her nose into investigations or sit out in coyote country with snack food. New me would embrace low-stress hobbies like landscape painting or herb gardening or perhaps yoga.

Flori was eyeing me expectantly, tugging at my resolve.

I didn't want a cheater to win either, but there had to be a better way to reveal Gloria's deceit. I needed to squelch this plan before it got started, or at least change the subject. I looked around for another distraction. This time, however, I was the one distracted.

A silhouette approached us, backlit by the afternoon sun and framed by the covered walkway along Palace Avenue. The scene was straight out of the Old West, from the cowboy hat and boots to the flash of a silver belt buckle and hint of a swagger.

"Oooo . . ." Flori elbowed me. "Here's a handsome sight. Put your flirting eyes on, Rita. Loosen up that scarf a little too." She reached over to fiddle with the chevron-print scarf looped around my neck as protection against the late October chill.

I grunted in irritation. As I'd also been reminding Flori, flirting—like sneaking over walls—was not part of my immediate plans. Flirting could lead to dating, something I wasn't ready for yet. I'd never be ready for online matchups, blind meetings, or beautifying tortures involving hot wax and lasers, all of which well-meaning friends and nosy acquaintances kept urging me to try. To ward off such pressures, I'd set a one-year moratorium on dating. The moratorium, I assured myself, could be extended.

My irritation wasn't with Flori. She's an irrepressible flirt. No, I was ticked about my heart doing a two-step. My emotions clearly hadn't gotten the no-romance/no-stress memo from the sensible rule-setting side of my brain.

Flori yanked my scarf into a noose.

"Moratorium!" I gasped as she chattered on about how I should "show some interest."

"What?" she demanded, yanking harder. "I can't understand you. Your scarf is so tight you can't talk, let alone flirt."

I wouldn't be able to breathe at this rate. I set down the box of skulls, pulled free of Flori, and loosened the noose as the cowboy silhouette morphed into the real-life form of Jake Strong, lawyer, gentleman rancher, and all-around hunk.

"Ladies. May I be of assistance?" He tipped his hat. I wished he wouldn't do that. As an expat midwesterner, I find hat-tipping way too sexy.

"Rita's loosening up," Flori replied, with her usual knack for sounding inadvertently inappropriate.

"I see that." Jake's smile, accompanied by a wink, didn't help my composure. A blush flared across my cheeks. If scientists ever discover the cure for blushing, I'll buy it, whatever the cost. My red-faced reaction wasn't merely because of Jake's twinkling eyes or hat-tipping or good looks, which definitely lived up to the Strong name. Think George Clooney only more chiseled and rugged, with hair the color of espresso, steel-blue eyes, and the feature I loved most, a warm smile that triggered well-hewn laugh lines. Yes, Jake was a hunk, but he flirted mildly with Flori too. I'd told myself that he was simply nice to everyone. Flori, however, had dispelled that illusion.

She's the one who pointed out that Jake had been stopping by Tres Amigas a lot more since my divorce. Flori also subjected the tough attorney to questioning. She discovered that he can bake biscuits from scratch, has an English bulldog named Winston and a family ranch along the Pecos, and grew up in Las Vegas. Las Vegas, New Mexico, she'd specified approvingly, not that flashy Vegas over in Nevada. I love biscuits and wrinkly bulldogs, and a cowboy on his ranch is the stuff of fantasies, but they weren't what rattled my moratorium resolve. It was Flori's confirmation that Santa Fe's most handsome lawyer was, indeed, feeling out my interest.

Beside me, Flori rooted around in her shopping bag. "I can't find anything in all this baggage," she complained, hauling out a scarf, a stop watch, and a pair of binoculars.

Baggage, I reminded myself. I certainly didn't need to tote around anyone else's emotional baggage. Flori additionally reported that Jake became an eligible bachelor when his wife left him to pursue Hollywood filmmaking about five years ago. That he didn't date for several years, hoping for her to return, sounded sweet. That he then engaged in several short-term relationships with tall blondes resembling his ex-wife sounded like big-time baggage. Not to mention too much competition. I'm five-foot-five with curly brown hair that the dry Santa Fe air turns into a static-charged hazard. I patted my curls, which had gone vertical in a gust of wind. Chunks of icing fell out. Not only was I not a statuesque blonde, I was likely splattered in multicolored sugar paste.

Jake smiled down at me. "I stopped by the café, hoping for some of your fine and fiery green chile stew. It's a nice consolation that I ran into you here."

I stammered something dull about chile peppers and chilly weather for Halloween. It was this kind of nonscintillating small talk that I'd have to give up if I started dating again. How I was going to become scintillating, I had no idea. I supposed I'd visit the library and check out some self-improvement guides.

"Aha!" Flori straightened her small frame and held out a Ziploc. "Here, you're a discerning man, Jake, try out this bread and tell us what you think. Rita decorated this one so it's extra sweet."

"It does look awfully sweet," he said, admiring the contents. "Nice teeth too." Inside was a golden skull complete with a toothy grin and crossbones dusted in colored sugar. Jake opened a corner of the bag and sniffed. "Heavenly. I can tell already that this is a winner."

"And you are a sweet man." Flori patted him on the arm. "If we weren't in public, I'd pinch your butt."

"And I'd haul you into court for sexual harassment," he countered.

Flori whooped in delight and picked up her bag.

"Wish that Rita and I could stay and flirt with you, Mr. Strong, but we have a delivery to take to the Galisteo Gallery."

I took this as my cue to avoid more blushing and reached for the box of skulls. What I grabbed onto were two warm, masculine hands.

"Oh," I said, continuing to show off my sparkling conversation skills.

"Please, let me." Jake managed to dodge my forehead, which in my haste to straighten up came close to head-butting him, another move to avoid in future dating.

"What do you have in here?" he asked, after righting his hat and handing me the box. "Boulders?"

"Skulls," I said, suppressing a groan. I cracked the lid and extracted a skull painted in swirls of vibrantly colored icing. Purple suture marks formed grim lips. Red flowers filled the eye sockets, and yellow and orange swirls decorated the cheekbones.

"Sure hope that isn't someone I know," he joked, flashing his wonderful smile.

Flori was already bustling down the sidewalk. Wind swept up her words, making them sound like they'd been carried in from far across the deserts. "No one you know," she said. "Not yet anyway."

A shiver rocked me. Flori claims to have a sixth sense. I didn't realize it at the time, but I'd caught it.

Chapter 2

A bad vibe is hard to keep under a New Mexican sunset. Orange flared across the sky in brilliant citrus hues. Thick sunbeams, like those in a child's drawing, spoked from clouds the color and shape of dusty plums. I was on my way home, on foot and determined to enjoy it.

No martyred mom thoughts, I chastised myself as a dust devil swirled across my path. Sand pin-pricked my face as I pictured my daughter, Celia, zipping around town in our shared car, which wasn't all that shared anymore. She'd be playing the radio too loud and blasting the heat while hanging her arm out the window, a questionable driving skill she learned from her dad. I hoped that wasting heat was the worst she was doing.

Meanwhile, a tote bag of library books dug into my shoulder as a bag filled with Flori's breads bumped against my knee. I felt like a weary pack mule. But wasn't walking the best exercise? And who could complain about a commute along Canyon Road, Santa Fe's renowned art district? I walked this way regularly, yet couldn't resist glancing in the brightly lit galleries, admiring panoramic paintings and fanciful figurines. I stopped by a giant statue of a horse head to re-adjust the tote bag. The statue, bronze turned to minty patina, stood as tall as an upturned van, with flaring nostrils and wild eyes. A nearby plaque named it as Helicon, cast from the mold for the world's largest equestrian bronze. Impres-sive, for sure, but for me the horse marked the best leg of my commute, the part that feels like an in-sider's secret.

Beyond the colossal horse, the galleries peter out, as do the tourists, few of whom make it as far as my address on Upper Canyon. It's too bad, as they would surely enjoy the picturesque land-scape as much as I do. The narrow road follows a gentle creek valley and its ribbon of cottonwoods and willows. Silvery sage, flowering cactuses, and rabbitbrush, which blooms in golden puffs in autumn, are more common than the manicured lawns of my midwestern youth. Even more en-trancing is the architecture. I still marvel at the high adobe walls with their bulging buttresses and massive gates trimmed in metalwork and flicker-ing gas lamps. I also adore the peekaboo views of the homes behind the walls, their windows deep set in thick adobe. Some, like my new home base, started out as simple farmhouses and remain as modest family compounds. Others have become luxury estates. I've spotted my neighbors' houses in design magazines, and realtors lucky enough to snag a listing in the area gush adjectives such as "extraordinary," "incomparable," and "priceless," all while assigning million-dollar-plus price tags.

And now this was my address. I still pinched myself, hardly believing my good fortune. Best of all, the desirable location came with a wonderful landlord, Victor. As I turned the final bend, I saw him waving to me from our mailboxes. I raised the bag of bread to show that I'd brought treats.

"Mmm . . ." he said when I reached the driveway. "The dead must be talking to me because I sensed Flori's *pan de muerto* before I saw you."

I handed him the bag and he stuck his face in it, making more *mmm* and *ahhh* sounds. When he emerged, purple sugar smudged the tip of his big nose, complementing the turquoise paint above his ear and dotting his apron. Although supposedly retired now that he's sixty-eight, Victor spends many hours running art workshops at his nonprofit for at-risk kids. In his spare time he creates his own art, primitive paintings of saints done on reclaimed wood and metal. Saint art is more common than horse sculptures in Santa Fe. In other words, there's a whole lot of it. Victor's work, however, stands out and is sought by collectors both locally and internationally. In fact, Flori heard from one of her sources—a keen-eared and loose-lipped museum docent—that Victor's saints will star in the Christmas exhibit at Santa Fe's Museum of International Folk Art. When I offered congratulations, though, Victor had shrugged them off. He's as humble as a teddy bear and resembles one too, with big ears, dark button eyes, and a round belly to boot.

I walked down the gravel driveway with Victor, charmed, as always, by the setting. The spacious gardens resemble a park more than a yard. Heirloom apple trees, planted by Victor's grandfather, still droop with ruby-red fruit in summer. Tall grasses wave against bristly cactuses, and stone pathways lead to hidden benches and peaceful resting spots. My favorite path meanders downhill to a pretty patch of forest and the burbling stream, which is actually the grandly named Santa Fe River.

Victor's family home blends into its natural surroundings. The sprawling, earth-hued adobe, built over multiple generations, is now occupied by Victor and his younger brother Gabriel. The bachelor brothers value their privacy and claim separate wings and entrances. Celia and I rent the adobe cottage on Victor's side, nestled at the top of the back garden. In other parts of the country our place might be called the mother-in-law house. Here, it's a casita, or "little house."

By urban apartment standards it's not that small, although tell that to my sixteen-year-old daughter. If Celia's home to complain about casita claustrophobia, that is. Lately, her after-school activities and study sessions were lasting late into the night. Curfew threats and cajoling on my part hadn't done any good, especially with her dad taking her side.

As I expected, the lone car in the driveway was Victor's vintage VW Beetle, painted shiny goldenrod yellow with red Zia sun symbols on the roof and mirrors. If Celia had come home, she was already gone. At best, she'd have written a note. As usual, I'd probably end up leaving unanswered messages on her phone and waiting up. I sighed.

"Cheer up," Victor said, guessing my mood. "No one should be sad around this time. We want the departed to come back and visit. We have to remind them there's good in this world. Come on in and I'll show you my altar."

I readily accepted. Visiting Victor is always a treat. He rivals Flori in his culinary skills and always has goodies on hand. Plus, his house is filled with amazing art. In addition to his own creations, he collects a wide range of the wacky and wonderful, like landscapes created from tin scraps and crosses decorated in straw inlay, as fine and lustrous as gold filigree.

A display I'd never seen before caught my attention. Clay figures, rustic in form but raw in their emotions, mourned in front of an open casket. They were joined by wooden angels and backed by a papier-mâché skeleton holding a sugar skull.

I shivered, despite myself. "So many skeletons . . ."

Victor turned and grinned. "Yeah. We get into the true holiday spirit around here. Those clay figures, they're from Oaxaca, made by a family of famous female potters. They're known for their wake and funeral scenes."

I told him they were lovely. They were, although they tugged at my emotions a whole lot more than the fake tombstones and cartoon vampires of Halloween décor.

"I think they're lovely too," Victor said fondly. He rearranged a kneeling mourner and smiled at me. "And wait until Christmas. I have a whole manger scene by the same potters."

Surely Christmas came with fewer bones. Carefully maneuvering my bags past art and a few more skeletons, I followed him into the main living room. "Wow," was all I could say. Even in this house of wonders, the shrine stood out.

"Yep," Victor said, sounding a bit embarrassed. "Pretty impressive, eh? This altar has been in our family for generations. I keep the main structure in a back room and bring it out to decorate every year."

A three-tiered stairlike structure sat atop a wooden table. On the top tier, an ornate silver cross gleamed, flanked by statues of the Virgin Mary and various saints. The other tiers held photographs. Most were formal portraits in black and white and all were surrounded by an array of foods, flowers, candles, and skulls.

"That's my dad," Victor said, pointing to a sepia print of a serious-faced man wearing a suit coat and a bolo tie that resembled the turquoise one around Victor's neck. "And this is Mom." He picked up a photo of a smiling lady with a wide nose and broad cheeks like his own.

As he pointed out other relations, I made appreciative sounds and told him how much I admired his family's sense of history. I did admire it, although it pressed a guilt button. Could I name my great-aunt's cousin, let alone find a framed picture of her? I probably couldn't recall all of my great-grandparents' names, and last year I'd proved that I couldn't pick a first cousin out of a police lineup. Worst of all, I was shamefully behind on calling my mom and sister. Mom had left a phone message and several e-mails. I vowed to e-mail her. I knew she'd prefer a call or better yet a visit, but I dreaded her worries, which often morphed into critiques. *How is Celia coping? How will you cope, alone? You're a cook. Why don't you come* home *and* cook?

I'd given up trying to explain to Mom that Santa Fe, not Bucks Grove, Illinois, was my home now. Sure, I hadn't lived here long, and I only moved to try to save my marriage. I'd thought—incorrectly— that Manny's discontent arose from big-city-cop burnout, potentially curable by reuniting with his small-city roots and family. After all, he always said he wanted to return to Santa Fe someday. When we met in Denver two decades ago, I was in culinary school and Manny was a dashing patrolman with urban-detective aspirations. After Celia came along, we moved closer to my mom and sister, choosing a suburb within driving distance of both Bucks Grove and Chicago. Manny earned a detective's badge in the city, while I took care of Celia, worried about my crime-fighting husband, and cooked part-time at a French restaurant. I liked our town and my work well enough. They were fine, though not enthralling or enchanting. Manny, meanwhile, never meshed with his jobs or the Midwest. He switched departments and positions and became increasingly restless with work . . . and with me.

Although Santa Fe failed to save our marriage, it transformed my life for the better in other ways. Flori hired me even though I'd never put hot peppers in my breakfast waffles and couldn't distinguish an ancho chile from a chipotle. She claimed that she sensed a shared spirit between us. Maybe it was our mutual knack for snooping. Then there was the place itself. The vast landscapes, the special light, the scent of roasting chiles, and, yes, even the painted bones enthralled me. I understood but couldn't quite articulate what Georgia O'Keeffe and others have felt. I belonged here. I had found my true hometown, the place I was meant to be. Mom didn't get the special light and breakfast chiles, but she usually conceded that I shouldn't tear Celia away from her dad and final years of high school.

Tuning back into Victor's explanation of his altar, I thought of other aspects of Santa Fe that I loved, namely the wonderful people and vibrant traditions.

"In Spanish this is called an *ofrenda*, an offering," he was saying, waving his big hands to encompass the whole structure. Candlelight reflected off the thick silver rings and turquoise stones adorning his fingers. "The idea goes back to the Aztecs, who gave their dead food for their journey to the netherworld. Now we celebrate the older beliefs together with All Saints' and All Souls' Days and Halloween too. This weekend, before the spirits return, I'll add more drinks and foods that my relatives liked. We don't expect that they'll actually consume it, of course, but it's said that the spirits can smell and taste the food. I'll put out other special things too, like this deck of cards for my Uncle Alejandro."

I wished I could taste some of the food already in place, especially the candies and sweets.

"These are beautiful," I said, pointing to a bowl of marzipan peaches that looked like the real fruit, except better, with a glittery sugar coating. "And the flowers and candles are so pretty too."

"Candles light the way for the spirits," Victor explained as he adjusted a wreath of marigold tops. "These marigolds, they're the flowers of the dead. The spirits can smell them. That's why we line our sidewalks with marigold flowers, to lead the way to our doors."

Victor took out one of Flori's breads, a grinning skull with doughy crosses as eyes. He set it on his altar and stepped back to admire it. "Perfect. Now, do you have time for a snack?"

I didn't need more snacking, that's for sure. I work with food and spend my days nibbling and taste-testing at Tres Amigas. On the other hand, I wasn't in any hurry to get back to the lonely casita. I gratefully accepted.

Victor refused my offer to help in the kitchen. I was dozing off in a comfy chair, lulled by the flickering candles, when he returned with what he called New Mexican hot chocolate.

I took a sip. "I'll never want instant hot chocolate again!" I exclaimed. In the six months I'd lived in the casita, Victor had treated me to several drinks that made my best-ever list. *Horchata*, a cool, sweet drink that tasted like rice pudding in a glass. Spiced cider pressed from tart heirloom apples collected in our backyard. Homemade chai, milky and scented with cardamom. This chocolate hit the top of the list. Rich, slightly bittersweet chocolate was balanced by the warmth of cinnamon, vanilla, and a surprising hint of hot pepper. Utterly delicious. If I were a spirit, this would lure me back.

"Wait until you try it with some of my *bizco-chitos*. I made them this morning." Victor headed back through the maze of art toward the kitchen. I eagerly awaited the official state cookie of New Mexico. Basically, a *bizcochito* is a shortbread cookie flavored with anise. But it's a lot more than that. The cookie is history and culture rolled into one sweet treat. Some say the *bizcochito* has roots in sixteenth-century Spain. Others point to Scotland or to crypto-Jewish settlers who hid their faith during New Mexico's early colonial years. Whatever the origin, the cookies are revered and grace special occasions from baptisms and weddings to sweet-fifteen *quinceañeras* and, especially, Christmas celebrations.

Victor returned with a cookie-laden plate and I was reduced to moans at my first bite.

"My nana's recipe," he said, a note of pride sneaking through his humbleness.

"You could win contests with these!" I exclaimed, before clamping my mouth shut. Flori would bristle like an angry horned toad if another top competitor entered local contests.

He shook his head. "No, it's enough that special people enjoy them."

"Lard," I said, determined to wheedle out the recipe. "You have to use lard to get them this delicate."

Victor liked to share treats, yet rarely gave up family secrets. I'd begged, unsuccessfully, for the recipes behind his green chile stew and skillet corn bread with brown butter and red pepper.

He rewarded my guess with a little smile. "Yes, lard. Of course."

Okay, lard was too easy. It may not be the go-to ingredient in modern cookies, but *bizcochito* purists swear by the melt-in-your-mouth texture lard imparts. I got Victor to reveal a splash of wine, a somewhat unusual ingredient, and dashes of anise, cinnamon, and ginger. I was lobbing other guesses when I noticed that my host had zoned out. He stared at the altar, his mug of chocolate raised to his lips but not sipped. I wondered if he was sad, thinking of lost family members.

"Flori says this is a time to celebrate," I said, sounding like a perky cheerleader for the dead.

My landlord nodded, eyes still fixed on the altar. "She's right. The spirits of the peacefully resting will be welcome visitors. It's the others that haunt us."

Worried, I put down my cup, prepared to ask him what he meant. However, his look had morphed to one of panic. Angry voices echoed through the house, followed by Victor's pounding footsteps running toward them.

Chapter 3

Showing surprising speed for a retiree weighed down by a big belly and heavy metal jewelry, Victor ran down the dark corridor leading to his brother's side of the house. I hesitated, unsure of the etiquette of charging through someone else's home and into an argument. Then I heard Victor yell, "Stop! No!" and I sprinted down the dark hall.

I'd never been in his brother's side of the house. In fact, I'd rarely made much more than small talk with Gabriel at the mailbox or the rare times he stopped by the café. A hospital administrator, Gabriel always seemed polite yet hurried, a habit I assumed he had acquired in his earlier career as an emergency room doctor.

The open door at the end of Victor's hallway led to another world. There were no bones here, no eclectic folk art. Instead, oil paintings in gilt frames hung on pale plaster walls, lit by museum-style lighting. Three doorways opened in different directions, all dark. Unsure which way to head, I stood for a moment beside a life-size portrait of an Indian woman collecting water, wishing she could tell me what to do. Then I heard Victor's voice rising above the rumble of an argument. Moving tentatively through the dark, I followed the sounds down a short arched hallway.

It led to a bright kitchen. I glanced at the white marble countertops and the pounded copper vent hood over a gorgeous Lacanche range. Under other circumstances, I would have studied the kitchen details and especially the French fantasy range, with its shiny dark blue enamel and array of burners. Not now. A man stood next to it brandishing a butcher's knife. Victor was in front of him, sandwiched between the blade and the shotgun held by his brother Gabriel.

"It's okay, Rita," Victor said, not taking his eyes off the man with the knife. "A neighborly spat over fence lines. My brother here is a little upset, that's all."

Gabriel looked a whole lot more than a "little" upset to me. His eyebrows, dark and thick like Victor's, furrowed into a scowl. Erasing the scowl and adding a handful of years and thirty pounds, he could have been Victor's twin, although I doubted that Victor ever wore pressed khakis and a button-down shirt without a speck of paint on them.

Glancing at me, Gabriel said, "You best leave, Ms. Lafitte. This is none of your concern. You too, brother. I'm going to handle this now. This man is threatening us and I'll have none of it."

No way was I leaving, unless I dashed for a phone. My cell phone languished in my purse in Victor's side of the house. That was too far away, and I feared that a sudden move might startle the weapon wielders.

"Please," I pleaded to the man with the knife. "Let's talk this through."

He made a scoffing sound. "Ha! Talk? I'm done talking, except through my lawyer and bulldozer driver! You'll be meeting them soon."

He raised the weapon, holding it in the classic horror-movie stabbing pose. I felt queasy. If he slashed downward, his first point of contact would be Victor's broad chest.

"Please," I begged again, trying to keep my voice from dissolving into sobs.

The scary visitor fixed me with pale eyes, then turned and stabbed the knife, hard, into a nearby cutting board, keeping his hand on the handle. Through the blurriness of fear, I realized that I knew him. Broom, I thought his name was, or maybe Broomer. He was the neighbor to our west, the relatively new owner of a rose-hued adobe hidden behind high walls. I'd seen him a few times at the café. Once, I'd seen him tearing up our narrow, no-sidewalk road in a baby blue Porsche convertible, his strawberry-blond hair whipping in the wind. He waved but never slowed down, forcing me to jump into whatever cactus or other hazard happened to be beside the road. I'd always suspected I didn't like him. Now I knew for sure.

With the knife out of his face, Victor turned to his brother. "Put the gun down, Gabe," he said, placing a steady hand on the barrel and lowering it gently.

Gabriel's hands remained shaky. He sputtered in anger. "Get out of my kitchen, Broomer. Send your lawyer if you want, but if you or that bulldozer touch our property, this'll be waiting for you!" He swung the gun upward. For a moment I thought he was going to fire it, straight into the wood beams and a crystal chandelier . . . or a person.

Broomer had the bravado to laugh. "You don't scare me, Gabriel. I know what I bought. My lot extends beyond your fence and that's exactly where I'll be digging. No more delays."

He yanked the knife from the cutting board. As he passed me, gripping the blade by his side, he leered, his pale eyes roving my body. "Sorry I scared you, honey," he said, putting his lips uncomfortably close to my ear. I could sense the knife blade and feel his hot breath as he whispered, "I'll drop by and make it up to you sometime."

I was still shaking after Broomer left and Victor pointed out the least of our problems. "Hey, Gabe, did he steal your knife?"

I know an awkward silence when I'm in the midst of one.

"Right," I said, adding to the awkwardness. In the absence of the knife-wielding neighbor, neither brother was saying anything. Victor stared at Gabe, who glared out the window in the direction of the disputed fence.

I shifted from foot to foot. "Okay . . ." I said, drawing out the word. "I should be going."

"You know what we have to do," Victor said, eyes fixed on his brother.

Gabe sighed heavily. "Vic, go back to your spirits and let me handle this world and Laurence Broomer."

"The spirits are what I'm worried about!" Victor's voice wavered. He seemed on the edge of tears. I moved to comfort him, but he rushed from the kitchen, mumbling prayers in a jumble of Spanish and English.

His brother didn't appear eager to chat about fences or fancy French stoves.

"Ah . . . okay . . . gotta go," I stammered, backing away.

Gabe set the weapon on the kitchen island and rubbed his temples. "Thank you," he said, halting my retreat. "You're kind to my brother. It's good for him to have you living here. He struggles, you know, with his depression and his fantasies. I want him to get help, especially now with all this talk of spirits."

I didn't know that about Victor, and I didn't know what to say either. Gabe hardly seemed to care. He picked up the gun and walked off down the dark hallway.

Alone in the kitchen, I had two choices. The logical one was to get the heck out. The self-indulgent one was to check out the kitchen details. Still feeling creeped out about armed men in murky corridors, I chose to stay in the kitchen. I toured the island, noting the built-in wine chiller and the deep sink, perfect for filling pasta pans. I lingered a moment by the stove, trying to calm my nerves.

"Someday," I told the Lacanche, and imagined it

mocking me in a French accent. *Yeah, right, some-day.* My fantasy range cost around $10,000. To get one, I'd have to win the lottery (which I don't play) or gamble Celia's meager college fund at one of the tribal casinos (which I would never do).

I took a final look and then quickly retraced my way back to Victor's comforting world of eclectic art.

"Victor?" My calls brought no response. He probably wanted to be alone. I understood that. I blew out a melting candle on the altar and found my coat and bag of library books. Inside the tote was a plastic sack tied with a red ribbon and filled with *bizcochitos.*

The casita was dark and chilly when I let myself in. And empty. In the old days I'd have been greeted by a cursing parrot or griping husband. I sometimes missed the bird. I thought again that I should get a pet, preferably one in the feline family. Who was I kidding? I barely had the time and money to take care of myself and Celia, let alone a furry bundle of vet bills.

I switched on the overhead light, illuminating the main living space. Santa Fe takes its architecture and its architectural terminology very seriously. Flori, insisting that I'd never be considered a local if I didn't talk like one, coached me in vocabulary. The round logs extending across my ceiling were *vigas,* not beams. Similarly, the small finger-width branches that lined the ceiling between the beams were not lathe or thatch or ceiling twigs. These were *latillas*. By any name, they were some of the first things I loved about this place, after looking at many bland apartments and seedy duplexes. I also adored the beehive-shaped kiva fireplace tucked into a corner. Adobe benches called *bancos* curved out from either side of the fireplace, perfect for lounging with a good book and cup of tea.

I rarely went to the trouble of lighting a fire, except when friends came over, but after the night's strain, I craved something warm and comforting. I placed a hickory log in the kiva and topped it with chunks of piñon for a piney perfume.

The piñon lit easily. I watched the wood spark for a few minutes before fixing the fire guard and walking the few steps to the kitchen. There, I found something surprising.

Mom, the note read. *Studying at G's. Back by 10??*

A note. My daughter had actually left a note. I felt absurdly buoyed. Celia is a good kid and smart. However, her teen years have strained all of us, especially since her dad and I split. Some of her rebellion is typical, like dyeing her hair black and getting a cut that looks weed-whacked. She's also mastered surliness, one-word conversations, and resisting curfews and mealtimes and pretty much anything with a time requirement, although she never misses school.

Her other rebellion is creative. She paints pictures of wide-eyed fairy girls. The fairies are the cute, doe-eyed kind that might populate Japanese comic books, only hers exist in desolate southwestern landscapes and are in perpetually bad moods. They're often weeping black or red tears and can be rather disturbing, as confirmed by her school counselor who called me in a few months ago. Ms. Dean showered me in pamphlets on depression, anxiety, low self-esteem, divorce stress, bullying, and gang membership. When I broached these possibilities to Celia, she'd laughed until she began hiccupping, and then proceeded to merrily paint anxious fairies loitering by graffiti-tagged cacti. Since then I've worried less about her art.

I poured myself a glass of wine, another indulgence for the night's stress, and settled in by the fireplace with new cookbook finds from the library. As I flipped through pictures of Tuscan landscapes and mouthwatering pastas and almond cakes, I wondered who "G" might be. I couldn't think of anyone with a G name, but then I didn't know all of Celia's high school friends.

I sipped and flipped, vowing to stay up until ten to greet—or track down—my daughter. By nine-thirty the warm embers and zinfandel had lulled me into a head-bobbing sleep, broken occasionally by pops of firewood. By ten I'd stopped resisting and let sleep take over, my head wedged into the wingback chair, the cookbook sprawled across my chest.

"Mom!"

I woke with a start. The fire had turned to glowing charcoal. I had no idea what time it was. For a moment I wondered if I'd dreamt my daughter's cry.

"Mom, help!"

The cry was real and coming from outside.

Shaking off sleep confusion, I dashed out the door. Stones and twigs jabbed my socked feet as I sprinted through the dark.

"Celia! Honey? Where are you?"

A response came from up the hill. I ran toward the main house, where a jacked-up orange Jeep idled next to Victor's VW.

"Over here, Mom, look!" Celia and a twenty-something woman I didn't know pressed their faces to the picture window that looked into Victor's sunroom and beyond to his living room. I joined them, smooshing my nose against the already steamy glass.

"Oh no, no . . ." I grabbed my daughter and twisted her away from the view.

"God, Mom," Celia sputtered. "Be careful."

I didn't have time to deal with her manners or what might have been a whiff of alcohol on her breath. I pounded at the window, praying that Victor would get up, even as I knew he wouldn't. He was slumped in the flickering lights of the altar candles, a wreath of marigolds around his chest, a gun in his hand and blood trailing down his temple.

Chapter 4

W e've gotta call Dad." Celia punched numbers into her phone.

My mind spun. I couldn't fully comprehend what had happened, but I knew I couldn't cope with Manny. Not now, not for Victor.

"No!" I said, too loudly, and then registered the hurt and anger on my daughter's face. "I mean, call 911, honey. The dispatcher will send an ambulance and whoever's on duty. It's fastest."

"It's okay, Cel," the young woman standing beside us said. A streak of blue ran through her cascade of shiny black hair. A tiny jewel sparkled on her left nostril and a curvy tattoo peaked out from her cleavage. "I just texted him."

She texted Manny? Manny texts? What sort of person texts a suicide? Suicide. My whole body trembled. Poor, dear Victor. I should have checked on him after the argument. Gabriel outright told me that Victor was depressed. *Why hadn't I checked?*

"Go over by the car," I urged Celia and her text-ing companion. "Keep together and wait for the police."

My daughter narrowed eyes lined in thick, Egyptian mummy-style makeup. "Where are you going?" she demanded as I started toward Vic-tor's door.

"I'm going to check on Victor . . . I have to check."

"There's nothing *you* can do, Mom. I should have called Dad first." Celia's shoulders heaved in the motions of exasperation, but her voice cracked and tears glistened behind her harsh eye makeup. She and Victor had talked art together. He encour-aged her to paint, morose fairies or anything else she wanted to. She'd be crushed by this.

I hesitated, torn between helping my daughter and helping a friend who was likely beyond help. I had to know for sure. Hoping that my sock feet wouldn't land on a cactus, I cut across the rocky garden to Victor's front door. It was locked, as I expected, but I twisted the knob and pounded the wood anyway until my palms throbbed.

Then I remembered Gabriel. Maybe he could get in. When I reached his side, I rapped the metal knocker and held down the doorbell, pausing oc-casionally to listen for movement inside. I heard none. *What if something had happened to Gabe too?* Thinking of Broomer and his threats, I banged harder, gripping the metal door handle to brace myself. Surprisingly, it moved, and not merely a wiggle. The latch opened and the door swung inward silently.

"Hello?" I called, stepping into the foyer. "Ga-briel?" When no one answered, I tried the door to Victor's hallway. It was locked, but why was the front door open? Had someone broken in? Fear buzzed through my body. It wasn't the only buzzing. From the other side of the foyer came the fuzzy sound of an off-air TV station.

I followed the noise across the living room and down a hallway to a closed door. Although I tried to tell myself that Gabriel probably fell asleep with the TV on, my brain churned awful possibilities, especially when I cracked the door and peeked inside. I could make out a bed and on it a figure that had to be Gabriel. He was flat on his back, arms straight down at his sides as if laid out in a coffin. The blur of noise harmonized with the blood swooshing through my head, and I fumbled to find a light switch. Finding none, I took a deep breath and tiptoed toward the bed, stealing myself to feel cold, unresponsive flesh.

Tentatively, I reached for Gabriel's neck to check for a pulse. To my relief, he turned out to be very much alive. To my horror, I'd discovered that he slept with a white noise machine and a gun on his nightstand.

At my touch, he jolted upright. His hands flailed, pushing me away as he yelled like a zombie Clint Eastwood. "I'll shoot! Holy Mary, Mother of our Lord, I'm armed!"

I fell backward, grasping for the nightstand. Instead, I latched onto the noise machine. I punched its buttons, frantic to turn it off. Not a good idea. The white noise changed to the roar of a flooding stream and screaming crickets.

"Gabriel, it's me—Rita, your renter," I yelled above the raging chirps, pressing more buttons.

Crashing ocean waves filled the room. Another press brought the thump of a single heartbeat. *Dum dump, dum dump, dum dump.* My sister had used a mechanical heartbeat to soothe her newborns. Here, it sounded like the dreaded heart of Edgar Allan Poe.

My own heart outpaced the mechanical one. In the din, I imagined I heard the cocking of the gun. I screamed and scrambled toward the door. Despite the darkness, I squeezed my eyes shut, dreading the imminent blast, thinking of my daughter. Would she have to find my body too? Would she paint *I told her so* on my grave? She'd have the right to. If I got out alive, I vowed I'd be a better, unshot mom.

"Rita, you fool, what were you thinking?"

Blinding light and a hand came from above. A handsome face frowned down at me. It wasn't a heavenly helper with a five o'clock shadow. It was my ex and he wasn't happy.

Manny dragged me upright as his partner, a muscle-bound woman named Bunny, calmed and disarmed Gabriel.

Gabriel was swearing and demanding answers as he yanked pink foam plugs from his ears and mercifully pulled the plug on his infernal noise generator.

"Gabriel, I'm so sorry," I said. "It's Victor, he's—"

Manny clamped a hand over my mouth. The hand smelled gross, like fried food, a major component of Manny's diet.

"Quiet," he demanded. "Stay out of this." To indignant, sputtering Gabriel, he said, "Sir, I apologize for this woman. There has, however, been an *incident* involving your brother." That said, he pushed me out the bedroom door. "Go outside and don't even think about meddling. I'll take your statement later at the station."

Flashing lights illuminated the pathway and Celia, flanked by a small cluster of hand-wringing neighbors. She wiped her eyes quickly when she saw me coming and stiffened when I hugged her.

"Dad's here," she informed me, unnecessarily.

"Yeah, I saw him." I dreaded seeing more of him. I released her, feeling my limbs sag, heavy from the realization that Victor would never serve cookies or make beautiful art again.

"Oh Rita!" Dalia Crawford, a neighbor from across the street, stepped up and enveloped me in a bone-crushing hug. She didn't let me go until I'd sobbed out the barest explanation of what I'd seen.

"Sorry," I said, wiping at the soggy spot I left on her shoulder. Dalia didn't care. A forever flower child with a tech-wizard's income, she wasn't one to worry about her clothes, which she wore in floaty tie-dyed layers.

"I warned him . . ." she murmured. "I said there was danger . . ."

Her words stopped me mid-dampening of my own sweater sleeve. "Warned him?" *Why was Victor in danger?*

Dalia stared up at the night sky, sparkling with

constellations you only see away from city lights. "I sensed a negative aura," she said, her tone as dark as the heavens.

I let out the breath I hadn't realized I was holding. Dalia and her divinations. She was a certified tarot master, as she pointed out frequently, and a little too eager to offer her celestial services. I tended to politely fend her off. So did Victor. Perhaps we should have listened.

Dalia tugged her long chestnut braid across her chin. "He should have let me read his cards. Maybe I could have foreseen his inexorable forces."

Maybe I should have seen them myself. I might not be certified in anything but pastry, but why didn't I notice that my friendly neighbor was hurting? Dalia's husband Phillip moved in to comfort her, giving me the chance to slip away. Celia stood in front of the ambulance. Its lights flashed, but the siren and engine were silent. There would be no desperate race to the hospital.

"Hey," I said, touching my daughter's elbow.

She flinched.

"Come on, sweetie, let's wait inside. The police will know where to find us if they need to."

"I want to see what happens," Celia said, without conviction. She stared toward Victor's house. The living room was bright with lights and camera flashes.

No you don't, I thought, and I didn't want to see either. I made her an offer that even her teen self usually can't resist. "We'll have some cookies. Your friend can come too if she wants."

My daughter twisted her spiky hair. "Okay, if you want, but you, like, know who she is, don't you?"

Your father's girlfriend?" I failed to keep a snarky emphasis off *girl.*

The woman in question sat in her orange Jeep a few yards away, seemingly texting and singing along to music. This is not how you behave at a tragedy, I thought. Then I acknowledged that at least she hadn't barged in and terrified the victim's brother.

"Yeah, whatever," my daughter said, in classic teen understatement. "She's cool."

She might be cool. She was definitely young. I'd guess she was a good fifteen years younger than Manny or, put another way, not that much older than Celia.

"Oh," I said, to avoid saying something I might regret.

"You're not weirded out by this, are you, Mom?" Celia asked, her tone changing from weepy to well-honed defiant. "You're the one who wanted to divorce Dad."

The latter was true. And no, I assured myself, I didn't give a pancake's flip that Manny was dating again. Why should he stop now, after he'd had such an active social life during our marriage? I was, however, a bit weirded out by the thought of him dating someone so close to Celia's age. I also didn't like the idea of Celia becoming best friends with her father's girlfriend.

"No," I said, for the sake of her feelings and my pride. "I'm not weirded out. But it looks like she's busy, so let's go inside by ourselves."

"Okay, I'll tell Ariel where we're going."

Ariel? Celia jogged off past the cluster of neighbors, leaving me to come to terms with my ex dating a young, cool, Jeep-driver with a cleavage tattoo and a Disney character's name.

I set out a few of Victor's *bizcochitos* for Celia as the clock inched past midnight. A new day, the first without Victor. I didn't think I could taste the cookies without tearing up so I made a milky decaf for myself.

Celia came in, thankfully alone, and dropped her backpack by the fireplace, where a few embers glowed.

"Have some cookies, honey. Then let's try to get to bed."

Celia nibbled a cookie and poked at her smartphone screen while I took a stab at grief counseling. "A loss like this is hard to understand."

This platitude was met with sniffles and heightened tapping on the phone. I persisted. "We can't always know how others are feeling, their pain."

"It sucks," my daughter said, turning away to wipe her eyes. Celia took after her dad in hiding emotions. I handed her a tissue and we sat for a few minutes in silence, until pounding on the door rattled us and the house. I didn't need Dalia's psychic powers to guess who it was.

"Open up!" Manny yelled in his cop voice.

I took a deep breath, hoping to squelch my own

emotions. Whatever Manny said, I was done arguing with him, I told myself. We were done.

"Hold on," I said, unlatching the heavy oak door. Manny pushed past, followed by his partner, Bunny, who politely but belatedly asked if they could come in.

I agreed, also politely, although I wished the invitation could exclude Manny. He stood in the entryway/living room, fingers looped around his weapons belt, legs apart in what I imagined was his movie-cop pose. Manny is very conscious of his looks, and there's no denying that he's good-looking. He works out, wears trim shirts tight across his muscular chest, and sets his shaver high to achieve an intentional scruff. If cast in a soap opera, he'd be the guy you know the heroine shouldn't fall for but does, taken in not only by his looks but his charm. Although I'd seen little of it since the divorce, Manny can be truly charming. Too charming, when it came to other women. Manny also thinks he's irresistible. That's what probably upset him most about our divorce: that I'd been the one to ask for it. Like me, he was probably also a little sad, not that he'd ever admit it.

He snorted, scanning the room. "Small place you've got here, Rita. What is this, a converted garage?"

"Nice *vigas*," Bunny said, towering behind my ex.

That's another one of Manny's problems. Height insecurity. He and Tom Cruise could wear the same pants.

"Thank you, Bunny," I said, ignoring Manny. "Would you like a cookie?"

She patted the flat front of her jacket. "Can't, I'm in training. Listen, Rita, we have to talk to you about what you saw."

Manny grumbled that I wouldn't be able to tell them anything useful.

Bunny also ignored him. She had that serious cop look on, the one that mingles mad and suspicious. Bunny looks this way a lot.

"We're exhausted." I gestured toward Celia. She sat in the kitchen, still ostensibly messing with her phone. A pile of wadded-up Kleenex lay beside her. "Can't I make a statement tomorrow? I'll come in after work, at the start of your shift."

Bunny shrugged. "That's fine. Looks like there's not much to investigate here. The medical examiner will be able to tell us definitively."

I knew what she wasn't saying directly. It looked like suicide. It likely was suicide. Rightfully or not, I mentally berated myself again. *If only I'd stayed to check on Victor. If only I'd had time to ask what was bothering him when we were drinking cocoa.*

Bunny and I set an appointment for three the next day for what she called "routine follow-through."

"It's not a closed case yet," Manny said, in the contrarian attitude he'd taken throughout our divorce. "Celia's coming home with me. If there was any funny business involved, I don't want her alone here tonight."

"She's not alone, Manny. I'm here."

"You, the woman who breaks in and terrifies some guy sleeping? Poor judgment, Rita." He shook his head as if disappointed in me and started for the kitchen.

"I didn't break in," I protested. "The door was open." I stepped in front of him, hands on my hips. "That's something you should be investigating. Along with a fight the brothers had with their neighbor tonight."

Manny smiled. "We already know about that. Gabriel mentioned the disagreement. Now let me talk to my daughter."

I held my ground. "You can talk, but you can't take her tonight. That is not part of our custody agreement."

"Our agreement is that the terms can change in exceptional cases and Celia can decide where she wants to go at any time. She discovers a dead guy? That's exceptional, Rita. She needs to be home." He pushed by me.

"This *is* her home," I sputtered, but he was already in the kitchen, talking to Celia.

"Honey," I said, joining them at the table. "There's no need to worry about staying here. We're perfectly safe, but if you're concerned, we can go over to Flori's."

My daughter twisted her black-straw hair. "Yeah, whatever," she said, putting up a stoic face in front of her dad. "Sure, maybe I'll go home for the night. Sorry, Mom."

She'd said sorry, but her words stung. Home. Did she not think of this as her home too? She was a kid, I reminded myself. A kid from a broken home.

I opened my mouth to protest, but thought better of it. Celia was hurting. She didn't need to see me and Manny squabbling on top of her pain. I hugged my daughter, telling her that I'd call the school in the morning if she wanted the day off. She shrugged, declined, and left.

Manny dropped a parting shot. "Stay out of this case," he growled. "I'm done with your snooping."

I'd snoop if I wanted to, I thought, but held in my retort. Hadn't I told myself I was through? Through with sniping at Manny and through with sleuthing. What was there to discover anyway? That I'd missed signs of a friend's agony? Or maybe there was more. I pushed this thought aside as I watched the police cruiser pull away, followed by the bouncing Jeep driven by cool Ariel. Was she going home with Manny too? I felt very alone. Then another thought struck me. Celia had driven back with Ariel. I had no idea where my car was.

Chapter 5

The driver at Pacho's Pickup, open twenty-four hours, sounded sleepier than I did. "You're calling for when, ma'am? Six-thirty tonight?"

No, I explained to the groggy voice on the other end of the line. I hoped for a ride twenty-five minutes from now, which would still make me late for breakfast prep at Tres Amigas. A taxi was an extravagance, but I didn't want to plod across town in the dark. Meanwhile, my bicycle had a broken gear shifter, my aged Subaru hadn't magically appeared, and it was too early to roust a neighbor.

As I waited, I tried to focus on lesser worries, like where Celia had left my car and what she'd been doing. I hadn't questioned her about the hint of alcohol on her breath, not with the bigger trauma to worry about. It was good that she got a ride, I told myself. That was responsible, if you could call any part of underage drinking responsible. And where did cool Ariel come into the pic-

ture? Was my teen daughter out drinking with
my ex-husband's young girlfriend?

To funnel anxious energy, I made notes. I stuck
a yellow sticky tab on the back of my hand, a reminder to pick up milk, nonrotted fruit, and food
in general, so that Celia and I wouldn't live on
café leftovers. Other notes involved calling Celia's
school, calling Celia herself, and finding the car. I
fantasized about sticking a GPS tracker on the car
once I found it, and another on Celia's backpack.
If she ever found out about my GPS fantasies, I
would definitely be an uncool mom.

By the time Pacho's Pickup beeped in the driveway, yellow tabs fanned across my hand. I tore
them off in a sticky mass, stuffed them in my coat
pocket, and hurried up to an old-model sedan
painted a sparkly purple.

The young taxi driver raised his chin in the direction of the house. "What's with all that police
tape?"

"An accident," I said, not feeling up for chitchat
about this or any other topic. I sank into the white
leather seat to avoid his gaze in the rearview
mirror.

"Looks like more than an accident to me," he
said. Mercifully, he tuned the radio to bouncy
borderlands music so I didn't feel the need to say
more.

As we pulled out onto pretty Upper Canyon
Road, I craned my head and stared back at the
police tape sprawled across Victor's garden. The
driver was right. This wasn't any accident. It was
far worse. It was intentional, an act designed to
end a precious life. I thought of Victor, preparing

to welcome back the spirits, setting out treats for their return. Had he decided to join them early? Had Dalia sensed a destructive vibe the rest of us missed? No. I couldn't believe it. He might have been upset by Broomer, but the Victor I knew would work for compromise. Most of all, he'd never abandon his beloved arts workshops and the kids he helped. There had to be more to the story, more to Victor's suicide. The landscape outside the taxi window blurred and my mind swirled, dancing around questions that had haunted my restless sleep. *What if this wasn't suicide? What if it was murder?*

The cab sped across town, weaving down side streets and surging on the mostly deserted main drags. To save my nerves and a bit of money, I asked the driver to let me out at the nearest corner.

"You be careful, ma'am. You know, with all that police tape around your place and whatnot," he said, after I tipped him generously for the early morning pickup. "And call Pacho's Pickup anytime. Ask for me, Pacho."

He swung into a U-turn and sped off in a flash of purple.

I zipped my coat to my chin to fend off the chill and hurried up the block, past adobe homes turned into commercial buildings, including a baby clothes boutique, a Western-wear shop, and Jake's law office. Tres Amigas Café commanded a prime corner spot at the end of the street. The little café might look modest from the outside, with its squat figure and reddish adobe coating. Inside, however, it was an extravagance of colorful artwork, delicious scents, and, most of all, warmth. Over four decades ago Flori and two friends—one younger and the other much older—started the café and worked together as the three *amigas*. Eventually her business partners retired. Flori could have retired as well. Instead, she placed an ad for an *amiga* who could cook, and I lucked out. Manny had been skeptical that a New Mexico newbie like me could hack it. An outsider could never master the nuances of chile sauces, he contended, let alone proper pronunciations of local delicacies. The learning curve was steep, I'll admit. But it was also thrilling to learn from a culinary master like Flori. Most of all, though, I was grateful for her friendship and all the new friends I'd made at the café.

I let myself in the back door and followed the spicy, earthy aroma of roasted chiles through to the kitchen. Flori stood by the sink, peeling and seeding dark green poblano peppers, the star of our popular chiles rellenos breakfast plate. Beside her was her eldest daughter, Linda, her dark hair wrapped in a net and her hands protected in clear plastic gloves.

As soon as she saw me, Linda peeled off the gloves and rushed to envelop me in a wordless hug.

Flori shot me a frown. "What are you doing here?" she demanded, after I released myself from Linda's comforting embrace. "You should be home in bed."

She sounded stern, a tone that meant she was worried. Or mad, or mildly irritated, or unsuccessfully attempting sarcasm.

"You heard?" I asked, knowing full well that of course she'd heard. Why else would Linda be here? She usually spent mornings in her own kitchen, steaming vats of tamales for the lunchtime food cart she ran on the Plaza. And why else would Flori want me home in bed instead of teasing me about sleeping late? She probably heard as soon as the police call went out. The keystone of her gossip network was a ninety-year-old wheelchair-bound man with a police scanner. He had chronic insomnia and spread news faster than high-speed Internet.

"Mom heard last night from Mr. Hoffman," Linda explained, naming police-scanner guy as she pulled on a fresh pair of gloves. "She called me right away so I could come in and help. Poor, dear Victor."

Beside her, Flori crossed herself with a char-blackened chile. "Victor gone . . . I truly *don't* believe it," she said, her stern tone cracking.

I could hardly believe it myself and I'd been there. Flori and Linda seemed to understand that I wasn't ready to talk yet. They recalled happy memories of Victor as we worked.

Flori managed a chuckle, recounting how he'd led her seniors' social group in a finger-painting class. "Finger-painting, at our age! He was right, though. It was such fun." Their tales gradually traced his life backward, reaching into Linda's youth. All the stories touched on Victor's kindness and gentle, artistic spirit.

"And that time he rescued me and my girlfriends when we got stranded out in the Pecos Wilderness . . . remember that, Mama?" Linda said. "My car was stuck in all that mud and I called Gabriel, but Victor arrived in a borrowed tow truck. Pulled me right out and all the way home."

Flori smiled. "I remember you girls coming back from that cabin, covered head to toe in muck. That seems like yesterday to me. You were so young."

"I was nearly twenty by then, Mama. An adult," Linda gently retorted.

Linda, at sixty, sometimes sounded like a defiant teen when talking to her mother. I tried to imagine myself and Celia at their ages. Hopefully we wouldn't still be arguing about car sharing and curfews. I checked my watch. Celia should be on her way to school. She'd answered her phone with a sigh this morning, followed by more sighs to report that *of course* she was okay and *of course* she was going to classes. "Why wouldn't I, Mom?" she'd asked, although we both knew why.

Flori reminisced about Victor, Gabe, and their little sister Teresa as kids as we formed a pepper assembly line. "Their mother loved those boys," she said. "And Victor, he was always such a protective big brother to Gabe and Teresa."

She handed skinned and deseeded chiles to Linda and me. For several minutes we fell silent, concentrating on the methodical work. First, the chiles are stuffed with shredded cheeses, a mixture of Monterey Jack, cheddar, and a fresh farm cheese that becomes wonderfully gooey when heated. Right before serving, the bundle is dipped in a batter and fried. Most cooks use a simple flour and egg batter and drop their peppers in a deep fryer. We pan fry ours in a soufflélike blanket, producing amazingly fluffy chiles rellenos that have won Flori awards and sparked jealousy among her competitors.

I love the cheesy chiles for any meal, but especially for breakfast, when we drape them in green chile sauce and top them with an egg, sunny-side up or over medium. On the side we serve saucy pinto beans, roasted tomato salsa, and a dollop of sour cream. My stomach rumbled. If we finished the prep before the breakfast rush, I vowed to make myself a plate.

"So?" Flori said, after we'd tucked the peppers in the fridge to await frying. "How are you doing, Rita?"

I was preparing the dry ingredients for our blue corn waffle batter, swirling in the key ingredient: purplish cornmeal. "I have the dry and wet waffle mixes ready," I said, my mind engaged in its own swirl. "And I'll add the waffles to the specials board."

Flori put down the knife she'd been using to dice tomatoes, peppers, and onions into the fresh salsa we served with our savory breakfast dishes.

"I mean about Victor," she said, concern etching into the wrinkles of her apple-doll face. "You've been awfully quiet about what you saw. You want to talk?"

I fluffed the blue cornmeal mixture again before answering. "I think I'm still in shock," I admitted. "I know that Victor's gone, but I can't get my mind around it. You know I visited with him last night?"

"I know," Flori said quietly, resuming her be-heading of tomatoes.

Her gossip network was good, but how did they know about my activities? Had the elderly guy with the police scanner upgraded to satellite sur-veillance? I almost didn't want to know. I asked anyway.

She shrugged. "No. No spy satellites, but Bill is awfully interested in personal drones. My friend Marie told me. Her cousin was one of the EMT first responders. He overheard the police talking to Gabriel, who said that you were visiting Victor last night right before he died. The EMT cousin saw you getting kicked out of the scene too." She gave me a look of pure pride. "Good job getting in there."

Linda frowned. Linda is a worrier. She obeys the rules and frets about safety and looks four times before she crosses the street, all probably apt re-sponses to growing up with Flori's hijinks. In this case, I agreed with her. What had I accomplished other than terrifying Gabriel and upsetting my al-ready distraught daughter?

When I told Flori this, she waved away my wor-ries. "Nonsense," she said. "You had to check, *cariño*. What if someone else had been hurt? You had to go in there. Isn't that right, Linda?"

Linda didn't look like she agreed entirely, al-though she tactfully switched the subject. "Ga-briel's door was open? That's so dangerous. Who does that in these times? Anybody could walk right in . . ." She eyed me, an anybody who had walked right in.

Flori continued to guillotine tomatoes, discarding their pulp and seeds before slicing and dicing them faster than any food processor. "I'm mad and sad at the same time," she said. "Victor was my friend and a good Catholic too. We sat together at mass last Sunday and then visited Our Lady of Peace. I wish I'd known he was feeling so sad. I wonder if he told Our Lady?"

I could picture them in front of the seventeenth-century statue of Mary, also known as La Conquistadora for her time among the early Spanish colonists. Although not Catholic, I also occasionally visited her chapel to enjoy its peaceful beauty and admire her seasonally changing outfits, selected from her sacred wardrobe of over two hundred items. I thought of the sticky-note reminders I'd written earlier. I had one to add—not that I was likely to forget.

"We should go to the cathedral later and light some candles," I said, my voice starting to shake with emotion.

"We'll buy the big candles at the gift shop," Flori agreed, emotion cracking through her stern tone too. "No twenty-five-cent ones for Victor. And I don't care what the Church says about . . . well . . . about taking one's own life, if that's what actually happened. He's in heaven no matter what, in my book."

"Mine too," I agreed, as did Linda, who sniffled her way out to the dining room.

Flori and I chopped mounds of onions as an excuse for teary eyes. She commandeered some of the onions for her stew pot. "Chorizo and corn chowder for the soup of the day," she said, before starting up her questioning again. "So what did you and Victor talk about?"

"That's the thing . . ." I'd replayed the conversation in my mind for hours, trying to come up with any clue or hint in his words. "He told me all about his Day of the Dead altar. He showed me pictures of his ancestors and talked about the special food he was going to put out."

"His father loved rice pudding with mangoes on top," Flori said, shaking her head sadly at another friend lost.

"Yeah, and a deck of cards for his uncle and marigold wreaths to attract the spirits. He said something similar to what you told me. The Day of the Dead is a happy time, that we're to celebrate life and those who've gone before us. He had a lot of plans to welcome them back."

Flori's mouth was set in a firm line. I could imagine her mind turning.

I smashed garlic for her soup and tried to explain what kept running through my head. "There was this odd bit too. I didn't understand it. He said that some spirits haunt us."

Flori's dark eyes narrowed. "Haunt us, he said? Which ones?"

"Those not at rest." I repeated his words exactly as I remembered them. "And there's more . . ." By the time I finished describing the fight with the neighbor, Broomer, Flori was drumming her fingers on the table. When I stopped talking, she thumped her fist down, sending cutlery clattering.

"I knew it! I knew Victor wouldn't kill himself!"

I'd had the same thoughts, though suspicion didn't make them true. But I had no time to tell Flori so. Our short-order cook had arrived, the griddle was sizzling, and Linda was unlocking the front door, letting in a stream of customers begging for coffee.

Chapter 6

ell," Flori demanded, mid-breakfast rush. "How should we go about this? I have time to break into Victor's place this afternoon." She pointed to her wrist, where a plastic sports watch dangled. It was neon orange, matching her sneakers and the grinning pumpkin ornament stuck in her bun of silver hair.

I didn't care what time she was free for a break-in. I wasn't coordinating watches or breaking into a possible crime scene. Luckily, I had an excuse.

"Sorry, I have an appointment with the police this afternoon." I suppose I sounded rather righteous. In truth, I dreaded this task and the likely encounter with Manny.

Flori tapped her small, sneakered foot. "That might work," she replied, ambiguously.

The less I knew, the better, I decided. Anyway, I had more immediate concerns, like balancing the waffle special on my wrist. I've waitressed off and on since high school. In all that time, I've never mastered the art of plate balancing. Splay your fingers, a frustrated front-of-house manager used to yell at me. Splaying makes no difference. As soon as I take on more than two plates, I tense up and begin to wobble. I also tend to forget orders moments after they're uttered and have been known to refill water onto diners' laps and grate cheese on their heads. Let's just say that serving isn't my greatest culinary strength.

A sausage rolled toward the precipice of the waffle plate. I overcorrected, sending a little pitcher of blueberry syrup crashing into the waffle stack.

Flori took this moment of weakness to quiz me on the time of my appointment and potential points of entry into Victor's place. A window? A vulnerable glass door? A chimney?

"Let me get this order out," I said, trying to heft the burrito plate with my oven-mitted hand. It was a dangerous move. Our egg, potato, and chorizo burritos must weigh in at several pounds and are smothered in molten sauce and melted cheese.

"Well go on and get back here fast. We need to establish our plan." Flori put the finishing touches on a plate of *carne adovada*, succulent chunks of pork slow-braised in an earthy red chile sauce. *Carne adovada* is a New Mexican favorite at any meal, in burritos, tacos, or as a star on its own. For breakfast, Flori serves the spicy dish with hash browns, guacamole, and a fried egg. Pretty much everything can be topped with an egg at Tres Amigas.

"Here, as long as you're going out, take this

with you. Table one." She plopped the plate on my oven-mitted wrist.

Poised for hot chile disaster, I backed out the swinging door, saying my usual waitress prayers. *Please let me locate the right table. Please let me not throw chile on a customer.* My destination was the far side of the room, beyond hazards including a baby carriage, stray chairs, and a framed painting, likely some priceless work of art. I added, *Please don't let me harm precious infants and artwork*, and carefully made my way across the room. Customers took advantage of my slow-motion advance to ask for stuff.

"Miss? Can I get more coffee?"

"Me too. And some water."

"I'd like the check."

"I want a muffin. Are they gluten free?"

With a plastered-on smile, I promised I'd be right back. Did customers think I had a coffeepot and muffins of any kind balanced on my head? I caught Linda's eye and managed to nod in the direction of the needy diners without spilling anything. Then I made my way cautiously past the baby and her carriage, reaching the waffle and burrito table first. I didn't recognize the two ladies and figured they must be tourists, especially after one frowned at the burrito.

"This plate is really hot, so please be careful," I said. I say this phrase so much that it appears in my dreams.

"Why is my burrito covered in sauce, and why is it two colors?" the burrito lady demanded.

I pegged her accent as upper Midwest, likely somewhere west and north of Illinois. Her fashion was over-the-top Santa Fe, from the mother lodes of turquoise and silver jewelry to the crinkled peasant skirt and purple cowgirl boots with rhinestone sparkles.

I upped my perky voice as I carefully placed the waffle special in front of her friend. "The burrito has red chile on one side, green on the other. Christmas, we call it here. You made the perfect choice."

Now, however, the friend frowned. "Why's this waffle a funny color? I think there's dirt in it."

I have little patience for food fussiness. I don't like it when customers complain before tasting, and I never understood Manny's refusal to eat green vegetables and most ethnic foods other than New Mexican and Mexican. Since I don't have to live with customers, though, I can usually handle their demands with a smile. Today was another story. I had to force a pleasant response. "That's blue corn," I said through a clenched-toothed smile. "Organic and grown right here in New Mexico. It has a delicious nutty flavor and is higher in iron and zinc than typical yellow corns."

"I don't eat blue foods. They're unnatural." This lady had gold accessories layered across a ruffled Western shirt.

"Oh, these blueberries and blue corn are all natural," I said, feeling my lip twitch. "Why don't you ladies try them, and if you don't like something, we'll be happy to fix you a different dish."

The woman in silver and turquoise sliced her burrito open and speared a forkful of fluffy eggs and spicy chorizo sausage. "This *is* delicious," she conceded, already digging in for a second bite.

"But here, take this with you. You have an embarrassing typo on your menu." She thrust it at me. I guessed the issue before I saw the red marks slashed across the laminated page. The chili vs. chile spelling debate. Indeed, she had scribbled out every *e* and added *i* and armies of exclamation points.

"You'll want to correct this," she said snippily. "I don't like to patronize restaurants with sloppy errors, and I know others who feel the same way. I'll try to hold off my Yelp review about this, but . . ."

She let the "but" hang ominously. A red marker lay beside her tapping right index finger.

I summoned the last dregs of perky. "Actually, here in New Mexico, we spell 'chile' with an 'e' because of the central role of the chile pepper, spelled with an 'e.' Like the famous Hatch green chiles, which I'm sure you've heard about. Our chile sauces and stews focus on the pepper, unlike say chili con carne in other parts of the country."

"I like Cincinnati-style chili," her friend said, glancing up from the cell phone that had attracted her attention throughout the chili vs. chile discussion.

Thank goodness Flori wasn't here to see the vandalized menu or hear New Mexico chiles mentioned in the same sentence as ground-beef chili on top of spaghetti. Once, a customer had asked for the Cincinnati version. After the full details of the dish emerged, Flori nearly evicted the man for blasphemy.

The lady in gold dumped syrup on her waffle. Although she didn't seem to care about spelling grievances, she continued to have color concerns. "I've never had such a blue breakfast. Do you have any whipped cream to cover it up? I'll need more plain syrup too. And a refill on coffee and more Sweet'n Low and fat-free creamer—hazelnut, if you have it."

Grateful for an excuse to leave, I commanded my sleep-deprived brain to remember her requests and headed to table one, hoping the *carne adovada* hadn't turned tepid. I immediately recognized the figure behind the newspaper. His cowboy hat hung on the back of the chair and his legs, in dark blue jeans, were crossed elegantly, one cowboy boot swinging over the other.

"Incoming *carne*," I said brightly to alert Jake to my presence. I'm not the only person to blame for throwing around plates of hot food. You can't trust customers, including respectable ones like Jake Strong. Customers make sudden moves that send their own plates flying. The kicker is that they get rewarded with a free meal.

He quickly folded the paper and cleared a wide spot for me to land the plate in. Okay, so I once spilled a bowl of soup—more specifically, red chile posole—on handsome Jake Strong. It was right after my divorce and I'd just talked to Mom. In her usual fashion, she'd infected my mind with thoughts of *If you don't start looking for a man now, you'll end up old and lonely*. When I saw Jake, those thoughts turned to, *Here's a decent, employed, and gorgeous man; sure hope I don't do something horrible like spill posole all over him*. At that moment, another customer bumped into me and the embarrassing vision came true. Flori had wiped off

Jake's jeans with a wet towel and flirted brazenly with him. That's when I got serious about the no-dating moratorium. No worrying, no pressure, no spilling of hot soup or overheated emotions.

Now, a hint of Jake's cologne—a delicious mix of bergamot and cedar—wafted toward me. He pointed to his paper, snapping me back from cologne enjoyment to gloomy reality. "Such terrible news," he said.

Victor's smiling face graced the front page of the *Santa Fe New Mexican*, right below the headline, RENOWNED LOCAL ARTIST FOUND DEAD.

Tears welled in my eyes. To hold them in, I raised my face to the ceiling, pretending to study the multicolored skeleton parts and flowers hanging from the beams. Flori had instructed Juan, our griddle master, to arrange each paper tibia and severed hand ornament just so. I'd insisted on the flowers because, despite what Flori says, not everyone loves so much bone décor.

Jake must have noticed because he turned over the paper, hiding the picture. "I'm sorry, Rita. Victor was truly a good man. One of the best. They say here that the police aren't looking for suspects."

I nodded, trying to hold my emotions together. I did not want to start weeping in front of Jake and the entire breakfast crowd. "Yeah," I managed. "It looks like suicide." I saw no use in telling him that Flori and I felt otherwise. Her sixth sense and my feelings would not impress a lawyer. Or the police. Manny would automatically disagree. I hoped that Bunny would listen.

Jake pierced his egg, and golden yolk cascaded

over the brick red pork. My stomach rumbled, reminding me that I hadn't eaten yet. Would it be breaking my moratorium to join Jake and pig out on comforting chiles rellenos? What if I put a cheesy chile and an egg on a mound of crispy hash browns and topped them all with green chile sauce? I decided that neither the moratorium nor the breakfast crowd—not to mention my dieting aspirations—would allow this fantasy.

"Suicide sure doesn't seem like Victor," Jake said, composing a perfect bite of pork, potato, and egg. "I had a meeting set up with him. He was so adamant that I rearranged my schedule to fit him in."

"Aha! More evidence of murder! You're one hot tipper, Jake Strong. Isn't that right, Rita?"

This exclamation, followed by the smack on my right shoulder blade, startled any lingering tears and fantasies away. Luckily, I wasn't holding anything spillable.

"Ack! Flori! What are you doing sneaking up on me like that?"

My diminutive boss stood behind me, a coffeepot in one hand, a canister of whipped cream in the other.

"Well someone had to come do the refills, what with you out batting your eyes at handsome lawyers. I sprayed cream all over that tourist woman's waffles and her coffee while I was at it. Can't tell what they are now. Good thing I keep this stuff on hand for emergencies. Good thing I came moseying by here too." She brandished the cream can, looking ready to unload it onto anyone else who might complain. Jake leaned away from us both.

"Yeah," I said, sarcasm creeping into my voice. "Good thing."

If Flori noticed the sarcasm or that she nearly startled me out of my socks, she ignored it. Investigating, she always says, demands rule-breaking for the greater good. She's also a firm believer in the persuasive powers of sugary praise and food.

She poured Jake more coffee along with a heaping helping of flattery. "You're an astute man, Mr. Strong, and you smell good enough to put on the dessert menu. Now, tell us what you think Victor wanted to talk about."

Jake knows Flori well enough to know her tricks. He leisurely chewed some *carne adovada* and shrugged in an exaggerated gesture of helplessness. She waited him out, a trick she learned from an old friend in law enforcement, the same person who taught her to operate a Taser and tail suspects.

"Sorry, can't tell you," Jake protested in between bites. "Attorney-client privilege."

"Was he an actual client yet?" I asked. My legal knowledge doesn't extend far beyond *Law and Order*, although I did learn a few things about lawyers and their ways during my unpleasant divorce proceedings.

Jake's response was cautious. "He wanted to become a client . . ."

"Ha!" Flori raised her whipped cream can triumphantly. "So, he wasn't a client yet. You can tell us, then. Don't worry, it's all for the good. Victor's good."

"Technically, privilege can still apply." Jake studied his plate.

Flori waited, fiddling rather ominously with the can of pressurized cream.

"I suppose I can tell you this much," he said, eyeing the spray can warily. "I don't actually know what he wanted. Like I said, we never got to meet."

Across the room a customer waved his coffee cup in the air. Flori ignored him. "Why would Victor need a lawyer?"

"The property line dispute?" I postulated. When Jake looked at me questioningly, I filled him in on the argument with the neighbor. "What else would there be, unless it was something about his art center or one of the kids he helped?"

Jake frowned over his coffee. "I wish now that I'd asked. All I know is that he wanted someone immediately and with . . . er . . . my 'specialty,' is how he put it. I told him I wasn't sure if I could fit him in right away. He said it was urgent."

Flori disregarded restless customers and took a seat across from Jake. "Your specialty, you say? Now that is disturbing, no offense, dear."

Jake shrugged slightly and recrossed his legs, looking elegant and handsome and in no way offended.

What was his specialty? I was ashamed that I had no idea. I was pretty sure it wasn't divorce, given that I'd Internet-researched all divorce lawyers in the greater Santa Fe region. Perhaps something to do with finances or real estate? He certainly did well, to judge by his posh office, fancy car, and designer suit coats, not to mention his great-looking jeans and flashy silver cowboy accessories. I risked looking foolish and asked.

He leaned back in his chair, eyes twinkling. "Well, let's see. Maybe an example will suffice. Flori, you'll be pleased to know that last week I negotiated an out-of-court settlement involving Gloria Hendrix's poodle. Not my usual type of client, mind you, but Gloria offered to pay double my usual rate if I'd make an exception."

"You evil man!" Flori said, slapping her hand on the table. "What was the charge?"

Jake grinned devilishly. "Twinkle Belle the Third was charged with menacing and ankle biting. All unprovable, I'm happy to report."

I frowned, not comprehending.

Flori shook her index finger in my direction. "There you have it, Rita. You want to know his specialty? He's Santa Fe's best criminal defense attorney. A defender of the guilty! Thieves, dirty politicians, murderers, and now a cheater's own poodle . . . he gets them off, free as the wind."

"'A strong defense,'" Jake said, quoting an ad I now remembered. "I defend the presumed innocent." His wry smile implied that he knew otherwise.

My thoughts were stuck on Jake's job. Setting the guilty free was not part of the noble cowboy/lawyer image I'd constructed. Still, surely some people and pooches were wrongfully accused and needed his help. That was pretty noble. No, incredibly noble. I'd reassured my fantasies when the full implications of the conversation hit me.

The coffee-desperate man across the room let out a whistle. Another table made gestures for their bills.

"Fiddles," Flori muttered. "Okay, Rita, let's go

tend to the masses." She filled Jake's mug again and added, "You've been very helpful. If you have room after that *adovada*, I'll give you a chocolate chip muffin on the house. Gluten, sugar, and whipped cream included." Then she leaned over and kissed him on his cheek.

I was too distracted to envy her boldness. I was thinking of Victor and why he sought out a lawyer known for saving the guilty. I'd said I wouldn't investigate, but I had to find out.

Chapter 7

Jake collected his muffin, tipped his hat, and headed back to his office. Moments later, a moment I'd been dreading became reality. The chatter in the dining room fell to a hum. Heads turned. Even the visiting lover of whipped cream halted her cell phone conversation to follow the gaze of the locals.

Gabriel stood in the door. His mouth sunk downward, taking the rest of his big facial features with it. Red rimmed his eyes and emblazoned his nose. For once, he wasn't rushing anywhere. A few regulars got up to offer condolences.

"Oh that poor man," Linda whispered, wringing a dish towel in her hands.

We stood behind the counter. My hand hung frozen over the cash machine. I yearned to apologize and console, yet how would I start? Linda sensed my anguish.

"Let me talk to him first," she said, patting my

hand. "We've known each other since we were kids. He was two years ahead of me in school."

She squeezed through other well-wishers and gave Gabriel a long hug. Then she took him by the elbow and led him to a cozy table by the window. They sat, and as they talked, Linda reached out and placed a hand over his.

A *tsk-tsk* alerted me to Flori's presence. I looked down, noticing the whipped cream canister strapped to her hip by apron ties, six-shooter style.

"Makes you wonder . . ." she said.

"Wonder?" I punched the button to open the cash register. The drawer remained firmly shut. I jabbed some more buttons, prompting the drawer to slam into my stomach and receipt tape to erupt.

"You charged those tourist ladies $33,920," Flori chuckled. "Tell them it's extra for all that whipped cream." She patted the loaded cream canister on her hip.

I hit the button labeled V, supposedly for void.

"Ha! Now you've doubled it." Flori nudged me aside and with a few clicks had the machine working again. Cash registers may rank lower on my professional skill set than serving.

Handing me the corrected bill, Flori completed her thought. "I mean, all that reminiscing and seeing Gabe now. I wonder what things would have been like if Linda had stuck with him."

"Stuck with him? They dated?" Linda was a widow. Her husband, Santos, died from a heart attack a few years ago. Flori, however, can barely mumble out the requisite "rest in peace" when his name is mentioned. By all accounts, Santos was no saint. He was a mean bully, especially to

Linda. For her part, Linda rarely speaks of Santos or her love life, except to insist to her matchmaking mother that she'll never date again.

Flori gave a little shrug. "Long ago. Gabe doted on her in high school, and she liked him well enough, until she met Davy Donaldson at a pig roast and liked him better. She fell flop-hearted in love with that man. He seemed like a good one too, at the time." Then she muttered something under her breath that sounded like a curse.

I looked up, shocked. Flori never cursed. "What happened?" I asked.

Flori's face darkened. "That Davy proposed. They were planning the wedding and then a few weeks before, he ran off. A postcard from El Paso, that's all he sent, saying sorry, he'd moved on. Sorry wasn't enough. He broke my poor baby's heart. Made her easy prey for that devil Santos. I don't attribute any of it to God's will. No. It was bad chance, that's all. If the Gonzalezes hadn't had that pig roast . . ."

I was surprised that devout Flori would put so much on chance. She punched numbers into the cash register, which beeped angrily in protest. Figuring they both needed space, I volunteered to deliver checks to tables. My path took me close to Gabriel and Linda. I had to say *something*.

"Gabriel—"

Before my second word, I was enveloped in a bear hug of heavy cologne. "I'm so very grateful for your friendship with my brother," he said. "You and your daughter, you both meant so much to him. You mustn't ever blame yourselves for what happened. None of us should."

"It's true, Rita," Linda said, her brow rippled. "Gabe and I have been talking about dear Victor. Inner demons can get anyone, including those of us with strong faith and love."

"He never seemed depressed to me," I said, tentatively. Who was I to say? Me, who hadn't finished reading all the brochures from Celia's school counselor. Me, the mom totally okay with mopey fairy drawings. I vowed to pay more attention to everyone I loved.

"He hid his depression well." Gabe stared into his coffee cup. "I'm afraid that he rarely confided in anyone. I wish more than anything that he'd said something last night. With the fight, I was so edgy that I took a sleeping pill and went straight to bed. I didn't remember to check my front door, as you know." He managed a slight smile.

I blushed and apologized, which he waved off.

"You did the right thing," he said, stirring a black abyss of coffee. "I do blame myself. I know I shouldn't. But if I hadn't let Broomer in last night and let the argument get heated, Vic might not have gotten so upset. I blame the dead too. All my brother did lately was talk about spirits. It's not healthy."

Murder wasn't healthy either. Could I bring up Flori's and my doubts to a freshly grieving relative? Manners would say that I shouldn't say anything. As Flori says, however, good manners won't dig out the truth.

I tried an indirect approach. "That Broomer guy, he scared me. Why is he so angry? Is it all about the fence line?"

Gabe frowned. "I don't like to say bad things

about people, but he's trying to steal from me and
Vic. Our fence has been there for decades. The
exact date is right on the property records down
at the assessor's office. Broomer, he says he owns
the land nearly four feet into our backyard. Says
he has a new survey."

Linda murmured about newcomers ruining
Santa Fe. "The pushy kind, I mean," she specified
for my sake. "Not nice people like you, Rita."

"Exactly," Gabe said. "Broomer was pushy. And
he has no respect for history, what's already here.
He got all furious last night, but I told him, 'I'm
protecting that land. Victor has his garden there.
You can't bust that up.' We were going to get another survey. I'll have to get at that too. Victor's
garden is more precious than ever now."

Linda sniffled into a napkin. Everything of
Victor's was precious now. I ached at the thought
of Broomer and his bulldozer razing the pretty
winding paths of pebble mosaics and cozy sitting
areas watched over by Victor's painted saints. I
had a favorite bench there, one carved from huge
cottonwood logs. It offered views of a busy hum-
mingbird feeder and the burbling stream, and
was the perfect place for an afternoon cup of tea.

"Has Broomer seen the garden?" I asked. Surely
any reasonable person wouldn't harm something
so pretty. Or maybe not so surely. All sorts of gorgeous places fell to chain stores and parking lots,
even in Santa Fe with its zealous historical protection groups.

Gabe clutched his coffee cup, his knuckles whit-
ening. "Yeah. He's seen it. He says he's putting in

a Zen pagoda in his garden and needs those extra few feet to get the proper dimensions."

My mouth fell open. I imagined Zen as peaceful and, well, Zenlike, not bulldozing and threatening.

Linda patted Gabe's hand, seemingly also at a loss for words.

"We'll get through it," Gabe said sadly, then corrected himself. "I'll get through it."

An hour later I finally sat down for breakfast. "I need a drink," I groaned, slumping before remembering that Flori's chairs have been handcrafted to punish poor posture. The wooden swallows carved into the seat back pecked me in the neck. I reluctantly sat up straight and settled for a sip of tepid coffee.

My best friend Cass sat across from me and smiled sympathetically. "My Swedish grandmother always carried a flask of vodka. Medication, she called it. She liked a well-medicated coffee."

"I could use that kind of medication," I said. After a shot of vodka, though, I'd be out cold. As it was, I was setting myself up for a food coma. It was 9:45 and I could have taken down the entire breakfast menu. In lieu of total gluttony, I'd made myself a plate of chiles rellenos with sides of beans and rice. It wasn't exactly a light snack but it wasn't the worst I could do. I'd forgone topping it with an egg or guacamole or steak and waffles.

Cass retied her long platinum blond hair back in a ponytail, looping the band around to approximate a bun. The bun came out looking elegant. So did Cass, despite her workday outfit of faded jeans and a slightly singed wool sweater.

"I'm glad you could sit for a bit," she said. "What a horrible thing. I miss Victor already. He was supposed to have the booth next to mine at the Christmas market." She shook her head sadly.

Outside the window, gray clouds rolled in from the north. Cottonwood leaves, big as brown paper lunch sacks, danced with mini dust devils in the street. Customers had reported that a storm was broiling and might powder Mount Baldy in snow by evening. Usually, I thrill at the first snow, taking it as an excuse to bake cookies and roast pretty much anything. Today, my mood was as dark as the sky.

Cass sipped hot chai and nibbled a chocolate muffin studded with chocolate chips. Like me, she buys into Flori's claim that the sweet chocolate treat is a health food because it's made with olive oil.

"You should come over to the shop and we can fire off some bad feelings," she offered.

She meant the firing part literally. Cass is a silversmith with a studio near the Plaza. I'm envious of her skill, although a nervous, jumpy mess around her tools. Recently she's been teaching me to solder using the one fiery device I can handle: a common kitchen crème brûlée torch. I've been reciprocating, showing her how to turn sugar into glassy caramel.

"I'd love to," I said, after savoring a gooey bite

of pepper, "but I have to help with lunch and then go give a statement to Detective Bunny. I hope it's her, not Manny."

"I could call in a fake alarm at a sleazy bar," Cass offered. "I bet he'd take that call."

I bet he would too. "He's probably already there," I said. "No, scratch that. He's not on shift yet. Maybe he's lounging around at home with his new girlfriend." I told her about my surprise meeting with Ariel.

"Poor girl," Cass said. "I almost feel sorry for her." Cass can be counted on to take the anti-Manny side in any situation, although as a supportive friend, she held off telling me so until I announced my divorce intentions. She always credits Manny with one good thing, though. Inadvertently, he was the reason she and I met.

It was a few months after Manny, Celia, and I moved to Santa Fe. I'd worried about Celia adjusting to not only high school, but also a school in a new place with all new people. Would she fall in with a bad crowd? Feel isolated or out of her element? Nope. Celia quickly found friends in the art crowd, including a boy named Sky whom she talked about a lot. Sky knew how to weld, Celia reported with awe. He made steel statues and won art competitions and wanted to take her to Bandelier to see cliff dwellings and petroglyphs. He wanted to show her the "real" New Mexico.

My daughter was happy. Manny was not. The boy had long hair, Manny informed me sourly. He was a grade older than Celia. Moreover, he sounded like a pyromaniac and had a funny name and his parents had never married. This boy, Manny concluded, should not be taking our daughter to caves or exposing her to the unlady-like craft of welding. Manny wanted to frighten Sky off. He proposed tailing him in a police vehicle or citing him for violating fire codes.

I was curious about Celia's new friend too, but suggested that we take the more reasonable approach of getting to know him and his parents. That's how Celia and I ended up meeting Sky and his mother, Cass, in her soldering studio. Our kids had fun pounding metal and we had a great time talking, so much so that I eventually revealed Manny's concerns about teenage romance. Sitting amidst torches and tanks of gas, I didn't dare bring up the welding.

I still remember Cass's wink. "I don't think Sky's interested in girls in that way," she'd said. "But he says he can tell Celia everything. I think your daughter's really good for him."

And he was good for her. I told Manny that Cass and I would chaperone. What we were really doing was having fun too. We took the teens to fascinating archeological sites at Bandelier and Chaco Canyon. We hiked picnics up mountains and visited art studios, including the painting studio of Sky's Native American dad. Along the way, I gained a friend and a Santa Fe insider connection unconnected to Manny.

"We should go out tonight," Cass proposed, plucking up a stray chocolate chip from the health muffin. "I made a big sale this morning. A new client nearly bought me out of earrings and ordered a bunch of matching necklaces and bangles."

And I had a Mason jar full of tips, which combined wouldn't buy one of Cass's rings.

"My treat," she said, encouragingly. "Drinks tonight at Small Plates? Their happy hour is super cheap and it'll do you good to get out."

I loved Small Plates, a tapas bar tucked away in a courtyard off the beaten tourist path. I thought of my evening plans. Make that my nonplans, like sitting around an empty house flipping through cookbooks or mindless TV. Celia had called earlier, buoying my motherly hopes until she said that she'd stay a few more nights with her dad. I couldn't argue with that. To tell the truth, I wasn't eager to return to our place either.

"Okay," I told Cass, "but I'm buying the first plate of croquettes." I couldn't go to Small Plates without ordering the wonder that was cream, ham, and cheese, fried into crispy rounds.

Cass beamed. "Mmmm . . . then I'm getting the artichoke dip. Oh, or maybe that fabulous grilled Catalan sausage they do."

"And wine," I said, anticipating my post-police mood. "Lots of wine."

Chapter 8

I suspected that something was up when I returned from a late lunch delivery to the courthouse and found Addie in the kitchen. Addie's presence itself wasn't unusual. Flori has a soft spot for the twenty-something singer/waitress and lets her work flexible hours. I suspect that Flori is drawn to Addie's fanciful dreaming, namely that she's a New Mexican double of the British songstress Adele. Addie's real name is Adelina. Other people might brush that off as mere similarity. Not Addie, especially since there's more. She also shares a birthday with the Grammy-winning Adele, as well as a love of belting out soul songs. To further reinforce her Adeleness, she has been working to acquire a British accent and a curvy figure. I can't decide which attempt is going worse. What I do know is that the world isn't fair when Addie can eat mounds of New Mexican delicacies and remain a stick-skinny size four.

Addie stood by the stove munching on an entire head of *pan de muerto*. The first clue that something was amiss was that it was Friday, Addie has singing gigs on Friday evening and thus spends the daylight hours "lying in," communing with her Adele collection, and pampering her vocal cords. Second, and more important, Addie's a champion waitress, a meticulous cleaner, and an all-around nice person. But as a cook? She's mediocre at best. At worst, she's burned soup and set her Adele wig on fire. Flori, although certain that Addie's culinary skills will someday blossom, doesn't usually leave her unsupervised.

Now, Addie stood at the stove, her faux blond beehive wrapped in a Union Jack tea towel. She tentatively sprinkled red chile powder into a pot.

"More chile, Addie. Pour it in!" Flori's coaching was muffled by the turtleneck sweater stuck midway over her face. She tugged and rolled the fluffy mass down to neck level.

"Are you cold?" I asked, suspicious. The café felt like a summer afternoon in the desert, thanks to our ovens and the glowing embers in the little dining room fireplace.

"I'm not cold now, but did you hear? It might snow." She reached for a scarf.

"Right horrid weather, this," Addie agreed in full faux British. "Reminds me of Liverpool at Christmastime."

As far as I knew, Addie had never ventured farther east than Texas, and that was only because she took a wrong turn in Los Cruces. "Right . . ." I said, hoping that I was misinterpreting the situation. I made like nothing was up. "Okay, thanks for covering for me, Addie. 'Bye you two. I'm off to meet with Officer Bunny."

Flori stepped between me and the back door. "Not so fast, Rita. I'm coming with you." She grabbed a bulging gym bag emblazoned with the words EXTREME SPORT. "Addie, throw more chile powder in and stir that *adovada* once in a while. Tell customers they'll have to eat what's already fixed. Don't try to make anything new unless Juan can stay and cook it."

My suspicions were confirmed. "Flori," I said, hedging for polite ways to resist. "It's really sweet of you, but you don't have to come along. There might be a late lunch rush."

It wasn't that I didn't want Flori to come along. Okay, part of me wanted her to stay put. The last time we went to a police interview together, Flori kicked a state trooper in the shin. New Mexico state troopers do not take well to shin kicking. He almost arrested us both. In fact, he probably would have if Flori hadn't reminded him that he was her first cousin's nephew-in-law and shouldn't arrest his elders.

"No worries, me loves," Addie chirped. "Juan and I will hold down ye old tea house."

Juan, a master of perfectly fried eggs and made-to-order steaks, stood in front of his griddle clutching two spatulas and looking worried. I felt for him. It wouldn't be pretty alone in the kitchen with Addie.

Flori only saw the positive in this case. "Good girl," she said to Addie. "See, Rita, Addie and Juan are here, and we won't get many customers in this weather. Now let me get some gloves and tuck this tape recorder into my sweater. They wouldn't dare frisk an old lady."

"Don't forget your Wellies!" Addie warbled. "Ta!"

I gave in to the inevitable and told Flori I'd wait outside.

She joined me a few minutes later wearing a red wool coat with wooden buttons and a peaked hood, like an elderly Little Red Riding Hood on her way to bully the police. "Now stop giving me that sour face, Rita," she chided. "I thought you needed a friend along."

My irritation melted to guilt and gratitude. I did need a friend and would certainly welcome her company if it turned out that Manny was there. He would put on his charm and behave relatively well in the presence of others. There was another benefit too: if Flori was with me, she wouldn't be breaking into the crime scene.

"Thanks," I said, meaning it.

"You're welcome. Now where's your car?"

The parking lot stood empty except for a bumbling tumbleweed. I felt like a fool. I'd been so distracted I hadn't considered the logistics of actually getting to the meeting. "Celia," I explained to Flori. "She left the car parked over on Hillside last night. She was going to pick it up this morning and drive to school." And then straight to her dad's place, or so she promised. I would have to resign myself to walking or arrange a payment plan with Pacho's Pickup.

Flori nodded sympathetically. "I don't have a car today either. Bernard, the old fool, took ours to his hip therapy."

Flori and her husband of over sixty years, Bernard, live a few blocks from the restaurant. She routinely absconds with their car keys to stop him from driving. He might be half blind, but he errs on the side of caution. Flori stomps on the gas while claiming she can't reach the brake pedal.

"I'll call a cab," I said.

"A cab? They cost a fortune and they're reckless. I'll find someone to give us a ride."

"We're not hitchhiking to the police station." I tried to block Flori, who already had her thumb up, jabbing it toward a rusty, white-paneled van. "Ack! Put your thumb down. Didn't your mother ever tell you not to get in creepy vans?"

"My mother told me not to wear pants, and look, I've survived this long." She defiantly thrust both thumbs in the direction of a fast-moving frozen foods truck.

Didn't she watch those TV shows where the psycho killer trolls for victims in his white-paneled van and/or ice cream truck?

The truck roared by. Flori remained resolute. "If we stand here a minute or two more, someone I know will come by."

I didn't doubt that. Flori knows everyone in Santa Fe, which is a village at heart. What I doubted was that we'd find someone happy to detour out to the police station, located off a busy road riddled with strip malls and more potholes than pavement.

A beat-up station wagon slowed, likely to avoid hitting Flori, who stood near the intersection waving her arms. With her red hood covering her face, she could be mistaken for a garden gnome carjacker. I prayed that the driver wouldn't call 911.

The side window rolled down. Flori said hello,

followed by a scream that sent my heart into flip-flops. "Get out of the car! I've gotcha!" she yelled.

Flori lurched forward, grasping at the door. Horrific possibilities flashed through my imagination. She'd spotted an ax murderer, an abduction in progress, a drug smuggler, a migrant smuggler, a—

"Armida Alvarez, you dirty bread cheat, open the door this instant and face the music!"

So much for the ax murderer. I reached Flori in time to yank her red gloves from the automatic window before it closed. Tires squealed. Armida swung wide and veered into oncoming traffic to a chorus of blaring horns.

"Did she flip me off?" Flori demanded.

In the distance, Armida, at the wheel of the station wagon, raised a hand. She definitely wasn't waving.

"Come on," I said, turning my bristling little boss back to the sidewalk. "Time to call that cab."

Flori scowled. "Not yet. I have a better idea and it involves your hot lawyer friend." She took off down the street.

"Where are you going?"

"Going to ask for a loaner car from Mr. Strong and Handsome. I'll drive. You flirt."

Begging a loaner car to visit the police didn't seem like a flirting-appropriate situation to me. Not like asking Jake to rub suntan lotion on my back or joking about whether he wanted his chile extra spicy. I started to tell Flori as much but she was already halfway down the block.

Beyond Flori, a silver Audi—Jake's car—backed out of his driveway. Relief outweighed disappointment as I pawed through my purse, seeking my cell phone and the number for Pacho's Pickup. An ear-piercing whistle interrupted my search. Flori again stood in the middle of the street, one thumb outstretched, her other hand waving for me to join her.

By the time I reached her, the Audi had stopped. A tinted window descended, revealing Jake's handsome face. He tipped his hat and grinned, his laugh lines crinkling devilishly. "Ladies . . . looking for a ride?"

My small-town Midwest upbringing comes with a fair amount of repressive guilt and an extra helping of manners-imposed inhibitions. I automatically backpedaled. "Oh no, sorry Jake, you're obviously on your way somewhere. We're fine. I was about to call a cab."

"Why do that when I can take you? I'm on my way to the police station to meet a client, but he can stew a little. It'll make him more amenable to my good advice."

Flori clapped her small gloved hands. "Perfect. We're on our way to see the cops too."

I insisted that Flori sit up front, where she raved about the heated leather seats and offered Jake some treats from her gym bag. *"Pan de muerto?"* she asked, as if hosting teatime. The scent of the freshly baked, buttery bread and anise filled the car.

He politely refused, citing driving safety. I added politeness and safety to the positive column of my Jake Strong mental assessment sheet.

"Sure smells good, though," he remarked.

"It'll be fantastic once I reheat it on these hot

seats of yours." The sounds of rustling winter clothes and bags came from the passenger's seat.

"Are you taking those baked goods as a bribe?" Jake chuckled. "Bribing an officer of the law is illegal. Good thing you found yourselves a lawyer."

"I'm not going to bribe the police. Rita and I are going to insist that they get going on their investigation, and fast. You tell him, Rita."

"You know what they say about a trail going cold," I said. I caught Jake's steel-blue eyes in the rearview mirror.

He raised an eyebrow. "Does this mean what I think it does?" he asked.

"Murder," Flori declared amidst the rustle of bags. "That's what it means. Victor was murdered and Rita's going to get him justice, with my help, of course."

Her confidence was contagious. We *would* get to the bottom of this. We would help Victor. Then I spotted Jake's frown. A frown of worry from a man who knew criminals and crime. My confidence crumpled into fear. If we were right, a murderer was on the loose and too close to home.

Chapter 9

Flori and I sat on hard metal chairs at a table too sticky to touch. The otherwise bare interview room sported walls the color of rotten pear. It smelled like decaying fruit too, along with notes of stale coffee and despair. I fanned myself with a flyer for a take-out place that put tacos on pizza. The fanning did little but stir the stuffy air around, and I didn't want to think about taco-topped pizza. I fought back a wave of claustrophobia, the kind I get when jammed in a slow, packed elevator. There's enough air, I told myself as my stomach jolted, as if bumping along with the imaginary elevator. I wanted to flee. Was Manny making us wait on purpose? He knew that I had issues with gross surfaces and enclosed spaces.

"Do you think they're watching us through the mirror like on TV?" Flori asked, looking around. She seemed perfectly content to sit in the smelly little room. She'd even broken out some of her bread to snack on.

I scooted my chair back to avoid accidental contact with the table. If "they" were watching, all they'd see was me fidgeting and Flori nibbling. "I thought you were going to bribe someone with that bread," I said.

"Shhhh!" Flori jabbed a finger in the direction of the mirror. "Don't say the B word. Besides, I'm not bribing the police. I'm going to give one of my breads to Elena Dickenson. She works in police records and is the sister-in-law of one of the *pan de muerto* judges. Take that Armida! Flip me off, will you? Ha!"

"And how will this help?" I wondered if the stuffy air was affecting my thinking or Flori's.

"Buzz," my elderly friend said, tapping her index finger to her forehead. "Elena will share this with her husband, who'll love it and tell his sister who lives on the other side of their duplex, and there you have it—buzz. That's partly why I've been baking so much. I'm spreading the word. By the time those judges get to the contest, they'll be salivating for my death bread."

"Speaking of death . . ." Bunny appeared in the doorway holding a tray of steaming cups.

I nearly jumped out of my chair.

Bunny, in contrast, personified cool calmness. She also didn't have my problem with balancing drinks. The tray remained steady as she handed Flori a hot cup, along with creamer and sugar.

I stood to accept a cup too, despite fears that afternoon caffeine would stick with me past bedtime.

"Sorry for the room," Bunny said. A scrunchy held back her pale brown hair. Her beige, button-down shirt had POLICE embroidered on its pocket and strained against the width of her shoulders. Standing above Flori, she looked like a giant. "Sit," she said, nodding in my direction and failing to add "please."

I sat back down. Bunny placed a police tape recorder on the table and seated herself as well.

"Bread?" Flori asked, tearing off a hunk of skull and offering the rest to the policewoman.

"I can't accept that." Bunny had her eyes fixed on me. "Now Ms. Martin—"

"Lafitte!" Flori and I corrected in unison, earning the hint of a smile from Bunny.

"Where is that cheating partner of yours anyway?" Flori demanded. "If he's not coming, can I have that extra coffee?"

"He'll be here," Bunny said. I thought I detected displeasure in her voice, although I could have been transferring my own feelings. She turned to me. "Now, Ms. Lafitte, this shouldn't take long."

"Oh yes it should," Flori mumbled.

"Looks pretty cut and dry," Bunny continued, without missing a beat. She produced a notepad and a tape recorder.

Flori fumbled with her sweater and probably the tape recorder underneath it. Had she stuffed it in her bra? Taped it to her chest? I didn't want to know. I had enough to figure out, like what tactic I should take. Could I demand they investigate? But based on what? All I had was a bad feeling, which would be as unconvincing as Flori's sixth sense and Dalia's star predictions.

"It's not cut or dry in our minds," Flori said loudly in the direction of her chest.

"Shhh . . . You're going to get kicked out," I whispered to my elderly companion. Then I said, for the benefit of Bunny, "Flori, I'm sure Bunny's going to tell us all about the progress the police are making in their investigation."

Bunny clicked her tape recorder on. "First, I need your statement," she said. She instructed me to go over the evening's events in detail.

I started with hearing Celia yell and discovering the horrific scene.

"And what were your first thoughts on cause of death?" Bunny asked.

"Initially I thought suicide," I said, starting to add a "but."

"That corresponds with our findings." Bunny made some notes.

"Except it wasn't!" Flori pounded an open palm on the sticky table. "Tell her, Rita. Victor had plans for Día de los Muertos! No man with plans for the dead kills himself!"

Bunny raised a pale eyebrow and addressed Flori. "Mrs. Fitzgerald, I let you join us on the condition that you remain quiet."

She clearly didn't know Flori, who had stood to her full five feet and a few inches, barely taller than the height of Bunny sitting. "I will not remain quiet when my friend has been murdered. He laid out cards for his uncle and marigolds to guide the spirits. Does that sound like a man who'd do himself in?" She stabbed her arthritic index finger on the table. I cringed, for the abused finger and its contact with table germs, not to mention its role in antagonizing the police. Still, I agreed with her. Victor was not a man to kill himself.

Bunny rubbed her forehead and sighed. "Marigolds do not prove murder. I will hear you both out, but first let's finish Ms. Lafitte's account. Rita, skip to the part where you enter the victim's brother's home. Why did you do that?"

"Good question." Manny entered the room, his face screwed up in a frown. "Rita's famous for meddling. Can't keep her nose out of things." He took the remaining cup of coffee and sipped it with a scowl.

"I was concerned about both brothers," I said, determined to remain calm. I clenched and unclenched my fists, a technique I'd learned in a relaxation workshop with Cass. I didn't feel relaxed.

Manny wasn't helping. "So you broke in and nearly scared the living brother to death? Not to mention nearly getting yourself shot in front of our daughter?"

"Celia was out front," I said, clenching my toes.

"Oh, so you left Celia alone." Manny put on an expression of an aggrieved parent.

"She wasn't alone. She was with your girlfriend," I said, "although I admit, I probably shouldn't have left two such *young* girls there on their own."

My dig at Manny backfired, as I should have expected. He flashed a wolfish grin. Bunny saved my composure by taking over the questioning. "I know it's disturbing, Rita, but can you describe how the body was positioned when you looked in the window?"

"Slumped by the altar." The police-station coffee rolled in bitter waves in my stomach, and I had to pause to keep my composure. "There was a gun beside him and a marigold wreath around his neck. Poor Victor, he looked . . . well . . . gone, but I had to be sure."

Manny looked through me to Bunny. "She makes rash decisions," he said with snarky righteousness.

I practiced some nonrelaxing clenching of my teeth. "I had to see if there was any chance to help him. And what if Gabriel needed help too? Victor's door was locked so I knocked on Gabriel's side. That's when I discovered his front door was open. See, that could be a clue."

"A clue to what?" Manny demanded. "That people need to lock their doors so you don't break in?"

I couldn't hold back this time. "No," I said with exaggerated patience. "A clue that someone else could have gotten in there and hurt Victor. Something that the *police* should investigate."

"It's a fair point," Bunny said.

Manny scowled like a sulky kid.

"Someone who fought with him earlier in the evening," I continued, taking advantage of Manny's silence. "Have you talked with the neighbor, Mr. Broomer? He was threatening the brothers with a knife last night."

Flori chimed in. "This wouldn't be the first time someone murdered over a fence line in this town. Victor had an appointment with a lawyer too. This afternoon, in fact. Does that sound like someone about to kill himself?"

Manny grabbed the file folder in front of Bunny and began pulling out pictures. "An appointment with a lawyer might drive anyone to suicide. And, yes, we talked to the neighbor in length this morning. He admits that he and the brothers had words, but that's all."

"He could have come back later that night," I pointed out.

Manny wasn't buying my argument, probably because I was the one making it. "You're trying to tell me that an art dealer who sells overpriced Buddhas gets mad over a fence, so he breaks in, kills someone, and stages a suicide? Oh, and that he kills the brother he's least mad at and does it with an antique gun owned by the victim's family that has only Victor's prints on it? Yeah, Rita, we checked the prints. We know how to do our job. We're not *Law and Order* wannabes like you."

Doubt and confusion engulfed me. *How could this be?* I'd hoped that the gun would point to someone else. I'd assumed that sweet, peaceable Victor wouldn't touch let alone own a gun.

"No evidence of forced entry," Bunny was saying. "Not at the brother's door or at the door that separates their sides of the house. Nothing suspicious in that. Only shows that people need to be more careful."

"Careful not to shoot themselves," Manny muttered. He dropped the folder of photos on the table. Some splayed out, allowing Flori and me to see. She gasped and turned her eyes heavenward, crossing herself. I wanted to turn away too, but I couldn't. There was something wrong, something I couldn't quite place. "Wait . . . no . . ." I said, reaching out.

"Yes, it's hard to accept suicide," Bunny said,

sounding like one of the pamphlets from Celia's school counselor. "We often try to look for signs in retrospect but that can't help." She started to gather the photos into the folder.

"Wait!" I grabbed one of the terrible close-ups and forced myself to study it. Beside me, Flori paused in her prayers.

"What?" she whispered.

"The gun . . . do you see where it is?"

"Aha!" Flori exclaimed, slapping me on the back. "Now there's your evidence! We knew it! Murder!"

Chapter 10

Manny sputtered. "So the gun's in his right hand. That's your big clue? So what?"

"So what?" I demanded, turning to Bunny. Surely she'd see the point. "You pick up a gun to shoot yourself, your last act, you're scared . . . are you going to use your nondominant hand?"

Bunny flipped through the pages of her file, not responding but not blowing me off either.

"Do we know for sure he was a leftie?" Manny said. "Even if he was, maybe he used his right hand to shoot. I know a guy, he's left-handed but he plays golf right-handed. Jimmy. Good old Jimmy Marks. You used to know him, Rita. He's one of *my* friends."

"Victor was definitely a southpaw," I said, ignoring yet another attempt by Manny to claim one of our mutual friends. "He painted left-handed. He used left-handed metal cutters to make tin frames for his artwork. Ask Celia, she's left-handed too.

She and Victor joked about all the great artists being lefties. Ask Gabe for confirmation, if you want, but I know I'm right."

"It would be unusual to shoot with your non-dominant hand," Bunny said over Manny's snorts of disapproval. "I suppose it's possible that someone else was involved. They could have come in the open front door at Gabriel's—"

"And then what?" Manny interrupted. "The door between the brothers' wings was locked." He leaned back in his chair, shooting me a guess-I-told-you look.

Bunny missed his look. She was flipping through her notebook. "I asked Gabriel about that," she said. "He said the interior door locks automatically on Victor's side when it closes. Said that it's a pain and that Victor occasionally locked himself out by accident, but it's some kind of fancy antique—like everything around there—so they didn't want to change it out." She turned to me. "Rita, when you followed Victor back to his wing last night, did the door close fully behind you?"

I tried to imagine myself back in the scene. I remembered hurrying through the foyer, feeling uneasy about Broomer and anxious to get back to Victor's side. The door had surely been open, or else how would I have followed Victor? Yes, I could see the door, about halfway open. I'd slipped right through. Had I shut it?

"I think I pulled it closed a little. I can't say for sure that it latched," I admitted. What if I could have prevented Victor's death by simply closing a door? Stress pounded out a staccato headache in my temples.

"It's something to look into," Bunny said.

"And fast!" Flori again slapped her hands on the table. When she pulled them off, they made a sticky sound. I made a mental note to bathe us in hand sanitizer the second we left the building, which I wanted to be soon.

I stood, nodding to Flori. "We'll help in any way we can with this *murder* investigation."

"Murder," Flori reiterated darkly. "We'll be sending you our list of suspects."

Bunny frowned at her notebook, flipping pages. She shut it with a snap. "We have a few things to check. We'll talk to you again." She looked determined to solve a murder. Or was she simply ready to get rid of us?

Manny, meanwhile, sounded like a kid who's been told he'll be cleaning his room rather than going out for ice cream.

"More work," he griped to Bunny, puffing out his bottom lip. "Just what we need with Halloween and Day of the Dead coming up. Holidays are nothing but a pain." To me, he put in a final jab. "If this is murder—which I doubt—you didn't help anything, Rita. Your fingerprints will be all over the crime scene. I should charge you with interfering."

"Go ahead and try," Flori said, heading for the door. "Rita has a hotshot lawyer, a hot one at that!"

Indeed, our hot lawyer was right outside the door. Jake leaned casually against the wall, cowboy boots crossed, as if waiting for the cows to come home. I hoped he hadn't heard Flori's "hot" description or her presumption that he was "my" lawyer.

He winked at me with those gorgeous steel-blue eyes before smiling at Bunny and Manny. "Officers? Is there a problem here?" The friendly words had a hard edge.

"No problem," Bunny snapped.

Jake, still smiling, extended both elbows, inviting me and Flori to loop our arms through. I basked in the gentlemanly gesture, as well as the scowl it produced on Manny's face.

Later, at the earliest bird start of happy hour, I recounted the moment to Cass.

"I wish I could have seen Manny's expression," she said with a grin.

"It was pretty sweet," I said. "He was definitely jealous."

"Good. All the jealousy he put you through, he deserves that." Cass unfolded her napkin and picked up her menu.

We'd snagged our favorite corner table at Small Plates, a little restaurant with a Spanish-meets-the-Southwest theme. The décor is modern in a dark, cozy way, with sleek cement floors, charcoal-hued walls, metal accents, and a hand-carved wooden bar that could be in an art museum. We took a moment to study our menus, featuring tapas-style dishes, and the specials scrawled in chalk across a blackboard wall.

"Maybe Flori's right," Cass said, reaching for the wine list.

"Right?"

"About you showing some interest in that hunky lawyer. I mean, Rita, come on. He's a dream to look at, not to mention I hear he's a wonder in the courtroom . . . and probably elsewhere too . . ."

I had been fixated on the menu and whether I could justify ordering smoked-paprika mac-and-cheese in addition to ham and cheese croquettes. I tore my eyes away long enough to roll them at Cass's suggestive suggestion. "Hey, didn't you agree to back me up on my moratorium? You're my spotter. Remember the one-year vow?"

My friend shrugged. "Just testing you."

I'd been tested enough today. I discarded any righteous thoughts of a light grilled radicchio salad and declared that I'd be ordering croquettes *and* mac-and-cheese.

"Perfect. And how about the fried artichokes? They'll count as a salad." Cass, never on a diet or worrying about one, mused at the menu a bit more, then asked if I'd also split some meatballs.

Would I ever. These were not just any meatballs. Small Plates served *albóndigas al azafran*, tender morsels of pork, beef, and Manchego cheese simmered in a white wine, saffron, and almond sauce as rich and exotic as the dish's name. Flori pestered the chef until he gave up the recipe. The yummy meatballs now appear at Tres Amigas with various New Mexican twists, like a spicy red pepper sauce and piñon nuts in place of almonds.

Donavan, our waiter, who strutted the restaurant like it was his personal catwalk, took our order and returned a few minutes later with our wine and complimentary olives.

"Let me know if there's anything I can do for

you," he said in a deep baritone, leaning in close to Cass's ear.

"Thanks," Cass said coolly. My gorgeous friend gets plenty of male attention, most of which she ignores. She claims to have no time for serious relationships. Plus, she says, she's happily raised a child as a single parent for seventeen years. Why should she add in a partner or husband now?

Donovan took the rebuff in stride and swaggered off. Cass and I raised our glasses.

"To Victor," we said in unison.

We sipped in silence for a few minutes. I thought of Victor making cookies, collecting apples in the backyard, and painting with Celia. Could I have helped him? Would it have been as simple as shutting and locking his door?

When Donovan deposited terra-cotta *cazuela* dishes filled with golden croquettes and meatballs, Cass broke the silence. "I've been thinking about what you said at breakfast. You know, about the possibility of murder." She looked around furtively at the tables nearby. The other diners studied their menus and chatted, uninterested in our conversation. "I have the perfect suspect for you," she said in a dramatic stage whisper.

I halted my fork midway to the croquette and waited.

Cass leaned across the table. "Jaylee Jantrell, Jay-Jay for short. Victor's ex-wife."

I searched my memory, which was coming up blank. Had I known of a wife, ex or not? I couldn't recall Victor mentioning her, though it's not like I'd go around mentioning Manny if I didn't have to.

"Jay-Jay's a witch," Cass said, then quickly revised her statement. "I shouldn't say that. I know some perfectly lovely witches. Switch the 'w' for a 'b' and a bunch of nasty adjectives. Mean, shrill, conniving, jealous, greedy . . ." She took a break from adjectives to sample the meatball. Then she said, "Okay, maybe she didn't actually do it, but she's mean, and the ex should definitely be on any list of suspects, right?"

"Sure," I said, distracted by the sight of Donovan strutting toward our table, bearing a steaming bowl of shellfish.

"Mussels in white wine," he said, practically cheek-to-cheek with Cass. "From the gentleman with the scarf." He scowled toward the bar, where a slender man in black jeans and a suede jacket dipped his chin in our direction. Cass flitted her fingers in a little wave and mouthed, *Thank you.*

I marveled. I've been the recipient of a few free drinks, mostly from dudes at sports bars when I waitressed in my twenties. But mussels? The shiny black shells swam in a savory broth, smelling of grapes and the sea. I also marveled at the man. Not only was he gorgeous in an elegant, artistic way, with chic black hair and clothes. He also wielded knitting needles and a skein of black yarn.

"Wow," was all I could say, not that "wow" did such a man justice. He could be a male model placed there to make the bar seem hip, upscale, and urban.

Cass smiled. "I know. That's Salvatore Dean. Such confidence, right? I mean, what man sends over seafood?" She put her nose over the mussels and breathed in happily. She added, as if this would explain everything, "He's a wood-carver."

I'd pictured him as a dancer in some avant-garde troupe. Or flamenco. I could definitely imagine him strutting around a dance floor in manly leggings with a rose in his mouth. I shook off the image. If I was serious about my moratorium, I had to stop reading romance novels.

"A wood-carver?" I said, knowing that Cass would eventually give up more details. "Who knits?"

Cass agreed that the knitting was a bit odd. "But kind of sexy too, don't you think?" she added.

She was right about that. He'd started knitting and purling, not in the tight, proper manner of elderly ladies, but loose and confident, like the knitting needles were a musical instrument.

Cass selected a mussel and expertly sipped it from its shell. "He's not any old woodworker. No carved bears like you see up in Colorado." She named a downtown store famous for its high-priced, handmade furniture. "They sold one of his coffee tables today for nearly $12,000. I guess it's the night to celebrate windfalls, not that mine comes anywhere close to that."

"Wow," I said again. My vocabulary seemed to be declining along with my early middle-aged memory. Maybe a meatball would help. I sampled one, reveling in the complex sauce, and then turned the conversation back to Victor's ex-wife, admitting I had no recollection of her.

"You probably wouldn't have met her," my friend said. "They split ages ago. She's an art

dealer. I say 'dealer' loosely. She's more like a professional swindler who undercuts artists and clients any chance she gets."

Cass picked up another mussel. "She gets
most of her inventory from desperate people.
For instance, I heard that she got a stack of Gus-
tave Baumann wood-block prints from a widow
facing foreclosure. She paid a couple hundred
for museum-quality originals and then turned
around and sold them for thousands. I'm telling
you, she's a prime one for the suspect list."

Artists, I knew, held a special hatred for anyone
who swindled their kind or anyone with a true
love of art. Jay-Jay sounded unpleasant and untrustworthy. That didn't make her a murderer. As
I'd learned, you can't assume anything in an investigation. The nicest grandmotherly type could
be a cold-blooded killer, while the biggest jerk
could be as innocent as a newborn.

"How did you know I had a list?" I asked, digging into the gooey mac-and-cheese. I took a bite,
luxuriating in the creamy, cheesy comfort and
watching as two twenty-something women sidled
up to Salvatore and his knitting. I wondered if I
should tell Cass. She glanced over her shoulder,
following my gaze.

"No worries," she said, guessing my thoughts.
"We have a date tonight, and he won't break it.
In fact, I worry he's getting a little too attached
to me." She rolled her eyes as if the attraction of a
swoon-worthy man with both knitting and wood-
carving skills was her burden to bear. "Anyway,"
she continued. "Of course you have a list, right?

And I don't care what you say. You're involved in this, Rita."

Cass knew me too well. I couldn't deny it. "Flori is making a list too but she won't share it yet," I told her. "She wanted us to write lists separately and compare. We asked Jake to make one, but he worried about client conflicts."

"See, he's thoughtful as well as handsome. So who else is on your list?"

I had to admit that she'd nearly doubled my tally with the addition of Jay-Jay. I had two main suspects. Number one was Broomer. The distant second was a random burglar/killer. However, as Jake pointed out on the drive back from the police station, Victor's home showed no signs of robbery.

"Jay-Jay's better than your unknown killer," Cass contended. "She has motive. Victor's art. She'd love to get her hands on that, let me tell you. You know the saddest thing? Now that he's gone, the value of his work will skyrocket." She caught Donovan's eye, holding up her nearly empty wineglass to indicate that she'd like another.

I considered my long walk home and decided to make my first glass my last. I nursed the drink, watching the restaurant fill up for the dinner hour. I realized that I recognized many of the people in the room. Some were fellow cooks and food workers. Others were regular or occasional customers at Tres Amigas or parents of Celia's classmates. It felt nice to feel like a local.

I raised my half-full glass to Cass's newly filled one and we switched to a happier subject, namely Cass's new superclient.

"She walked in off the street," Cass said, waving her hands heavenward in a hallelujah gesture. "I couldn't believe it, she was literally dripping turquoise and diamonds, and you know I barely do anything with stones or gems. Well, she saw my plain silver works and said she had to have some. She bought a whole collection, ordered specialty pieces, and recommended me to some of her friends."

I was about to ask the identity of this mystery woman when Cass clasped her hands together. "Oh look, there she is now." She rose, wineglass in hand.

I gawked. I knew this woman too. Cass's wealthy client was none other than Flori's baking nemesis, Gloria Hendrix. Cass and Gloria air-kissed. After three rounds of efficient cheek swaps, Cass introduced me.

"Rita, you know Gloria? Gloria, Rita is an amazing chef who works at—"

I cut in. "Oh, I've worked in a couple places around town," I gushed loudly, flashing a *Sorry* look at Cass. To cover my rudeness, I launched into compliments, all of them true. "What a gorgeous bracelet! And those rings!"

"By our fabulous Cassandra." Gloria held out her hands, which sported three sleek silver rings, all effortlessly graceful. Gloria's face was another story. Her lips puffed like overfilled sausages, a feature made more obvious by her otherwise taut, wrinkleless skin. I suspected she had indulged in extra helpings of Botox, eye lifts, and whatever made lips inflate.

"Cassandra, you *must* come to my Day of the

Dead cocktail party tomorrow night. I'm having a skeleton theme, of course, and *everyone* will be there." She drawled out the names of some upper-crust types and hotshot artists, including Salvatore the confident knitter.

Cass handled the invitation smoothly, saying that she'd love to stop by.

I knew that she'd be inwardly cringing. For all her poise and confidence around men and flames, Cass dreads large events. Yet no artist in this shaky economy can turn down a chance for publicity and schmoozing. She had to go. Gloria's frozen face turned to me. "Rita, I hope you'll come too. If you're part of the food scene, you'll absolutely adore what I'm serving."

I was speechless. She was inviting no-name me? Should I accept? Would Flori accuse me of cavorting with the enemy? No, she'd be thrilled that I'd have a chance to spy on Gloria's kitchen. This was much better than hefting myself over her wall to trespass. I recovered my manners as Cass was starting to cover for me, citing my busy schedule.

"Thank you, I'd love to join you," I said, effusing about Gloria's generosity and ending with "I've heard that you're a wonderful baker!"

"Why that is so sweet of you!" Gloria's eyes sparkled behind the Botox mask. "Not to toot my own horn, but I am the reigning queen of death bread. I can't serve it to everybody at the party, unfortunately. I need to wait for the contest. Besides, I'd have too many people begging for my secret recipe, now wouldn't I?"

I bet it was a secret. Armida's secret. I kept these thoughts to myself and my face in a beaming smile. Gloria left after issuing instructions that the party attire was black-tie skeleton.

Cass took a gulp of wine after Gloria left. "Ugh, I hate dress-up parties," she said. "And what the heck is black-tie skeleton?" She sighed into her wineglass.

"Salvatore will be there," I said encouragingly. Surely his presence made any party better.

My friend was not easily consoled. "Also dreadful. If I go with him, he'll want to drag me around to chat up all the socialites. I'll go with you, though, if you're really going and we can figure out what to wear."

I had no idea what to wear, but it sounded pretty fun. It was also an opportunity. I confessed my ulterior bread-snooping motive to Cass, half expecting her to warn me away from her client.

Instead she grinned. "Now that makes the party a whole lot more interesting."

Chapter 11

Cass invited me to join her and Salvatore at the gallery opening.

"He won't mind," she'd said. "But I warn you, the exhibit's paint-drip art."

Part of me felt tempted, especially when she mentioned the gallery's plans for a chocolate, cheese, and wine spread. Most of me, however, had no interest in paint drippings and being the third wheel. That part of me also wanted to get home, slip into flannel pajamas, and cuddle up under a blanket by the fireplace.

With my scarf bundled around my ears, I set off through the heart of downtown. Despite the chill, the place bustled. Tourists gazed in shop windows decorated in fanciful skeletons and skulls and strolled under the covered walkways, or *portales*, as Flori would insist I call them. As a shortcut, I crossed the Plaza, the centuries-old square at the heart of Santa Fe.

Tonight, like many nights, a band played on the raised bandstand. I heard a bluesy saxophone first, followed by a familiar voice. Addie sang about a fire in her heart as two skeleton-costumed backup singers crooned and danced behind her. A puffy down coat gave her the curvy figure she so desired, and she'd attracted groupies. A handful of teen girls and young guys in trendy tight pants swayed in front of the bandstand. Nearby, a few older couples danced a two-step complete with swings and dips. I stopped to listen. Addie spotted me and gave me a divaesque point-out.

"Sweet, isn't it."

The deep male voice at my shoulder startled me into again nearly head-butting its speaker. Jumpiness is like blushing with me, a characteristic I hate but can't stop or grow out of.

"Sorry to scare you," Jake said, his chiseled face suggesting more amusement than contrition. "Worried about the ghouls?" A group of laughing kids ran past us, dressed as various forms of the undead.

"Nice scarf," I said, changing the subject. He wore a gray wool overcoat and a loose-knit black scarf that could have come straight from Salvatore's knitting needles. "Did you happen to get that from a woodworker?"

When he looked puzzled, I tried to explain. "There's this guy my friend Cass is seeing. He makes $12,000 coffee tables and knits at bars, which seems to attract all sorts of women." I could have kicked myself. Here I was, in front of a man who supposedly liked me, and I was going on about male knitters. This is why I shouldn't date, not until I could overcome small-talk anxiety and jumpiness in the face of desirable bachelors.

As a couple waltzed in front of us, Jake held out a hand in a dapper leather glove. "I sewed a button back on this coat," he said, nodding to a mid-chest button secured with a lump of black thread. "Does that mean I can ask you to dance?"

"No!" I blurted out before thinking. Seeing the hurt look on Jake Strong's manly face, I back-tracked. "I mean . . . I don't . . ." My mind swirled through all the wrong things to say. Telling him about my dating moratorium would sound silly, not to mention presumptuous. You could dance without being on a date, I reasoned, as a mom-and-child dance pair twirled by us. My moratorium wasn't a prohibition against friendly, seasonal exercise.

"I mean," I said, after taking a deep breath. "I can't dance. Really, I'm bad. Horrible. I can barely clap in rhythm and I'll destroy your boots." This was sadly and totally true. I lag beats behind in group cheers at sporting events. I've fled step aerobics classes in shame, and I once managed to break my big toe while square dancing. With anything rhythmic, I'm a danger to myself and to others. I looked down at Jake's black boots, pol-ished to a gleam that would never last through any two-stepping on my part.

He laughed. "Okay, then. We won't do any clap-ping, and don't worry about these old boots. I wear them to the ranch. Cattle have stomped on them and they've been just fine. I can't see how a petite lady as pretty as you can do them any harm."

Petite? Me? I was glad that darkness covered my raging blush. From the stage, Addie announced a song request from "her mates." A song for romance, she said, and launched into a slow, sentimental croon in one of her actual native tongues, Spanish. My limited vocabulary picked up the words for love and parting.

Again, Jake held out his leather-gloved hand.

I hesitated before taking it. "Okay," I said. "They're your boots . . ."

He chuckled and moved his feet slowly. I stumbled along, making multiple stutter steps for each of his smooth ones.

"Does counting help?" he asked. "One two two, one two two . . ."

Counting was as confounding as clapping, I regretfully told him. Then I added, "I have *tried* to learn. I've taken dance classes. Two, in fact. Polka and Greek line dance."

"Very handy skills," he said. "Nothing sexier than the polka."

Now I started to worry my blush would stick, especially after he said, "Keep your left hand on my back and feel my movements. Shut your eyes, think of the music . . . you'll be dancing without thinking about it."

I pressed my hand to his back and he pulled me close. I shut my eyes. I tried not to think of dancing and then, all of a sudden, I was stepping, back and forth, foot after foot. *I was actually dancing.* As soon as I realized this, I faltered and tromped on Jake's boot. He brushed off my apologies and held his hand high, inviting me to spin. Above me, a beautiful swirl of string lights and stars twinkled. I spun until dizzy, finally wobbling to a halt when Addie finished her song and announced her plans to "pop out for a hot cuppa."

Jake looked down at my bare hands. "You must be freezing. I know a fine place to warm up with a drink. Will you join me?"

I hesitated, rationalizing to myself. Yelling no again would be rude, and I was cold, from my numb fingertips to my popsicle toes. I accepted Jake's invitation, which I assured myself was not a date.

"Where are we going?" I asked.

"You may think it's silly," Jake said as we waited for the crosswalk sign to give us our turn. "But I'm craving hot cocoa from La Fonda. They have killer margaritas there too, of course, if you want."

"Hot cocoa sounds absolutely perfect." So did the La Fonda, a landmark hotel and adobe marvel designed to resemble the ancient Pueblo architecture up in Taos. The interior is also fabulous, with colorful painted windows and wood carvings and quirky displays of local art.

Jake held the door for me and a group of happy tourists, laden with shopping bags. Once inside, he led the way to the casual lounge restaurant. I knew about the La Fonda's famous margaritas. Cass and I had indulged in quite a few, especially the night we celebrated my divorce. I'd also heard raves about their chiles rellenos, although I remained loyal to Flori's fluffy wonders. I had to admit that I'd never heard of their hot chocolate.

"It's a secret," he whispered close to my ear. "I have an inside source."

I loved the idea of that and the tingle his whisper shot through my body. We sat near a leafy potted ficus, far from a flamenco guitarist strumming madly on the other side of the lounge. Jake caught the attention of our server and asked for Ramando.

"You really have an insider for cocoa?" I asked.

"Yep. Don't tell anyone."

Ramando, when he tottered in, looked older than the hotel itself. He greeted Jake with a hearty handshake and an effusive exchange in Spanish. The conversation seemed to involve his and his family's eternal gratitude, the holidays, and chocolate. Was he one of Jake's clients? He looked nice enough, and he certainly sounded grateful. Maybe defense lawyering wasn't such a bad job.

Jake turned to me. "No whipped cream, right? Straight up chocolate?"

"No fluff," I confirmed, "I want pure chocolate."

"So," Jake said, in the slightly awkward silence that followed. "I left my knitting needles at home."

I laughed. "Me too. Although I can't knit to save my life." We chatted about other things we couldn't do and about our families, his now mainly in the high country outside Taos and mine who can't stand high elevations or aridity.

"No one told my mother that Santa Fe is higher than Denver," I said, recounting my mother's sudden onset of supposed altitude sickness the moment she realized we were more than a mile above sea level. "After that, she spent most of her time in the oxygen bar downtown."

It was a nice distraction from sad thoughts about Victor, until the cocoa arrived. The steaming mugs of dark deliciousness sparked a flashback of my last visit with my friend.

Jake sensed my shift in mood. "Is the hot chocolate okay? If it's not sweet enough, I bet Ramando has emergency whipped cream like Flori does."

I tried to laugh it off. Gloominess, even on a nondate, was not good, as Flori would remind me. Of course, she'd want me to be playing footsie and pinching Jake's butt.

"Victor served hot chocolate the last time I saw him," I explained, so as not to offend Ramando's delicious drink. "He made it with spices to go with his *bizcochitos*."

"A man of legendary cookies," Jake said, raising his mug in a salute. "To Victor. May he rest in peace."

I seconded the salute, wishing it to be true. "He won't rest, will he? I mean, that's what he'd say. He'd say that a murdered spirit can't rest."

Jake, a defender of at least some guilty souls, nodded seriously. "A lot of people say that the living can't rest either, not until there's justice. It's my feeling that eventually the guilty get the punishment they deserve."

Hoping for his insider's view on criminal types, I brought up Cass's suspicions regarding Jay-Jay.

"I've had some dealings with Jay-Jay," Jake said carefully. Then he smiled. "I kind of hope it wasn't her. I wouldn't want to defend her."

This from the man who recently defended an ankle-biting poodle. "I don't see what she'd gain by hurting Victor," I said. "I mean, if they were di-

vorced, it's not like she'd inherit anything, right?"
As I said this, a pang of worry hit me. Manny
and I made wills when Celia was born. I hadn't
thought about them in years, but mine left everything to him.

Behind his cocoa mug, Jake's face turned serious. I couldn't tell if it was lawyerly caution or a
personal cloud. "In the state of New Mexico, divorce revokes a will made during marriage." I
breathed a sigh of relief, until he continued.

"But, there's really no way to know until Victor's
will is submitted for probate. You'd be surprised.
The most ironclad will can be hit by claims from
third parties or disinherited relatives or a judge
set on picking out technicalities. Plus, you never
know. If he made another will after the divorce, he
could include bequests to whomever he pleased,
Jay-Jay included. Or maybe he didn't have a will at
all. That's always a fun bucket of rattlesnakes. In-
heritance isn't my specialty, but anything legal can
become complex, especially here in New Mexico."

I added will updating to my mental task list and
was about to change the topic when an exclamation through the ficus did it for me.

"OMG! It's you! Talk about fate!"

Fate indeed. Here I was, on a hot-drink nondate
with a hot man, and who interrupts but Manny's
girlfriend, Ariel. Wobbling on platform heels, she
trotted around the potted tree and leaned over
our table, cleavage straining against a tank top
that revealed more of her tattoo. It appeared to be
a greenish butterfly or maybe a flying dinosaur or
perhaps a leaf lettuce. Her eyes sported the same

Egyptian cat-eye liner that my daughter favored. I hoped that Celia wasn't emulating her father's girlfriend.

"Hi Ariel," I said, rallying my manners. "I didn't know you worked here." Of course, I hadn't known she existed before last night. She waved her fingertips at Jake. Manners demanded that I introduce him.

"Hey," she said, in a flirty voice directed at my handsome companion, "of course I recognize you."

I suppressed the urge to kick her. Instead, I cleared my throat in what I hoped was a meaningful way, and by meaning, I meant a shove-off.

Ariel didn't leave. She did renotice me. "Yeah . . . I've, like, never seen you here, Reba."

"Rita," I corrected.

"Yeah, that's cool. Anyway, I'm sooo glad you're here. Celia called. She got herself in a mess over in Tesuque and I can't go get her until I'm off shift in, what, two hours? Three?"

She reached over and grabbed Jake's wrist, twisting it to see his watch. "Yeah, almost three hours."

My head spun. Hot chocolate and wine did an unpleasant polka in my stomach. "Celia? What's going on? Is she okay?"

Ariel released Jake's arm to make an *I'll be right there* gesture to a finger-snapping man in a bolo tie and fringed shirt. "Oh she's fine. She made me promise not to call Manny, so I didn't know what to do, you know? Like, can I break a girl's confidence? But this is perfect. Now you can go get her."

I could understand not calling Manny. The time Celia got in trouble for drawing chalk graffiti/art at school, Manny went ballistic, threatening to ground Celia for life and charge her art teacher with harassment. But why had she called Ariel and not me? I rummaged through my purse, frantic for my phone.

"She said she tried to call you," Ariel said in response to my muttering. I interpreted Ariel's tone as smug with a dash of snippy, an interpretation surely influenced by my guilt.

Where was my phone? I'll admit, I'm not a fan of cell phones. I resent their cost and constant need for charging and intrusive buzzing. And, yes, I do often forget to carry my phone, but today I knew I had it. I'd used it to check on Celia earlier. I had it out to call Pacho when Flori wanted to hitchhike. "I never heard it ring . . ." I gave up rummaging and dumped the purse's contents onto the table. A notepad, enough chapstick for full-body coverage, and handfuls of old receipts, gum, and napkins fell out, followed with a thud by my phone. My heart dove when the screen lit up.

Five missed calls, three messages, all from my daughter. I felt like the world's worst mother. "The police station!" I cried, realizing too late what happened. "I put the ringer on mute when I met with Bunny and Manny."

"It's cool," Ariel said, now sounding generous as she and her tottery shoes turned toward the antsy customer. "Cel's with the police too. I don't think she's actually locked up or anything. Anyway, she's a kid, so a little drunk driving won't stick to her record."

Drunk driving? I felt ill. I was certainly a moving hazard. I jumped up from the table, tipping cocoa and nearly toppling the potted plant. Every nerve in my body urged me to run to my daughter. Trouble was, I didn't know where to go.

Chapter 12

D on't panic," Jake said gently.

I was already beyond panic. "The police? She's with the police?" Tension froze through my shoulders, working its way into my arms and hands until I could barely punch in my voice-mail code. Jake held out my chair and touched my arm. I sat back down, shakily. The phone took its sweet time describing how many messages it had collected. Three, its robotic voice declared, and again I heard judgment in the tone. The last message came in about thirty-five minutes ago.

I rubbed my forehead, pushing throbbing stress from temple to temple as I listened to the first message.

"Hey, Mom? It's me. What's up?" Celia's voice sounded perky, which if you know Celia in her teen years is nothing like her typical bored-yet-surly affectation. However, under normal circumstances I might have interpreted this as Celia being nice, not a tip-off to what came next. "Listen, Mom, this is totally messed up. I'm out with Sky over in Tesuque and I need you to call me, okay? Like, whenever, but right away. Call me."

The news that she was with Sky calmed me somewhat. I looked over at Jake. He'd leaned back in his seat, possibly to give me privacy. From under an arching ficus branch, he raised an eyebrow. I shook my head, waiting for the phone to move to message two. "Nothing yet," I reported, as my daughter's recorded voice started up again.

"Mom, did you get my message?" Celia had replaced perky with an angry whine. "Call me. Sky and I are with the *police*, the *tribal police* over in Tesuque. We're, like, driving around with them 'cause they won't let us go unless you come get us. It's stupid, so don't tell Dad or Sky's mom. It's 6:35 and you should be home. *Where are you?*"

Any reassurance I'd felt vanished. *The police?* My daughter and Cass's good, responsible son were in police custody? And where *had* I been at 6:35? Probably laughing and drinking wine with Cass, neither of us knowing that our children needed us. It made sense that Sky would call his dad, Walker, an influential member of Tesuque Pueblo, a Native American community about ten miles north of Santa Fe. Walker is also a well-known artist, and he and Cass would make a gorgeous, artsy couple if they both weren't committed to being friends.

Message three started playing as I tried to understand the last message, especially the driving around part. "Mom, geez, where are you? Sky can go home whenever but says he won't until I can. Whatever! I'm calling Ariel."

I took a deep breath and told myself to remain calm. Then I hit the speed dial number I'd programmed for Celia. She answered on the second ring.

"Mom! It's about time!"

I felt horrible. On the other hand, I was not in the custody of tribal police. Celia, not me, had a whole lot of explaining to do. I tried for a tone that would keep us both civil and calm.

"Celia, honey, I apologize. I forgot to turn my phone on. I'll come and get you right now, but I need to know what happened and where to find you."

My daughter muttered about the whole situation being stupid. "And I don't know where you can get me," she said in a pointedly loud voice. "We're sitting under the underpass at a speed trap. That's how they caught us! Here, talk to this guy."

After some rustling and a muffled discussion, a male voice came on the line. Officer Day, as he introduced himself, was a sergeant in the Tesuque Pueblo police force. He was also a very disappointed man. "Disappointed," he repeated to me. "Highly disappointed."

I assured him that I too was disappointed, although for what I didn't know.

"I told these same youths once before when they were speeding," he said, his words clipped and rising at the end. "I said, 'one warning, that is all you get.' Tonight I caught them again, Sky Clearwater driving, your daughter as a verbally combative passenger. It is only out of courtesy for Walker Clearwater that I do not throw them in jail for the night."

"Jail? For speeding?" I asked, hearing my voice go squeaky. Jake leaned in close. I held the phone out from my ear so he could hear.

"For an alcoholic beverage container open in the front seat. And speeding. Seven miles per hour over the speed limit on Pueblo lands. You may retrieve your daughter and pay her ticket, but be warned because now I have warned you too."

I've been warned," I said to Jake, trying to laugh off the situation. My attempt at a cavalier chuckle came off as a verge-of-hysterical hiccup. Part of me felt drained from relief. Celia wasn't hurt. She wasn't in the hospital or a jail cell or abducted. In another part of me, anger fed off the relief. Celia and Sky should have known better. Or maybe I should have known better and kept a closer watch on her. I would now.

"I'm sorry," I said to Jake, well aware that if this had been anything resembling a spontaneous date, it was now wrecked. "I have to go. The officer said that he's getting off his shift and will take the kids to Tesuque Village Market to wait for me."

I got up again and pulled out my wallet.

Jake beat me to it, putting down cash to more than cover cocoas and a tip. "Aren't you forgetting something?" he asked.

"Sorry! Thanks for the cocoa."

"You're very welcome. It was my pleasure. But what I meant was, aren't you forgetting that you're carless?"

I'm afraid I cursed, never the perfect ending to an evening of dancing and cocoa with a handsome man. Flori would be as disappointed as Officer Day.

"You're right," I groaned, giving up any hope of a dignified exit. "I'll call a cab."

"Oh no, you won't. I'm your driver today. Besides, you may need a lawyer."

I protested, but only a smidgen, enough to be polite. I did need a ride there and back. I wanted someone on my side too, although I prayed I wouldn't need Jake's legal talents.

Under better circumstances, I adore the winding pre-expressway route to the village of Tesuque, a rural oasis of heirloom apple orchards, historic ranches, and artists' enclaves. Tonight, however, the twists and turns heightened my anxiety. I involuntarily slammed on the air brakes as we neared a sharp, blind curve, made more hazardous by towering adobe walls crowding the pavement. Jake drove fast but not recklessly.

"Okay," he said as we turned at one of the few stop signs in the village. "Here we are." We parked on a gravel pull-off across from a squat adobe. Looking at the modest structure, you'd never guess it sold gourmet foods in its country store and served up a menu ranging from fancy pastries to local delicacies. I stepped out of Jake's car and breathed in the scents of a wood fire. The market was known for its wood-fired pizza. Inappropriate thoughts of a charred and cheesy pie popped into my head until maternal worries crowded them out.

Inside, the front-of-house manager greeted us with a bouncy, "Two for dinner?"

Didn't I wish. "We're meeting someone," I corrected, craning my neck. Several groups waited, squeezed between the bakery display, Day of the Dead décor, and the busy servers' route. Jake stood on cowboy-booted tiptoes to survey the dining areas. I backed up for a wider view. Feeling a finger poke my shoulder, I said "Excuse me" before realizing it belonged to a painted skeleton.

"Over there." Jake pointed to the other side of the room.

How did he recognize Celia? I supposed that he'd seen her at the café. Until recently, she'd been happy to hang out at Tres Amigas after school, scoring free meals and finishing her homework. That was before her black-straw hair and cat-eye makeup. I hardly recognized her some days.

I followed his pointing finger. There she was, at a back table by the general store room. Black bangs covered her eyes. She gripped a pencil and appeared to be drawing madly in her sketch notebook. Sky sat beside her, face stony. He wore his hair shoulder length, pulled back like his mother often did, except where hers was so blond it was almost white, his was shiny black. The teens were with Sky's father, Walker, and a tall, slender man in uniform. When the policeman saw us approaching, he stood, pointing at Jake and frowning deeply. My heart could have bounced off the old wooden floors. Great, here I'd thought that Jake could help, and this guy hated him. What cop didn't hate a snazzy defense attorney? I should have known better.

"Is everything okay?" I whispered to Jake.

"Absolutely," he whispered back. Then in a louder voice, he said, "Danny Day's no problem. I can crush this man before breakfast."

The tribal policeman's frown went full-facial before breaking into laughter. "You wish, hombre. Wait until next weekend, Strong. You're going down."

My heart returned to normal cadence as they hugged each other in a manly back-slapping way.

"You brought this man along to help you?" Sergeant Day said to me. "He can't even dunk a basketball."

"Yeah, but I can make more three-pointers than you any day, Day." Jake turned to me. "When Officer Day here isn't fighting crime, he and his basketball team are losing to the Legal Hoops. Team basketball, every other Saturday or whenever Day feels like losing."

Day was chuckling happily now, promising that the Legal Hoops would eat their words.

Everybody sat down and I relaxed. Too soon. Day abruptly turned from basketball to teenage misbehavior.

"You're lucky this time," he said, directing his words at me and Walker. Our teenagers stared at the table. "Driving with open alcohol containers is not taken lightly by the Pueblo. We're cracking down. It is only because of my uncle, Sky's godfather, that I don't charge these youths officially."

Walker, throughout, bobbed his head in agreement. When the policeman was finished, Walker agreed with everything he said, except for letting Sky off easily. "His godfather and I will ensure that this never happens again," he said.

I seconded his statement, adding my gratitude and saying that Celia and I were both very sorry.

"Why should I be sorry?" she muttered, scraping her pencil across a drawing of storm clouds looming over an angry fairy girl. "We didn't do anything. It's not like we were drunk or speeding that much."

Sergeant Day took a notepad from his front pocket and flipped it open. "Two cans of Santa Fe Brewing Happy Camper IPA were found open in the front compartment of the vehicle, a 1981 Ford F-series pickup truck, dark blue, driven by Sky Clearwater."

"Yeah," Celia protested, "but they were only open because we were doing a ceremony."

Sky nudged her, probably hoping to shut her up. I wanted her to shut up too, but my telling her that would backfire for sure.

"It was *my* idea," she persisted. "Sky was just helping out and driving 'cause I left our car at Dad's, like I said I would, Mom." I nudged Jake's boot with my shoe. Wasn't he supposed to be advising us all to remain quiet? That's what the lawyers on *Law and Order* all did.

He recrossed his legs, looking serene.

"We were saying a prayer for Victor," Celia explained, fixing me with watery eyes. "We went out and sat near Camel Rock, lit a candle, and ate some *frito* pie like Victor liked and opened his favorite beer. We took a sip and poured some on the earth, *that's all*! If we drank it, Officer Nosy here wouldn't have found any beer left in the cans. The rest of the six-pack is in the truck."

Officer Nosy looked ready to follow up on his threat to charge Celia. He had connections to Sky and Walker, but none to my daughter. I could imagine what he saw in her, an angry girl with bad hair and a worse attitude. I, however, could picture her and Sky visiting Camel Rock, a natural rock formation that resembles a flattened mushroom more than any animal. I could also picture them honoring Victor with one of his favorite naughty snacks: an individual bag of Fritos, opened and topped with canned chili, shredded cheese, and onions. If only they'd stopped at the snack. And where had they gotten the beer? Another serious talk with my daughter was needed.

"We're sorry," I said again, reaching out a hand to let Celia know that it was time for us to leave. "My daughter is grieving the loss of a dear friend, but that is no excuse for illegal behavior. Please give me the ticket and we will pay it."

Walker insisted on paying half, a generous offer, as was his promise to inform Cass. I appreciated both, but I firmly rejected any payment. I knew the memorial picnic hadn't been Sky's idea. Besides, how bad could one ticket be? I could make Celia work it off.

Sergeant Day tore off a ticket sheet. "You can

pay online," he said. "By the deadline or you'll be in court."

I was glad that he and Jake had started talking basketball again. I didn't want the fancy lawyer to see me gawping at the bill. One hundred eighty-five dollars? "Come on," I told my daughter grumpily. "We'll talk about this when we get home."

"What are we going to do, walk home? Our car's at Dad's."

"*My* car is at your father's," I corrected. "Where you'll no longer be staying unsupervised. You're coming home with me."

Celia, to her credit, didn't argue. She did put in a snipe when Jake said he'd be driving us home.

"Way to go, Mom," she said, sarcasm oozing. "Now I know why you didn't answer your phone."

Chapter 13

I asked Jake to drop us off at Manny's house, hoping Manny would be out working and that Celia could, as she promised, find the car keys in her room. Her spaces were messier than the interior of my purse.

"I can wait," Jake offered. We sat in his warm car, watching as Celia trotted to the front door of Manny's adobe-coated rancher. It had been his grandparents' house, and I'd never considered fighting for it in the divorce. The house was his, too much so for me to want to live there. Still, it did hold some fond memories. Celia lit lights, and I pictured the familiar rooms and hallways she was walking through.

I turned to Jake, noting again how good he looked in his scarf. "You've already done so much for us," I said. "It's okay. We'll get our car and go straight home."

"We should do this again sometime," Jake said as I reluctantly made moves to leave the heated leather seats and warm male companionship. "I mean, not *this* in particular. Perhaps coffee without any police involvement?"

I got out thinking of my moratorium, but mostly about Celia. She was clearly hurting. I had to focus on her. On the other hand, wouldn't it be rude to refuse coffee with the man who drove me to not one but two law-enforcement meetings in a single day? I agreed that coffee would be nice. "My treat," I insisted.

He smiled, his blue-gray eyes twinkling. "Shall I call you, then, or expect to find you hitchhiking on the street?"

Calling definitely seemed like a date, I worried, as I wrote my number on the back of a grocery receipt. As he drove off, I worried some more. What did that grocery store receipt reveal? A run for snack food and chocolate? I assured myself that it didn't matter. Jake wouldn't call anyway, not after reconsidering the day of driving me around. Moratorium or not, I realized I'd be disappointed if he didn't.

"Hey, Mom, snap out of it." Celia appeared beside me, dangling keys. She had a duffel bag over one shoulder and her favorite faux-feather pillow under her arm. "I left Dad a note. You know he's going to be ticked, 'cause I told him I was staying a few more nights."

She opened the garage door. There my car was, in my old parking spot right next to the moving boxes I'd never unpacked. At first I'd told myself I was too busy to fully unpack. I had to help

Celia adjust. I had to find my own way around
and learn my new job. Down deep, however, I'd
known that my marriage was crumbling. Part of
me had been poised to move back home, until I
realized my home was here, in Santa Fe.

I squeezed through to the driver's-side door,
glancing at box labels as I went. *Kitchen pans:
Bundt, muffin, popover. Books, crafts, gardening.
Albums, Celia.* Nostalgia hit me. I missed parts of
my old life, and I definitely missed my collection
of miscellaneous cookware. It's not like I needed
to make cakes shaped like pumpkins or churn
ice cream in winter or whip up golf-ball-shaped
Danish pancakes in my ebelskiver pan, but I sure
liked the idea that I *could* if I wanted to. I almost
regretted negotiating a year's storage of my stuff
as part of the divorce. I couldn't afford a private
storage facility, though, and the tiny casita could
never accommodate the mountain of cookware. I
peeked in one of the boxes.

"You know Dad wants to throw all this stuff
out," Celia said. "He wants to get a motorcycle
and maybe an ATV and put in a workbench and
a punching bag and stuff. I told him that he could
toss my old kid junk."

If he tossed my ebelskiver pan or sentimental
items from Celia's babyhood, I'd want to use him
as a punching bag. Feeling slightly panicked, I
grabbed the first thing I found at the top of the
box—my waffle maker—and vowed that as soon
as life got back to some semblance of normal, I'd
find a new storage option.

Driving is not the best time for imparting life

lessons. On the other hand, Celia couldn't tromp off and avoid me if she was buckled into the front seat. At the first stoplight, I turned to my daughter and asked her point-blank whether she was drinking.

She shrugged and stared out the window.

"Celia," I said, aiming to sound gentle but firm. "I smelled alcohol on your breath the night of Victor's . . . the night Ariel brought you home. Is that why you left the car parked downtown?"

I focused on the narrow street and avoiding pothole craters. In my side vision I saw Celia fidget. I waited her out, an interrogation technique I learned from Flori.

"Yeah, fine," my daughter said under my gaze at a four-way stop. "I was at Gina's place, and her sister's in college and some of her friends were there having drinks and gave us some. I only had one hard cider. Maybe one and a half."

Celia and I have had the no-drinking/avoiding-peer-pressure talk before, several times in fact. I struggled to find the right words, all of which were met with rote, "I know, I know" responses from my daughter.

"And the beer?" I asked. "Where did you and Sky get that?"

Gina's sister was again implicated. "I've been helping Gina study for her SATs," Celia said. "We were all hanging out there and I saw the beer and thought of Victor." Her voice wobbled and my sternness caved.

"You know how I feel about this, Celia. But you did the right thing getting a ride the other night." I glanced over to see her staring out the side window.

"Yeah, I know," she said again, before adding, "I ran into Ariel. She's the one who insisted on driving me back home. She's cool."

She was cool, I thought, feeling unexpected gratitude for Manny's girlfriend.

Our serious talk ended in the driveway. Celia jumped out before I'd fully stopped the car and bolted inside, hugging her pillow. I got out too, clutching the waffle maker and shivering from both the cold and the chilly darkness of the main house. No candles would light Victor's altar. I wondered if I should make my own altar. Maybe his spirit would visit. His haunted spirit. In the distance, the Japanese-style lanterns atop Broomer's walls flickered. Their prettiness angered me.

For a moment I considered a Florilike maneuver of hoisting myself over his wall to spy. Then logic took over. What did I expect? To catch him videotaping a confession or laughing about murderous deeds with co-conspirators? Unlikely. I was about to go inside when movement caught my eye.

"Hello?" I put down the waffle maker and fumbled to light the miniflashlight on my key chain. Swinging its weak beam into the darkness, I anticipated the glowing eyes of a raccoon or the toothy sneer of a coyote. The clang of glass and metal came from the area by Victor's back door where he kept his recycling bin.

"Is someone there?" I clapped my hands. "Shoo, get out of here!" Wildlife frequently visited our yard, following the creek downstream from a nearby bird sanctuary and open space. The sanctuary connected to pine and piñon-dotted hills and miles of forest, home to deer, foxes, coyotes, and even some mountain lions and bears.

This was no coyote, and it startled me more than a bear. A human form, hunched and massive, appeared in the thin beam of my flashlight and then quickly disappeared into the shadows.

"Hey! Come back here!" I yelled. I immediately regretted these words. A giant was skulking around a murder scene and I yell for him to come on over? To my horror, the figure reappeared under Victor's bluish porch light, where he stopped. I froze too, afraid to move but ready to bolt for the casita if he approached. The front door would likely be unlocked. That thought also filled me with horror. Celia was inside. What if he reached the door before I did?

"I'm calling 911!" I bellowed, reaching for the waffle maker and waving it wildly as I backed toward the door. "Nine-one-one!"

The figure spun and disappeared, leaving only the sounds of rustling brush. Celia appeared at the door, wide-eyed.

"Mom? What's going on?"

"Coyotes," I told her, pushing her inside and then locking the dead bolt and the chain lock.

"You told coyotes you're calling the cops? Gosh, Mom, Victor's death really is getting to you." The kettle, having called the pot black, made a huffy snort and returned to her bedroom.

If the police did drive by during the night, as the dispatcher assured me they would, I didn't notice. They surely didn't come down the driveway or I would have heard them. During the long night, I woke to the slightest groans of the old beams and rustlings of leaves. When I did sleep, my dreams morphed into anxiety nightmares. By five-forty, unable to keep my eyes closed any longer, I gave up and got up, pulling on jeans and a sweater. Bits of colored icing clung to the cuff. I brushed them off, wishing the laundry would do itself. It wouldn't, and neither would the grocery shopping, finding storage space in my tiny home, and sorting out the new me. My dwindling supply of clean clothes also meant that I'd have to visit the little utility room and laundry attached to the main house, exactly where I'd seen the creepy lurker last night.

I peeked out the living room windows, checking for anything or anyone unusual. The only eyes that looked back belonged to two ravens playing with an old apple. One tossed the withered fruit in the air as the other cawed, flapping its glossy black wings and dancing on springy toes. Some people disparage crows and their bigger brethren, ravens, as nuisances or bad omens. I've always admired these impressive, intelligent birds and was happy to discover that they're celebrated in New Mexican art and lore. However, as the two crows flew off to join others, a darker thought struck me. A murder . . . that's what a group of crows was called. The flock gathered in a giant cottonwood, directly over Victor's house, cawing madly.

Coffee didn't help my edginess. Nor did the

lack of food in the house. I was about to resort to an expired granola bar when I heard footsteps crunching on gravel, moving toward the kitchen window. Fear spun up the adrenaline of too much caffeine and too little sleep. Grabbing a marble rolling pin, I tiptoed to the window, ready to roll out some serious defense moves.

Through the cotton curtain, I spotted a blurry form moving near the window. What if last night's intruder was scoping out more break-in prospects? I decided to make the first move.

"Make my day!" I yelled, yanking open the curtain and waving the rolling pin. This was another move I immediately regretted. Not only did I sound like an idiot, I pulled down the curtain rod and tipped over a sugar canister and a potted basil. That, and Flori looked ready to wet her knickers from laughing so hard.

"Oh dear," she said, removing her glasses to wipe away tears of glee as I let her in the front door, the place most people would go instead of skulking around the windows. "I shouldn't be laughing, but surprises make me giggle."

"Is the doorbell not working?" I asked.

"Now now, don't be cranky, *cariño*. I didn't want to wake you up after your big date and all that police fuss over in Tesuque. I thought I'd peek and see if you were up. You're the one waving around that rolling pin and yelling like Dirty Harry." She carried a canvas shopping bag in one hand. Binoculars big enough to spy on Albuquerque swung from her neck.

"It wasn't a date," I muttered. The binoculars were an ominous sign. Flori was not a birdwatcher.

And I wasn't going to bother asking how she knew about my night. Dancing, drinking cocoa, and meeting with law enforcement in public places would be as easy as candy on Halloween for her gossip network. Still, I couldn't help being a little impressed. And a little suspicious.

"You don't have a GPS device stuck to me, do you?"

My elderly friend made a snorting sound, waving off modern tracking devices as if they were useless newfangled trinkets. "I could give you the details, but we don't have time." She brushed past me to the kitchen. I recognized the bakery box she pulled from the shopping bag.

Any lingering grumpiness vanished. "You went to Clafoutis! You're an angel, Flori!" I reached for the box, anticipating the treasures it held. The owners of Clafoutis, bona fide pastry chefs straight from France, made delectable goodies using sinfully perfect loads of butter. My savory favorite was their flaky, buttery croissant wrapped around ham and cheese. On the sweet side, I could barely pick a favorite because everything was so good. I loved the éclairs and the moist little almond cakes and of course their namesake tart. A clafouti is like a flan, but firmer and studded with fruit. Cherries are the typical choice, although the bakery also makes versions with plums, berries, or bananas.

My hand hovered over the box as I imagined the possible treasures inside. A firm slap ended the fantasizing.

"Not yet," Flori said, pushing the bakery box aside. "We'll get to that later. Right now we have to get going. I don't want the whole world up and seeing us."

"And what are we doing?" I asked, looking longingly at the pastry box.

"Snooping of course."

I should have known.

Chapter 14

Flori was out the door before I could ask the who, what, and where of our snoop. Aiming to set a good example, I wrote Celia a note: *Out with Flori. Back soon?* Realizing I should set a better example than that, I recorded the exact time and invited Celia to help herself to the bakery box. Then I grabbed my keys, locked the front door, and prepared myself for the battle over who would drive, feeling way too edgy and hungry for Flori's hair-raising pedal stomping. I expected to find her revving her old boat of a Cadillac. The white whale sat in the driveway, but no silver bun poked above the steering wheel. She wasn't impatiently tapping her foot by the door or sneaking around the wrong side of the police tape either.

"Flori?" When several more calls went unanswered, I began to worry. I should have warned her about the skulking figure. I should have insisted that we go outside together. A muffled voice came from the back garden. I thought I heard my name and the word "Help." Now I was scared. Regretting that I hadn't brought the rolling pin, I grabbed the first thing at hand on the porch, a decorative broom made of cinnamon twigs.

"I'm coming, Flori!" I took the most direct route, stumbling through Victor's rock garden, dodging agave spines, and hurdling over a small stone wall before skidding to a stop near the stream. Water trickled over smooth stones, creating a soft burble and blurring the muttered Spanish emanating from a thicket of creek willows.

"Flori? Hang on!" Willow branches whipped at my face as I forged in, one hand shielding my eyes, the other dragging the cinnamon broom. In a tiny clearing of trampled ground, I found her. She stood alone and perfectly safe, pointing to a line of red paint. Pushing up her Harry Potter spectacles, she sniffed the air. "What is that delightful smell . . . cinnamon? That reminds me, we have to get into Victor's kitchen. I want his recipe for *bizcochitos*. That man wrote everything down, and it would be a sin for a recipe like that to be lost to the spirit world if no one went and found it."

With a sigh, I put my broom into an at-ease position. I really needed a pastry. If she'd bought only one éclair, I was going to take it. No polite deferring until others made their choices. Boldly declaring what I wanted would be part of the new me.

"What are you doing with that broom?" Flori asked.

Any explanation about saving her from a hulking giant using a glorified potpourri stick seemed silly now. I asked what she was doing in the shrubbery.

"Following the trail." She pointed to the line of red paint. "See this? It's probably a surveyor's mark. I found a little mark against a tree up closer to the house, but mostly the paint line's been dug up or hidden under rocks. Except here."

Right, because who else but Flori and a Santa Fe surveyor would bother to thrash through a willow thicket to scout out a line? I needed to get my bearings. After holding back the branches for Flori to pass, I squeezed back out to examine the alignment of fences and yards.

"Up there." Flori pointed. "That pine tree has the other paint mark."

From where we stood to the pine, we were a good four feet inside Gabe and Victor's property, according to the fence line. I ran my hand along the rough bark still attached to the fir limbs that made up the attractive barrier. Coyote fencing, it was called around here. Sometimes the branches have different heights, a look that works well against a sprawling desert sky. Victor's fence had a neatly trimmed top, but the logs, slightly thicker than my arm, were lashed tightly together and ended about three feet above my head. Unless I boosted Flori onto my shoulders, there was no way we could see over.

Flori cupped her hands to her face and peered through small gaps in the logs. "We need to get over there," she said. "That Broomer man is number one on my suspect list. Which reminds me, here's my list so far. If you see any of these people around town, keep an eye out for suspicious behavior."

She produced a small day planner from her coat pocket and thrust it at me. I opened to the first page, New Year's day five years ago. The date sparked memories. Was that the day Manny and I tried to go into Chicago for brunch, but he got called on duty? Or was that the year when Celia and I went to Mom's on our own and Manny watched football with the guys? Images of Mom's New Year's staple—cold shrimp poised above bottled cocktail sauce—flashed through my head. She'd already invited me and Celia for every upcoming holiday, but I wasn't sure when we could go. Thanksgiving seemed too soon, Christmas too busy. Maybe New Year's, though I'd yet to broach the prospect to Celia, Manny, or Flori.

I shook my head to refocus.

"I've numbered my suspects by the day of the month," Flori explained, pointing to the number one.

I flipped through the days. On each, Flori had listed suspects and their questionable characteristics.

"Okay, you beat me," I said, reaching February third and the last name. "But the mailman, really?" I squinted, trying to read Flori's spidery scrawl. "He's unreliable, but I don't see him as a murderer."

"I heard that he tramples flower beds on purpose and delivers packages without postage," Flori said, sticking her nose in another gap. "Now I'll admit, most of those are long shots, but you can't be too careful. Friends, coworkers, relatives, neighbors . . . they all have to be checked and eliminated."

"Suspect number twenty-eight, Dalia Crawford, left a basket of jelly and tarot cards on my porch this afternoon," I said, wishing I had a pen to cross off Dalia's name. "Homemade jelly, no less. Made from organic currants she and Phillip grew themselves."

"There you have it. Shows that they're handy and know the layout of your property," Flori said stubbornly. "Anyway, they had opportunity, and I do not trust tarot readings. They try to tell you what to do."

This from a woman who followed her sixth sense, I thought, continuing to flip through Flori's list. "It's a wonder you didn't list me."

"Don't be silly. I eliminated you straight away along with Linda and Celia, and then Bernard, since I can vouch for his whereabouts. And the Espinosa couple next to the Crawfords. They're wintering in Florida, although why anyone would want all that humidity . . ." She listed a few more suspects to eliminate, including a school bus driver, the UPS man (despite his disturbing predilection to wear shorts in all weather), and Gabe, the out-of-town sister Teresa, and first cousins Albert and Lucinda, who were clearly distraught. "It's the first two that are my main suspects," Flori said resolutely. "The rest are backup, in case we get short on ideas."

I flipped back to January first and second, feeling quite pleased with myself. "These are the main suspects on my list too. Broomer is number one, and Jay-Jay number two."

Flori took her nose out of the fence and beamed at me. "Good girl! You found out about Jay-Jay? I knew you would. You're a natural at snooping, just like you are at chile sauces. Now, let's pay a visit to suspect number one."

I was glad I'd worn old sneakers instead of my usual leather Keens. On the other hand, the Keens claimed to be waterproof. The sneakers flooded instantly with water that felt like liquid ice.

"Ooo," Flori said, stepping into the frigid creek. "Now that'll get your blood flowing in the morning."

So would sugar and butter in French pastry form, along with a full night's sleep. "I don't know what we're expecting to find," I grumbled. Checking out the other side of the fence had seemed like a fine idea, until my toes turned to ice.

Flori made *tsk-tsk* sounds. "I should have let you eat first. You're light-headed and petulant. Of course we don't *know* what we're going to find until we find it. That's what investigating's all about, as you well know. You can also bet that your ex, Detective Do-Little, isn't going to come back here to investigate. It's up to us."

The part about Manny was likely true. Having set his mind on suicide, he'd drag his heels at any other explanation. Finding Victor's killer might be up to us, and maybe he was only a coyote fence away. But did we have to wade through ice water to get there? My grumpiness evaporated, however, when we reached Broomer's yard. An astounding Southwest version of a Japanese garden stood before us. Ink-black river rocks curved to a sea of pebbles, raked to perfection. Junipers resembled ancient bonsai trees. Sleek bamboo swayed gracefully, setting off a small raised teahouse featuring sliding glass doors and what looked like authentic tatami mats.

"Mmmm," Flori said. "Not much into the local aesthetic, is he? Very suspicious."

Awesome was more like it. I forgot everything my mother ever taught me about trespassing—as in, never trespass—and made my way up rustic stone steps to the teahouse, following the sounds of cascading water. Every so often the flow was interrupted by a hollow clack, like wooden cymbals.

"Wow," I said, assuming Flori was right behind me. "I've never seen anything like this."

"Like the view, do you?"

I jumped sideways and right into full-frontal view of a fully naked Broomer. "Oh my gosh, I'm so sorry!" I stuttered. I lurched backward but found myself blocked by bamboo.

"Come to join me for a skinny dip?" Broomer sank back into the steaming, rock-lined pool the size of an oversized hot tub. Rounded boulders lined the water. A waterfall cascaded over a rocky ledge, falling in sheets behind his blond hair. Slightly raised and off to one side, a bamboo tube fed another round, deep pool. This was the source of the wooden clacking. Water flowed through one bamboo tube to another that collected water until it reached a tipping point. Once emptied, the collector sprang upward, striking a rock. It would have been hypnotizing to watch, if Broomer hadn't been there.

"Want to slip into that cold pool first? Go for it. You'll jump right in with me after that." He laughed as the bamboo clonked behind him.

I kept my eyes on the view behind his head as I stammered out an explanation.

"We were . . . ah . . . looking for something down by the creek and we ended up on your side and—geez, your garden is amazing and, sorry, we couldn't help looking, I mean looking at the garden, not, I mean . . . ah . . ."

He was clearly enjoying my discomfort way too much. A wolflike grin spread across his face, broadening as my face turned hotter than Cass's molten metals.

"We?" he asked as my explanations fizzled out. "Did you bring along a friend? The more the better, I say."

Flori appeared beside me, not bothering to keep her gaze abovewater. "That bath looks pretty good, but at my age, I skinny dip only after dark."

Broomer laughed. "Sounds good to me, ladies. I'll set the mood lighting if you want to drop by tonight. But now, if you don't mind, I have to get to my gallery. Either one of you ladies hands me that towel, or . . ." He started to rise.

Flori stood next to the blue piece of cloth he'd motioned toward. "Towel!" I bellowed, sounding like a surgeon in need of an emergency clamp.

Time did not seem to be of the essence for Flori.

She dangled the dish-towel-sized rag between two fingers. "Not so fast," she said. "We have some questions for you. Let him have it, Rita."

"We can ask them later," I said, tugging at Flori's elbow. "When everyone has eaten pastry and put on pants."

"Ask away. I'm intrigued," our naked host said, dashing any hopes I had of extracting Flori. He adjusted his position, leaning back, both elbows resting on smooth boulders. I focused on the waterfall above his head.

He waved toward a rock carved out to form a seat. "If you won't come in, you might as well sit. Help yourself to some green tea if you want." He nodded toward a cast-iron teapot. "There are cups in the teahouse. My blend today is a roasted organic *sencha* from Kyoto, highlighted with premium Darjeeling tips."

We both declined tea. Flori plopped herself on the stone seat, sticking her wet feet out toward the heat. My own feet had frozen to numb in the sopping sneakers, but I wasn't about to remove any item of clothing in the presence of Broomer.

"Where did you go after that fight you had with the brothers the night Victor died?" I asked, trying to keep my voice neutral.

"Yes, where?" Flori said, playing bad cop to my neutral questioner. She held the towel in both hands, as if ready to snap Broomer into answering.

"Ah, so that's what you're poking around about? I'll tell you where I was. I was here, trying to relax after such a stressful, unnecessary encounter. You try dealing with a hard-headed, property-stealing neighbor like Gabriel. Victor, I had no big problem

with. He was willing to listen. His brother is cost-
ing me a fortune in time and legal bills."

Was this why Victor had contacted Jake? Maybe
he'd simply been mistaken about Jake's legal specialty or thought that since he got guilty people
off, he could do anything. "But all this is about
a few feet of land?" I asked. "Why bother? Your
yard looks great."

"This is a garden, not a yard. And why bother?
Do you know what property's worth in this
neighborhood?" He waved his hands, sending up
a splash that landed on my knee. "I'm going to
build a meditation hut over there and I need certain dimensions for proper flow. More than that,
it's the principle. You buy land, it's yours. Case
closed, except with those yahoos next door."

Fighting in the name of peaceful meditation
boggled my mind. I supposed I should have been
glad that Broomer wasn't into Asian stick fighting
or swordplay. I nudged Flori, hoping she'd leave
with me. Instead, she subjected Broomer to more
questions.

"So, no alibi," she said, brazenly eyeing Broomer
from head to naked toe.

"Alibi?" He stretched an ankle over the side of
the pool. "I need an alibi for a suicide?"

When neither Flori nor I said anything, he
frowned. "What are you implying? It wasn't a
suicide? Don't tell me someone else shot him?" A
stream of curses was followed by a whiny, "Why
does this always happen to me?"

How much more self-centered could this guy be?
"Victor's the one who's dead," I snapped, neither
confirming nor denying our suspicion of murder.

"Dead guys don't have to worry about their property values, do they? It was bad enough to be by a suicide house, and now it's a murder house?" He stood abruptly. I looked away but not before seeing Flori toss his towel into the far side of the pool.

Chapter 15

"You should never trespass," I told my daughter, ignoring Flori's rolling of eyes.

"Who said anything about trespassing?" Celia asked, her surly voice refreshed by a long night's sleep. Only the racket of me accidentally tipping cookie tins onto the tile floor had gotten her out of bed.

"I'm just saying," I said. "Trespassing leads to unsafe and unexpected encounters."

"Like naked men," Flori chimed in.

"Absolutely *do not* talk to naked men," I clarified, shooting Flori a glare.

Celia took advantage of my bungling attempt at motherly advice and snagged the sole chocolate-covered éclair. "Sure, Mom, whatever. No trespassing. What were you two doing this morning anyhow? You have forest stuff stuck in your hair."

I reached up and felt around.

"Over your ear," Flori instructed. "A bamboo leaf. And maybe a spider."

"Ahh!" I doubled over and pawed my hair frantically, feeling around for legs and worse. A leaf and several twigs fell out. The absence of a spider wasn't entirely reassuring. "We were looking into some things," I said, tentatively patting my hair and composure back into place and surveying the bakery box. I narrowed the choice down to a soft raisin bun wrapped around custard cream, and the éclair with a coffee-flavored glaze and filling. Loving anything with rich vanilla custard, I decided on the bun.

"We were trespassing," Flori admitted, again to my maternal dismay.

"Which you shouldn't do." I waved the bun for emphasis. "Never trespass. Obey all signs and speed limits too."

"That's where you saw the naked man, when you were trespassing?" Celia now sounded mildly interested.

I started to protest. Flori, however, had the floor and Celia's attention. "Yes, dear, your neighbor Mr. Broomer. Listen to your mother and never go over there. That man is untrustworthy and sits about naked in the morning when honest, hardworking people should be getting on with their day."

Celia polished off her éclair and washed it down with orange juice. "Broomer's a creep. I could have told you guys that. Victor and me, we hit a badminton birdie over there by mistake and

Broomer threw a fit when I went around through the creek to get it."

"A fit? He threatened you?" I'd worried about what my daughter was doing away from home, and look what was going on right outside our door: knife/gunfights, a likely murder, a skulker, and a naked creep/possible murderer.

"Maybe we should move," I said, ready to start packing immediately. "I could look into that El Matador condo complex by Fort Marcy Park. We could use the gym and sports fields across the street, and they have that nice secure entry gate with the metal bull and matador on it and—"

"Oh Mom, calm down," my daughter said, exasperation evident. "I meant that he's a creep, that's all. There're creeps everywhere. He had some guys over there and the whole yard stunk of pot. I told Victor. He said he'd deal with it."

Beside me, Flori rapped her fingers against the colorful Mexican tiles of my kitchen table. I could guess what she was thinking. Maybe Broomer was dealing in more than art. Maybe Victor found out. If she was having such thoughts, she didn't let on in front of Celia.

"I need a helper to watch my display table up at the International Folk Museum this weekend," Flori said, "so I'll be rested for the *pan de muerto* contest on Monday evening." She took the last croissant and smeared butter on the already buttery pastry. "You wouldn't know anyone who could help me, do you, Celia?"

When my daughter made a noncommittal grunt, I nudged her foot under the table. Flori knew about Celia's speeding/open container/surly attitude ticket. It was kind of her to ask. I mentally willed my daughter to be wise and polite enough to accept her offer.

"I guess I need some extra money to, ah . . . pay for something stupid," Celia said grudgingly.

"Fabulous!" Flori said. "I bet you're a great skull decorator."

Celia actually smiled.

S he's fine," Flori assured me later at Tres Amigas. "I did silly things when I was that age too, like cutting my own hair. I didn't go and dip my head in black ink, though."

I didn't reveal that Celia's weed-whacker hairstyle had been professionally and expensively inflicted. We stood in the café kitchen, watching as Celia and Addie, headphones wedged in their ears, applied colored icing to sugar skulls. So far Addie had produced a single skull decorated in smudged polka dots. Celia, meanwhile, was a skull assembly line, her artistic drive heightened by Flori's financial incentive. Flori had generously offered her half the day's profits from skull sales. Hopefully she'd make a lot. The folk museum, located on Museum Hill, was an ideal venue, stuffed with handicrafts from all over the world, including some of Victor's painted saints. Cass was right. Victor's art, already museum quality, would jump in value now that he was gone. Someone would be inheriting a fortune. The only question was who.

"I really appreciate your helping Celia out," I said to Flori, shaking off these thoughts. "Helping us out, I should say."

She smiled. "Sugar skulls won't put a dent in a Tesuque traffic ticket, I'm afraid. Bernard, the old fool, got three of those one summer. That's when I put my foot down about him gambling out at Buffalo Thunder. He lost more money driving there and getting tickets than he did at the infernal slot machines."

I asked about Bernard's bum hip and listened as Flori complained about her husband's ailments, real and imagined. She didn't fool me with her gruff talk. I'd seen her and big white-haired Bernard dancing on the Plaza together, cheek-to-cheek, sweet as can be. I'd even spotted them making out behind the bandstand one summer night. If you're making out in public in your eighties, you must be pretty darned in love.

The cowbell hanging from the front door clanged. I looked up, half expecting and hoping to see Jake's cowboy silhouette. Instead, short legs, a pair of arms, and a huge stack of boxes stumbled in. I rushed to help Linda.

"Boxes for packing up skulls," she said, out of breath.

"One hour until we pack up!" Flori yelled in Celia's direction. Celia nodded and picked up her pace. Linda, freed of boxes, sagged into a chair by the fireplace.

"I'm exhausted," she declared, accepting my offer of hot Earl Grey tea.

"Too many tamales?" I asked, pouring hot water into a teapot for us to share. Addie abandoned her skull, trilling happily about a "nice, proper cuppa." Only Celia, committed to continued skull production, declined a tea break.

"Hundreds of tamales," Linda groaned, twining her fingers in her thick, salt-and-pepper hair and tugging it away from her face. "Tamales for the museum event, tamales for my cart, tamales for the Día de los Muertos festival on the Plaza, tamales for the café. I wish the event coordinators had kept everything to Saturday and Sunday like they used to." She paused to take a sip of tea. "But I would have been okay for today. I had the timing right and my corn husks soaked and laid out, and then . . ." She took another sip of tea.

"Then what?" Flori demanded. She has no patience for suspense. It's the reason she's so driven to snoop and won't watch movies unless she knows the ending, and why she peeks at the final chapter of novels before page one.

Linda avoided her mother's stare. "Gabe. That poor man. He wanted to come over and visit, so I said yes and . . ."

"And?" Flori prompted. "Did you show some interest in that man?"

Addie, her pinkie finger raised above her teacup, backed up Flori. "He's a right nice chap that Gabriel."

"Mama! Addie!" Linda protested. "You know my feelings about relationships, and such talk is not appropriate at this time. Gabriel is delusional with grief, bless his heart and the soul of dear Victor." She made a dramatic sign of the cross and looked heavenward.

Flori made a huffy sound. "Well I didn't mean

for you to do anything sinful, dear." She shot me a pointed look, like I'd be taking her side on this. I held up my palms. Flori and each of her three daughters are strong-minded and stubborn in different ways. No way was I getting involved. I had enough to worry about with Flori's demands that I show interest in Jake Strong. However, I couldn't help being curious.

"What did Gabe want to talk about?" I asked.

Linda said something in Spanish, the gist of which I understood in my rudimentary *español* as "crazy talk." Switching to English, she said, "He says that it is like we are teenagers again. Like time has gone backward." She paused to scowl at her mother's and Addie's *awwww* sounds. "We are not teenagers. I am no teenager. I think he only says these things because he is all alone. He misses his brother."

"Poor man," Flori said, verbalizing my thoughts. "I hope you were nice to him, Linda."

Linda assumed a pout and a surly voice that could have come straight from Celia. "Of course I was nice, Mama. Too nice. I listened to all his talk and spent the rest of the night worrying that I'd given him the wrong idea. Such worries will affect my tamales. The masa felt heavy in my hands. The tamales will be tough." With a dire shaking of her head, she stomped off to take a seat by Celia, who acknowledged her with an upward nod and handed her a paintbrush.

Flori leaned in toward my ear, whispering so loud it reverberated off my eardrum. "Tamales, that's all that girl thinks of, despite being widowed and free. Rita, let it be a lesson. Don't get so wrapped up in tamales that you get old and miss out on something good. Pinch that strong and handsome Jake Strong on the butt next time you see him. Trust me, it's a pleasure."

Addie, snickering, topped off my tea. Flori tottered off to check the rise on her *pan de muerto* dough, a final test version before she started the contest batch tomorrow. I thought about what she'd said. Not only about Jake but about age too. Forty hadn't been bad, but now I was *into* my forties. According to women's magazines, this was the time when I should be reinventing my life in some fabulous way. Like discovering an innate knack for making goat cheese or inventing a bestselling cell phone app or becoming a pillow designer for the rich and fabulous. None of these prospects seemed feasible or what I wanted to do, except for the goat cheese, but that fell into the impossible-dream category. The rich and fabulous, however, reminded me that Gloria's Halloween/Día de los Muertos party was tonight. I had nothing black-tie skeleton to wear.

I called to Flori, saying I needed to run an errand and pretending I didn't hear her demand to know where. I knew one thing: I didn't want to be responsible for Flori crashing Gloria's party.

Chapter 16

I stood in front of Cass's studio, realizing that in last night's swirl of dancing, cocoa, police, and skulkers, I'd neglected something vital. I'd failed to tell my best friend about my daughter getting her son in trouble with the law, not to mention with his father and possibly his tribal elders. That surely broke all sorts of friend and mom codes of conduct. Feeling guilty, I peeked in her studio window, inset deep in thick adobe walls. Strings of white lights twinkled across the beamed ceiling of the cozy front room where Cass sold her jewelry. If customers aren't around, she works on new pieces in her attached studio room. Now, however, she stood behind the row of display cases, holding up silver chains. Two women in denim skirts and cowgirl boots pressed their noses to the cases, pointing out items to try on. I hovered outside, not wanting to interrupt a potential sale and worrying about what to say.

Walker had said he was going to call Cass. He seemed like a man of his word, so she likely already knew. This sparked a new worry. If she knew and hadn't called me, maybe she was mad about Celia goading her son into questionable activities. The worst before this was when Celia convinced Sky to help her graffiti-tag cacti for an art project. Her use of water-washable paint hadn't stopped her art teacher from giving both teens mandatory cactus restoration work. Cass brushed that troublemaking off as artistic license. But getting nabbed by the police was in no way artistic.

Cass looked up, saw me, and mouthed something I couldn't understand, holding up her index finger in a *Soon* or *Wait* gesture. Was she mad? I was worse at reading emotions than I was at reading lips. To avoid further speculation, I turned from the window and leaned up against the adobe wall, looking out over the postcard-pretty scene surrounding me.

At the nearby cathedral, bells rang out the hour and reminded me that I wanted to light a candle for Victor. Down the street, the ancient *portales* along Palace Avenue would soon be decorated with pine boughs and Christmas lights. Already, piñon smoke scented the air, turning my culinary thoughts to baking and hearty stews. To distract myself from worries, I focused on recipes for roasted winter squashes. I was pondering cheese choices for butternut lasagna when Cass's customers came outside, followed a few steps behind by Cass.

We watched as the ladies jaywalked toward the

cathedral, swinging Cass's brown-paper gift bags
with colorful ribbon handles.

"Good sale?" I asked, thinking that *So, my daughter and your son, hauled in by the police* wouldn't be
my best opener.

"Any sale is good these days. That one was
good, but not like the bounty of Gloria," she said,
and then groaned. "Gloria's party . . ."

"That's why I'm here," I said. "What to wear . . .
that and . . ." I let my sentence drop off, hoping to
feel out if Cass knew. When she only raised an eyebrow, I burst out, "You haven't talked to Walker,
have you? He said he'd call and so I thought I'd
let him tell you, not that there's much to tell since
nothing much happened, except that the open
beer can is unforgivable and surely Celia's idea.
I swear, she'll be paying for the ticket by making
sugar skulls for the rest of her teenage years if she
has to. Please don't be mad at us!"

I paused for air, my stomach turning as I registered Cass's deepening scowl.

"Sky's staying with his father this week," she
said, still frowning. "Walker texted me and said
the kids got stopped for speeding out at the
Pueblo. That area's a speed trap, so I figured it was
nothing."

"Oh," I said, and after more hemming and
umming, explained Celia's offering of Victor's favorite beer at one of his beloved spots. I finished
with, "She'll be grounded forever if I have to."

"It was a rather sweet sentiment."

"What?" I said. "Well, yeah, sweet but stupid."

"Indeed. Stupid about the beer. I'll talk to Sky
this afternoon," Cass promised. "He swears he

doesn't drink. His father has talked to him a lot about that. But how can we know? It's not like we can fix breathalyzers to their necks." She reached inside her shop and turned the door sign to BACK SOON. Then she gave me a quick hug. "I know you're worried about Celia, but she'll be okay. She's tough and smart and is getting to know herself."

Everyone except the school counselor kept telling me that. I was worried, but a little less, knowing that Celia had a good friend like Sky. Our talk turned to Gloria-appropriate attire as we set out in search of dress shops. The first stop did not go well.

"We have to get out of here," I whispered to Cass. We were trapped between an overenthusiastic saleslady and racks of brightly colored dresses, the flowery kind with lace and frills and velvet trim.

Cass flipped through a rack of velvet pants with price tags nearing my weekly income. "You're right. This is definitely not the black-tie Día de los Muertos look." She slipped between racks, me following, as the saleslady zeroed in on other shoppers. When we were back outside she said, "I have a go-to black party dress I could wear. That and some face paint should do it. In fact, I have a couple of little black dresses if you want to borrow one."

"Love to, but not unless you have one that's a size eight or ten or maybe twelve." I patted the extra padding on my hips and eyed her outfit, a slender orange and white striped sweater dress topped with a jeans jacket and big wooly scarf.

If I managed to squeeze into that, I'd look like a lumpy throw pillow.

When Cass didn't offer up a not-so-little black dress, I guessed that borrowing was not an option. I did another mental sorting of my wardrobe. Who didn't have a go-to black party dress? Me, that's who. I used to have one, several in fact, back in my pre-Manny days. But cop parties don't tend to require black ties or cocktail dresses, and Manny's criteria for going out focused on the availability of beer on tap, sports on TV, and wings on the menu. While I might feel like an interloper at Gloria's movers and shakers' party, I was looking forward to the excuse to dress up. As long as it didn't cost me a fortune.

"Double Take?" I said, naming one of our favorite consignment stores near the Railyard District. We were going to a glorified costume party, after all, not a dinner at Buckingham Palace.

Cass agreed readily, and we set off toward Aztec Street, weaving down side streets to avoid crowds of tourists. We could not, however, avoid meeting people we knew. I don't mind a bit of chitchat. Cass dreads small talk as much as parties.

"It's a problem of living here too long," she grumbled after we'd been stopped a fifth time by someone wanting to discuss the possibility of snow. "Sometimes I just want to get from one side of town to the other without any bother."

"Perhaps you could find some sunglasses and a ski mask at Double Take," I joked, turning the corner. I hadn't made it one step onto the next street when Cass grabbed my shoulder and yanked me back behind the corner building.

"I know them!" she said.

"You know everyone." I stepped back onto Aztec Street, Double Take and its potential treasures within sight.

"No, no, you don't get it." Cass tugged me back again.

I considered my hands pretty strong from hefting dough and heavy pans all day. I had nothing on Cass. Her hands could bend metal and command fire. I stayed where I was and listened.

"That's your suspect list out there!" she said. "That's Jay-Jay, Victor's ex, and look who she's chatting up."

I peeked around the building and immediately ducked back. "Broomer!"

Cass muttered about Jay-Jay and her penchant for tacky gold clothing as I punched in my cell phone's code, hoping that its randomly working camera would actually work. When it miraculously switched to camera mode, I took Cass by the elbow. "We're two friends walking down the street . . ."

"Right," she said, sounding dubious. "Isn't that what we were doing anyway? Look, I don't want to get stuck talking to that awful woman. Double Take has another entrance. Let's go around the block and avoid them."

I peeked down the street again. There they were. Main suspects one and two. Together and possibly colluding. I wanted a photo as evidence to take to Detective Bunny, I told Cass.

She grudgingly relented. "Okay, but don't say I didn't try to warn you."

I suspected that Cass would later have an "I told you so" opportunity. By appearance alone, I didn't like what I saw. It wasn't Jay-Jay's lemon-yellow hair that threw me. It was her wardrobe, dripping with dead animals, from a fur beret and fur vest to what looked like Ugg boots covered in a deceased fox. Gold spandex clung to her legs, and sunglasses the size of rhinestone-crusted pie plates covered her face. She was head-to-toe glitter and pelt and waving her hands dramatically in front of Broomer. He was—thankfully—fully dressed, and standing as still as a scowling statue in front of his art gallery.

"Okay," I said, as we neared. "I'm going to hold up my phone like I'm trying to make a call and . . . there!" I pushed the photo button a few times before holding the phone to my ear, acting out a call that didn't go through. The playback function confirmed that I'd achieved three blurry yet recognizable photographs.

"Cass Sathers! Where have you been hiding?" The pie-plate glasses turned our way, along with bejeweled fingers, waving as if to cast a spell on us. Cass greeted Jay-Jay through a clenched smile. She introduced me, and I made a show of introducing Cass to Broomer, who looked about as happy to see me as Cass felt about Jay-Jay.

"Well now," I said, beaming at the art dealers/suspects. "What a small world. How do you two know each other?"

"Art," Broomer said, sounding testy. "What

else in this town?" His attitude perked up as he leered over my shoulder at Cass. "Ah, now here's a friend you can bring around to my hot tub anytime." Getting a steely stare from Cass and a firm thwack from Jay-Jay, he shrugged. "I have to get back to work."

"Oh no you don't, you handsome beast." Jay-Jay grasped Broomer with manicured talons and turned to Cass, who edged back against me. "Cass, you know I would adore representing your work, especially if I could talk you into adding some gemstones and beads to your collection. And of course gold!" She cackled.

I noticed Cass's clenching and unclenching fists, our supposed relaxation move. She did not seem relaxed. Neither did Broomer. His pinched, red face looked ready to erupt. I'd seen the knife-wielding yelling side of Broomer and I didn't want to see it again. Hopefully he'd keep it together on a public street. Or maybe I should be hoping the opposite. If he showed his true character, others could see him as a suspect. I kept my cell phone ready, finger poised over the camera button. If he threw a fit, or a punch, I'd photograph and run. Cass would be ready to spring. She was already inching away.

Jay-Jay leaned into Broomer, practically reclining against his side. "I was telling Laurence here that he needs more local art. Tourists don't come all the way to Santa Fe for orange Buddhas." She pointed a fingernail, enameled in gold glitter, toward Broomer's showroom. Buddhas of all shapes and colors stood, sat, and lounged amidst gorgeous scrolls and porcelain vases.

Broomer made a huffy sound. "I have no interest in jackalopes and kachina dolls." He wrenched himself from Jay-Jay's clutches and stomped over to his gallery, yanking open the door. Incense wafted out along with the soft gong of door chimes. There was nothing soothing about the way he slammed the glass door and pointedly locked it.

"Remember our deal, sweet-cheeks!" Jay-Jay yelled after him. She probably meant to sound jovial. She sounded like the wicked witch of the Southwest.

Cass had edged her way off the curb and was taking up a coveted parking spot. A white mini-van beeped at her. She waved the driver off and motioned for me to join her. "We gotta go," she said. "Must get you that dress, Rita."

But I wasn't going anywhere. As Cass waited for me in the street, manicured talons sank into my forearms and the scent of musky gardenia perfume made my eyes water. "So you're Broomer's neighbor, are you?" Jay-Jay asked. "Which side? The old DeVale mansion to the east? The Chavez estate across the way?"

"Ah . . . the casita in the backyard," I said, feeling her grip loosen.

"Oh," she said, realizing I wasn't a rich potential client. "Oh!" she then repeated enthusiastically, digging in again. "Then you knew my Victor. My poor, flawed Victor. We were once married. Young love, so intense and fleeting."

Ugh. Your Victor, give me a break.

"Did he give you any of his artwork by any chance?" Under a rim of heavy mascara, Jay-Jay's eyes had the intensity of a hyena poised to leap on its prey.

"No!" I said, too loudly and not at all believably. "I mean, nothing I could ever part with, that is. Only a small item of sentimental value. A wooden plaque of a kitchen saint." San Pasqual, the patron saint of cooks, watched over my kitchen.

Jay-Jay shrugged, then switched to faux-morose. "I cannot believe he's gone. Somebody will have to sort out his estate." She sighed, sounding put-upon. "I suppose it will have to be me. Gabe will be of no use and their sister is out of state. I'll need a key. Do you have one?"

I told her truthfully that I had no key. "Besides," I said as pointedly as my inner politeness repressions would allow, "that will have to be sorted out by Victor's will."

Jay-Jay produced a tissue and crocodile sniffles. "Oh, I already know what his will says." She honked loudly into the tissue. "He left his art to me. Along with that junky downtown warehouse he calls his studio."

"What?" Cass demanded. She looked as horrified as I felt.

A smile brightened Jay-Jay's face, which was suspiciously dry of tears. "Yes, I know, isn't that sweet? Most divorced couples would cut each other out, but Victor felt so bad that he wasn't there for me. He put me right back in his will after our separation. Of course his art was hardly known then. Such a precious legacy to leave me."

A truck had set its sights on the parking space in which Cass still stood. The driver laid on the horn, covering Cass's exclamations of disbelief as she turned and stormed across the street, me following at her heels.

"That woman!" she exclaimed when we reached the doors of Double Take. "I can't believe it. I won't. Victor would never leave his art to such a scoundrel. He had to know her reputation. He, if anyone, would know her."

I agreed. "I thought he'd leave everything to his nonprofit. That was the most important thing to him."

Cass stomped off into the consignment store. "That 'run-down studio' she mentioned? I bet she means the warehouse where he ran his nonprofit art workshops. And he'd want his art donated to a museum," she said, dodging a salesclerk. "Or if it was sold, with the profits going to the nonprofit. Never to Jay-Jay. Never." She turned and looked at me earnestly. "Right?"

I hoped she was right. "How long ago did they get divorced?" I asked when Cass came to a stop in the women's section.

She estimated a date decades ago, long before my time here.

"Then it's fine," I said, trying to comfort us both. "Say Victor did feel bad for her immediately after the divorce. He's had years to reconsider and make a new will."

"Yeah," Cass said, sounding uncertain. "Yes," she said after a moment, this time with more conviction. "You're absolutely right. Someone will have his new will or know where to find it."

I agreed heartily. However, as I sorted through the dress racks, I couldn't help worrying. Flori said that Victor wrote everything down, but our friend wasn't the most organized person. Last month, for example, Victor had come to me, sheepish, saying he'd misplaced my rent check. Again. He'd speculated that he might have accidentally tossed it out with a pile of junk mail, or stuffed it in a filing box, or used it as sketch paper. What if no one could find his will? If Jake didn't call me, I was going to call him, not for a coffee date but for legal advice.

Chapter 17

You look awesome, Mom," Celia said, painting a swirl of bright yellow down my chalky cheek.

I looked terrifying. And, I had to admit, I did look pretty darned awesome, thanks to my artistic daughter. A black line ran down my forehead to my collar bone. On one side I was normal me, makeup-free except for a little mascara. On the other side I was death. Atop white face paint, a black circle cloaked my eye, ringed with a fringe of red. My cheek bore bright yellow swirls that twirled to meet the smiling black suture marks extending from my lip. A black circle representing the hollow of my skeleton non-nose, and a fun half flower in black on my chin completed the look.

I rechecked myself in the full-length mirror. My new black dress had a plunging neckline and fit like it had been made for me. Well, me about five pounds lighter. I gave thanks to the makers of Spanx and to the fashion gurus who had allowed ballet flats and tights to come back into fashion.

"The face paint's not too much?" I asked again.

"No, it's totally awesome." Celia must have liked the design because she'd painted her face similarly. The lack of cat-eye makeup lightened her look, and her attitude seemed bouncier too. Probably because I'd already relaxed her casita arrest. I hadn't totally folded. She'd wanted to go out with Sky and some other friends, including Gina, an idea I nixed. Then she suggested hanging out with Ariel, which I squelched. Manny would be working and I didn't want to leave her here alone. And I couldn't cancel on Cass. Deserting my party-dreading friend would not be a good-friend move.

"You *will* stay within sight of Flori and Bernard the whole time, you promise?" I confirmed for the third time.

"Yeah, Mom. I'm not going to ditch old people. Anyway, I texted Rosa and she's going too. We'll hang out."

"Don't let Flori hear you call her old," I said, giving my daughter a little hug. Sure, Flori could call herself old, but heaven forbid anyone else did. Her great-granddaughter, Rosa, was about Celia's age, and I was happy that she'd be there. Rosa had inherited the good behavior of her grandmother, Linda, minus Linda's worries.

Celia turned her death profile to me and touched up her black lipstick. "Flori's the coolest."

I thought that too and was grateful that she had invited Celia to accompany her and Bernard to the live music and dance event on the Plaza. I had a nagging suspicion, though. Was Flori up to something? She hadn't questioned me with her usual intensity when I returned to work with the black dress and told her that I had plans with Cass tonight. She hadn't demanded to know where we were going or if we were meeting hot men and how I intended to flirt with them. Did she have an ulterior motive?

"I mean it," I reiterated to my daughter. "Don't let Flori out of your sight. I don't want her slipping off to snoop. She's very sneaky."

This earned a snicker from Celia.

"And don't let her and Bernard make out behind the bandstand again either."

Celia giggled like the little girl I remembered. "Don't worry, Mom, I'll watch 'em."

You look fabulous," Cass said when I picked her up in my old Subaru.

"It's all Celia's doing," I said, feeling motherly pride. "You look stunning." She did, despite her sour expression. White makeup covered her entire face, broken only by black curves forming skeletal cheeks, nostrils, and eyes. The white set off the paleness of her hair, which she wore down and straight.

"I'm fine," she said, more to herself than me. "We go, we greet, then we get out before midnight." She sighed and then added hopefully, "Unless you have to get home early to check on Celia. I'm happy to leave early."

I had to disappoint Cass. "Celia's staying overnight at Flori's. It's part of her weekend work deal. Flori wants an early start tomorrow to get ready for her bread contest."

"I bet you'll be glad when that stress is over," Cass said.

Glad and sad. On the one hand, my thighs could use a reprieve from buttery sweet bread. On the other hand, I loved buttery sweet bread and could happily eat it year round. At least I had another sweet treat to look forward to. "After this, Flori's entering the *bizcochito* contests," I told Cass. "I sure wish we had Victor's recipe."

"Let's hope that Gloria's little helper Armida doesn't get her hands on it first."

We headed into the darkness of Old Santa Fe Trail. The twisting road looks deceivingly rural, until you spot all the homes hidden in the junipers and the mansions perched on the hilltops.

"Dancing Eagle Way," Cass said, snorting at the street name. "Should be close." She squinted at her phone. I slowed to read a road sign. "Laughing Coyote."

Cass snorted again. "Let's keep going out to Harry's Roadhouse. They have their fried chicken special this week."

Now I groaned out of wistfulness. Harry's, a roadside diner on the outskirts of town, has some of the best fried chicken I've ever eaten. Crispy, juicy, peppery . . . my stomach rumbled.

"We're both on missions," I reminded her and myself.

"More jewelry sales," Cass sighed.
"And snooping."

Dancing Eagle Way was a small dirt path that I
almost missed in the glare of oncoming head-
lights. In other parts of the country dirt roads and
mansions don't go together. In Santa Fe unpaved
lanes remain in some of the most desirable parts
of town, prized as symbols of history and southwestern character.

"No wonder she drives that tank of an SUV,"
Cass grumbled as the Subaru struggled across a
dip the size of a gully.

We pulled up to a solid metal gate that opened
automatically. A valet in a tuxedo and skeletal
face and white gloves directed us to drive to a
massive portico, where another skeleton waited
to park my car.

"We should have brought your car," I whispered
to Cass, mortified that duct tape held up my sun
visor and a hula-skirted bobble-head man danced
on my dash. My car was underdressed.

Cass made me feel better by making her car
seem worse. "My car's filled with flammable gas
canisters and a jug of used etching chemicals. The
valet would call in a Hazmat team and the DEA."

I smiled apologetically to the valet and handed
him a key chain laden with library and supermar-
ket quick-scan cards, the miniflashlight, and a
trinket shaped like a Japanese tea kettle.

"Okay," said Cass, her skeletal face grim. "Here

we go. Let's have a code word in case of emergencies, like if either of us wants to leave early. How about the word we used for that potluck a while back? 'Cupcake'?"

*C*upcake turned out to be a bad choice. Gloria, we quickly found out, was also known for her cupcakes. Cupcake towers the size of Christmas trees stood at either end of a great room that lived up to its name, from its floor-to-ceiling fireplace to its walls of windows. The room and cakes were impressive, but what entranced me was the kitchen beyond.

"Do you see that kitchen?" I marveled, before realizing that Cass was already being cheek-kissed by the moving-and-shaking set, including the handsome knitter Salvatore. I left her to her mingling and made a beeline for the kitchen, which was straight out of the pages of a magazine. I caressed the soft soapstone countertops. I coveted the industrial stainless steel range with double ovens, a grill, and six burners, reminiscent of my French dream stove. I adored the backsplash of translucent green tiles, each the size of a Scrabble tile.

"You like it?"

My jumpiness again got the best of me. I jump/turned to see Gloria, a martini glass in one hand and a black and white cupcake in the other.

"It's fabulous," I said, hoping to keep envy out of my voice.

"You're Cass's friend, the culinary expert?"

I nodded, surprised that she remembered me, in half skeleton attire no less. She was also in face paint, only hers covered her entire face and featured black swirls and red roses. It was much more flamboyant than my paint job, I noted with relief. According to my mother's code of manners, at costume parties, like dinner parties and weddings, one should never outdress the hostess.

"Here," Gloria said, putting down her drink glass. Her voice slurred a little, making me suspect she'd prefortified herself for her own party. "You have to try my cupcakes. I am the former cupcake queen of Amarillo. Blue ribbons three years in a row." She waved me toward a tray of cupcakes on the counter.

No one has to ask me to taste an award-winning cupcake twice. I bit in, savoring rich chocolate ganache icing, a moist yet airy white cake, and the surprise delight of cherry filling.

"This is amazing! Did you use mascarpone in the cake?"

She raised her glass to me and gave me a Botox-straight smile. "You're the first one to guess it straight off! Good girl! Now, y'all come with me and I'll introduce you around."

I was reluctant to leave the kitchen. I yearned to drool over the espresso station and what appeared to be the thousand-dollar Italian ice cream maker I'd ogled recently in *Food and Wine*. Most of all, I wanted to snoop for dough and evidence of Armida making it. Maybe she'd made the cupcakes too, although the integrity of Texan cupcake contests was none of my concern.

Gloria herded me back into the great room. "Here's someone y'all will adore!" she said, hands on my back, pushing me into a group of well-dressed ghouls. "Fabulous foodies, meet Rita. She's a chef at . . . what restaurant did you say you worked at again, darling?"

"Ah . . ." I stalled for time, worried about Gloria's feelings toward Flori but also the daunting chef talent standing in front of me. There was a James Beard award winner, a guy with a Michelin star, and the owner/chef of one of my favorite restaurants. And those were only the ones I recognized in their makeup. Compared to them, I was a culinary ant.

Luckily, or maybe not so luckily for my undercover aspirations, a familiar voice answered for me.

"Rita dishes up the best chiles *rellenos* in town and the best cherry empanada I've ever tasted. And her *carne adovada*? Divine."

The chefs turned to a dapper figure dressed in a chic black suit. His face might have been covered by a folk-art skull mask, but I recognized the voice, not to mention the espresso locks, steely blue eyes, and shiny cowboy boots. Jake continued to sing my praises to the chefs. "Tres Amigas Café. I assume you've all been there? It's always been good, but it's better than ever now with Rita's touch."

The makeup-free side of my face surely burned bright red, especially when the James Beard winner deemed our red chile sauce "stunning" and our baked goods "divine."

Gloria clasped her hands in pleasure. "I have a sense for the food stars, now don't I? I'll have to come try your chiles, that's for sure." She slapped me on the back in a jovial linebacker sort of way. "I won't dare come by for a while, though. Your little friend Flori is my main competition in the death bread contest." She turned to the chefs. "I'm sorry to say, she won't be getting the ribbon this year either. Y'all will be showing up and rooting for me, right?"

They agreed and slipped back into a conversation about cash flow. Their problems of cash flow were definitely not the same as mine. I listened with a mix of envy and awe, sneaking peeks at Jake as I did. It was impossible to tell what he was thinking under his mask. I was thinking that I should make my move back to the kitchen. When a waiter glided in and distracted the chefs with crab legs, I saw my opportunity to escape.

Jake did too, following me a few feet away to the buffet table. "Good move," he said. "All that talk of accounting makes law briefs sound like thrillers. Hope you don't mind that I talked up your empanadas." He'd lifted his mask, revealing a chiseled face better than any disguise. "I didn't know that you were friends with Gloria."

I explained my invitation via Cass and tried to find her. Partygoers crammed the room. I scanned, wondering if she'd already bolted outside and was waiting by my car. Then I saw her. She was backed into a corner by a figure in a gold body suit with familiar lemon-yellow hair: Jay-Jay Jantrell. Cass, her eyes flashing like those of a lassoed wild horse, spotted me and mouthed *Cupcake*.

Chapter 18

S he said 'cupcake'!" I cried to Jake. "I'm going in!"

"Cupcake?" He looked around, rightfully confused, before his eyes and hands gravitated to a nearby cupcake tower.

"Cupcake. It's our rescue word for bad social situations. I'll be right back." I made it two steps before he grabbed my elbow.

"That's Jay-Jay Jantrell over there. You think you're going to make any kind of graceful exit from that woman? You'll get stuck too and then I'll have to go rescue you and we'll all be trapped. Here, try a cupcake. They're really good."

I didn't admit that I'd already had one. I took the cupcake. I couldn't eat it, though, not with Cass suffering and trapped. Another yellow-haired skeleton had joined Jay-Jay. Both were gesticulating excitedly with their hands.

"Who's that with her?" I asked Jake.

"Her assistant and mini-me look-alike, Angelica. The name does not match the personality, trust me."

Cass shot me another desperate look, but when I mimed that I was coming over, she gave a quick negative head shake and glanced pointedly at the stage. A skeletal crew in mariachi attire had begun playing old-fashioned country music, and Gloria was on the microphone, inviting her guests to dance. Cass knew I couldn't dance. I steeled myself. I'd do it for her.

"I'm going to do it," I said. "I'm going to go over there and pretend that I need Cass as my dance partner. It's the only way." *And then we'd glide away.* Right. I'd stomp on her feet and we might trip over a waiter, but Cass wouldn't complain, not to escape Jay-Jay.

I was about to hand over my cupcake to Jake when he stepped forward. "I've got this," he said, and strode toward the yellow-haired skeletons.

I ate the second cupcake and considered having a third as I watched Cass and Jake spin expertly around the dance floor. I had to admit that I was slightly jealous. Okay, more than slightly. They made a gorgeous couple, she lithe and blond, he rugged and smooth. Not only that, they danced like pros. She dipped and twirled and two-stepped without any foot-stomping involved. He expertly glided them through the crowded dance space.

When the band switched over to a slow Mexican ballad, they parted. Jake tipped an imaginary cowboy hat to Cass and sauntered off to mingle with a well-heeled group. Cass, flushed, joined me.

"Thank you!" she said, grabbing one of the last cupcakes.

"Don't thank me. It's Jake who saved you." I hoped that I didn't sound bitter. I forced a smile. "You two looked great dancing together."

"That man is a fabulous dancer," Cass acknowledged. "But you know who we talked about the whole time?"

"Jay-Jay?"

"Heavens no. That woman is horrible. She was practically threatening me, wanting information on your 'relationship' with Victor."

"Relationship?" The way Cass said the word made it sound unseemly.

"Yep. She thought you must have been living in Victor's casita to seduce him and get at his art. When I shot that down, she suspected the same thing of you and Broomer."

I made a gagging sound.

"Don't let it worry you," Cass said. "She's a poisonous snake projecting her own nature. Oh no, speak of the viper." She tugged me behind a group of distinguished skeletons. Across the room, two yellow heads were making their way toward us.

"We have to get out of here before they spot you," Cass said. "Jay-Jay's desperate to get into Victor's place. She's convinced you have a key. You know, because of all that romantic manipulation you've been doing." My friend started toward the door.

"Wait!" I tugged her back. "We can't go yet."

My party-dreading friend grumbled about never understanding extroverts and pulled us behind a cupcake tower.

"It's not that," I protested. "I have to get back in that kitchen and look for evidence of Armida baking the *pan de muerto*. I owe it to Flori."

Cass couldn't deny the glory of Gloria's kitchen. "I expected gaudy," she said. "This is pretty darned gorgeous—if you want to live in a catalog, that is."

There were days—a lot of days—when I yearned to live in an Ikea display or the Pottery Barn catalog. Residents of Pottery Barn land, I imagined, never stored their treasured Bundt cake pans in their ex's garage.

I looked around the kitchen, not sure what I was hoping to find. A recipe for award-winning *pan de muerto* with Armida's signature and fingerprints on it? A home video of Armida kneading the forbidden dough? With Cass standing lookout at the doorway, I peeked in the fridge. Flori suspected that Armida let her dough rise slowly in the refrigerator to heighten its flavor. The double-door fridge was the size of my closet and packed with everything but dough. Gloria, it seemed, was a lover of fancy salsas, gourmet condiments, and high-priced cheeses. The fridge reeked of a

Parisian *fromagerie*. In other words, it smelled absolutely divine. I breathed in the scent of ripe Camembert and stinky blue.

Cass cleared her throat, snapping me back to my senses. "Please hurry," she said. "This is making me more nervous than the party."

"This from a woman who wields a blowtorch," I teased her.

"Fire is controllable," she said darkly.

I reluctantly shut the refrigerator. What else would Armida need to make the bread? Flour, that's what. I spotted fine dustings of white on the mahogany floor and tracked them, stopping every few steps to check cupboards and windowsills.

"Hurry!" Cass urged. "This is the last song before the band takes a break. If Gloria stops dancing, she might come in here."

Now that I was looking for flour, I saw it all over, in prints on doorknobs and smudges on canisters and drawers.

"I'm seeing a lot of flour," I reported to Cass.

Her response was depressingly logical. "Well that's no surprise, right? Someone did make towers of cupcakes."

She was correct, of course. Flour in a kitchen would not prove Armida guilty. I spotted footsteps in a dusting of flour by a closed door and went to investigate. My hand was on the doorknob when my phone vibrated. The caller ID said Celia. My heart jumped. Was she in trouble again?

"Honey, what's wrong?"

"Why? Does there have to be something wrong for me to call you?"

She had a point. "You're right, honey. How's the party at the Plaza? Fun?"

There was silence on the other end of the line. "Yeah," Celia said, after a beat or two. "It's fun. Rosa and I were dancing with a bunch of people and, well . . . I think we kind of lost Flori. You told me to call if she gave us the slip, so whatever, I'm calling . . ."

I breathed a sigh of relief. Calling was nice. Celia was extending an olive branch, and losing Flori was no big deal, as I assured her. Flori was certainly an adult and could take care of herself. Still, it did confirm my suspicion that she was up to something.

"When did you last see her?" I asked. Celia consulted with Rosa. The girls were unclear but estimated that Flori loudly mentioned "finding the old girls' room" about an hour and a half ago. I thanked Celia for the update, and hearing Cass's anxious toe-tapping, hung up to get back to my search.

"Rita," Cass whispered, "they're coming this way!"

"Gloria?"

"No, worse!" Cass skidded around the island to my side. "We have to hide!"

"No one will care that we're here. We'll say we're looking for the restroom," I said, thinking of a Florilike excuse.

"No, no! I mean, it's Jay-Jay and Broomer!"

Gloria's distinctive hyenalike laughter sounded near the doorway. I acted on instinct and pulled Cass into what I assumed was Gloria's pantry.

"Ouch!"

"Sorry, Cass," I whispered. Leave it to me to tromp on feet.

"Sorry for what?" she whispered. "Did I bump you?"

"Shush you two! You'll give us away!"

Luckily, Gloria's hyena hooting drowned out my yelp and Cass's gasp.

"Flori!" we both exclaimed in whispers.

"Great minds think alike," she chuckled in the darkness. "Now hush. I need to record what they're saying. I have to get this tape recorder out of my bra or it won't pick up anything."

I rolled my eyes in the darkness as Flori whispered about the recording detriments of wired, padded undergarments.

Outside, Jay-Jay's cackle had subsided, replaced by more disturbing sounds. Moans and loud lip-smacking sounds. Jay-Jay and Broomer either really liked cupcakes or they liked each other a lot more than he'd let on previously.

Cass nudged me and groaned in my ear.

"Laurence . . ." Jay-Jay's voice was right outside the pantry door and piercingly high. "You fox. No more of this, you bad boy, until you give me what I want."

"I told you. I can't get into Victor's place any more than you can. What do you think, they're going to let me walk in and haul out all his folk junk?"

Jay-Jay's response was breathless. "I don't need you to haul out anything, darling. Not yet. I need to get inside, that's all. Vic surely has a spare key hidden outside. You go and find it for me. He was a ninny about those things so it'll be obvious. Look under the doormat or a potted plant or behind those infernal saints."

Behind the pantry door, we endured another round of lip smacking before Broomer spoke again.

"And what will you do with that key?"

"Insurance," Jay-Jay cackled. "Ensuring my grieving widow's rights, let's say. And if you're good, you'll get some sugar too. Now let's go get ourselves some oysters. They're aphrodisiacs, you know."

Jay-Jay's cackle receded. Flori pushed by me, opened the door a crack and peeked out. I blinked against the brightness of the kitchen.

"All clear," she declared.

As my eyes adjusted, I fixed on Flori. She wore a black robe and cloak that would fit right in at a Hobbit or Harry Potter convention. In fact, the robe looked a lot like the Harry Potter wizard's outfit she'd made for her great-grandson last Halloween.

"What are you doing here?" I demanded. "Did you follow me?"

"I could ask the same of you," she said, rather righteously for someone found skulking in a pantry. "I saw you out there flirting with your handsome lawyer. Good job."

"Hardly flirting," I grumbled, feeling petty because of my feelings. "Cass is the one who danced with him."

"That was a rescue dance," Cass protested. "And anyway, I never told you who Jake talked about

the entire dance. You, Rita! Flori's right. That man
sure is interested. You can thank me later."

"Thank you for what?" Early after my divorce,
Cass dragged me out on a double date that turned
into a singular disaster for me. I didn't want any
more well-meaning setups.

She winked, smiled, and followed Flori toward
the kitchen door. We were almost out when an
arm blocked our path.

"You again. Where did you come from?" Broomer's voice was mean and hard, like I'd heard that
night at Gabriel's.

"Looking for the ladies' loo!" Flori crowed,
sounding like Addie in full faux British.

Broomer snarled. "No you weren't. I've been
standing right here and didn't see you come in.
What did you hear?" He stepped closer, backing
us into the kitchen island.

"Nothing," I sputtered, praying that someone
else would come looking for the loo in the kitchen.

"And what's that in your hand, old lady." He
reached to grab Flori's tape recorder.

"Old lady!"

I could have warned him. Flori landed a solid
kick on his shin. He buckled, cursing, as we
rushed by him and across the expanse of the great
room.

"Coat closet!" I commanded as we jogged past
a group of cocktail sippers that included Jake. We
needed my coat to get the valet ticket. I glanced
over my shoulder to see Broomer recover and
stride after us, his face stormy. As I waited anx-
iously for our coats, I anticipated a punch, a kick,
a curse. When none came, I dared look again.

Broomer was with the cocktail drinkers. Jake had his arm draped around the red-faced man's shoulder and was laughing heartily, as if they were old buddies. He caught my eye, his own eyes twinkling.

Chapter 19

My heart jitterbugged until we passed safely through Gloria's gates. No cars sped after us. No knife-wielding men sprang from the sagebrush. Dancing Eagle Way was moonlit and quiet, except for my car tires grinding over gravel and Flori humming happily in the front seat.

"You're way too pleased," I said, swerving to avoid a rock the size of a skull. "Go ahead, tell us. How'd you get in?"

"I can't give away all my secrets. Try guessing and I'll tell you if you're close."

I went first. "Please don't tell me that you scaled Gloria's wall. It's over eight feet tall. If Linda finds out, she'll worry herself straight into the hospital."

Flori chuckled.

From the backseat, Cass spoke up. "I know how you did it. The valet who got our car, isn't he one of your cousins?"

A huffing sound from Flori confirmed Cass's

quick guess. "Yes, I'll give you that. But he's not a cousin. He's my nephew Chago's cousin's boy, Andre. A fine young man, although easily bought off. We must remember not to trust him with any baking secrets, Rita."

"You bought off *another* relative?" I asked.

"Free chiles *rellenos* for the rest of the year plus New Year's day," Flori said. "If he says 'operation cheater' and taps his nose, that's the code for the free food."

Nearly every week another of Flori's informants showed up at Tres Amigas brandishing a code word redeemable for free food. Flori's system was getting too complex for me to remember. I suggested we keep a handy written chart, an idea Flori squashed, citing the need to avoid a paper trail.

"So, was it worth it?" I asked. "Did you find any useful evidence of bread cheating? All I saw was some flour."

"Good job!" She slapped me on the thigh, causing me to punch the gas and nearly careen into a juniper. I overcorrected into a jutting rock and she admitted to defeat.

"I didn't find any more than you did. I photographed some floury fingerprints. There's no time to get them analyzed, and it doesn't prove anything either."

"You make the best bread in northern New Mexico," Cass said. I peeked in the rearview mirror. She had her head back, her eyes closed, and was practicing her relaxation moves. I could tell by the deep breathing and occasional *om* chants.

"That's very sweet of you, Cass, darling," Flori said. "As I've told Rita, I actually wouldn't mind being beaten by Armida, if she'd put her real name to the bread. It's cheating. It's not right. And then there's all Gloria's money. Who's to say she hasn't bought off a judge?"

"Wouldn't put it past anyone around here," Cass said. She can say things like that. Although born in Sweden, her parents moved her to Santa Fe before she could walk. This makes her pretty much local. I say "pretty much" because local purists insist on a grandmother from the region.

No one spoke for a few minutes as we bumped onto Old Santa Fe Trail, headed for town. When we neared Cass's place, she said what we'd all been thinking.

"I keep wondering about Jay-Jay and Broomer."

Flori dug out her tape recorder and replayed the muffled, fuzzy recording. "We should take this to the police," she declared, switching it off before the final lip-smacking part.

"As evidence of what?" I asked. The tape only repeated the frustratingly vague innuendoes we'd overheard earlier. Jay-Jay never said why she wanted Victor's key, but I could guess. Maybe, like me and Cass, she suspected that Victor had made a newer version of his will, one that cut her out. If she found it, she wouldn't rush it to the probate judge. She'd destroy it.

I filled Flori in on Cass's and my earlier spotting of Broomer and Jay-Jay. In the backseat, Cass gave up on *om* and vented more disbelief that Victor would leave Jay-Jay anything.

Flori was silent for a while. Then she said something that shocked me. "I can see it," she said in a quiet voice. Her words elicited a not-so-quiet protest from Cass, who was still sputtering when I pulled into her driveway to drop her off.

"I understand your feelings," Flori said, twisting back to look at Cass. "I knew both Victor and Jay-Jay back then. I always thought those two were oil and water, but he was terribly upset around the time they split."

"Why'd they break up?" I asked this over Cass's muttering that she could guess why someone would break up with Jay-Jay.

Again, Flori's response surprised me. "I never did find out why," she admitted. "And believe me, I tried. I remember the day he told me about the divorce. Linda's wedding day. A terrible day anyway because I knew my baby was marrying the wrong man. Victor, he kept saying over and over how sorry he was and how bad he felt. It worried me. Later on I checked in on him, but he wouldn't talk about it."

Cass leaned forward and hugged Flori's shoulders before saying good night and going inside. I drove on to Flori's house. Candlelight flickered in her picture window and three shadows moved behind the lace curtains. I recognized the big one as Bernard and the two slender figures as Celia and Rosa. The spiky-haired silhouette raised her hand in a victory salute. They were probably playing games. Bernard likes obscure card games that we all suspect he makes up. He's so generous that his rules usually favor others winning.

"Come inside, Rita," Flori urged. "There's more than enough room for you. All I have to do is move

my exercise gear and surveillance equipment off
the other guest bed."

I was tempted. Very tempted. Flori's home
looked warm and fun. I imagined chamomile
tea and candlelight and Flori's pudgy orange cat
Zozo curled up on my lap. Reluctantly, I said no
thank you. It was nearly midnight. I wasn't worried that my Subaru would turn into a pumpkin,
but I knew I'd toss and turn in an unfamiliar bed.
More than that, I imagined the grumpy look on
Celia's face if I crashed her fun. Grounded or not,
she deserved an evening with friends, far from a
crime scene.

Back home, I regretted my decision. The adobe
compound was dark and lonely. A ribbon of
crime scene tape fluttered in the shrubbery, and
the motion-detector porch light struggled to
flicker on. I parked next to Victor's old Beetle. He'd
cringe to see his beloved car already accumulat-
ing dust and leaves. He'd also hate the yellow
police tape marring his lovely garden.

The tape barrier across his front window had
come loose. It waved, seemingly motioning me
inside. I skirted the fluttering tape and peered in,
trying to conjure happy images of Victor, cookies, and cocoa. The living room was dark. So was
the altar. I shivered and was about to leave when
something caught my eye. A flicker of light in the
kitchen.

For a moment the spirit of the holiday took over.

Had I seen a spirit? A ghost? Victor? Not unless ghosts needed flashlights. The beam flashed across the threshold before roving through the living room and sending me ducking for cover. I held my breath, fearful that the light could somehow hear my heart thudding. Murderers returned to the scene of the crime, isn't that what *Law and Order* and Flori always said? Was I within feet of Victor's killer? Or was this another kind of criminal? A common thief, who learned of Victor's death and came to rob an empty house? Anger crept into my fear, and I raised my head enough to sneak a peek. A large figure stood in front of Victor's altar, stuffing the offerings of marzipan and fruit into his pockets. Now I was really mad. Maybe this was the same figure I'd encountered lurking around earlier. Breaking in was bad enough, but desecrating a dead man's family altar was plain mean. I wanted to pound on the window and yell. Instead, I yanked out my cell phone and called 911.

The emergency operator sounded as sleepy as Pacho's Pickup in the morning. I rushed through an explanation, stressing the address and the urgency of a robbery and/or return-to-the-scene-of-the-crime in progress.

"Yeah," the female voice said through a yawn. "Okay. I'll send someone over when I get a free car."

I struggled to keep my voice level. "No. They need to get here as fast as possible. He's in the house now."

"Right, okay," the voice said. "You say he's where?"

I let out an exasperated sigh and risked a look over the window ledge. "He's in the . . . oh my God!"

The figure had left the altar and was approaching the window, looking out and hopefully beyond me. I froze, every muscle tensing. It wouldn't matter that I was hunkered under the windowsill. All he'd have to do was look down and he'd see me.

The voice on the other end of the line sounded more awake now. "Ma'am? I can have a car there in ten minutes or less. Go to a safe place and wait for an officer to arrive. Do not put yourself in any danger."

Too late for that. I clutched my keys. If I sprinted, I could probably reach my car before he got out of the house. But if he didn't try to catch me, he'd flee. I wanted this guy caught. My other option was to cower like a cornered rabbit and pray for invisibility in plain sight. Inside, I heard the thud of something falling. It sounded far away and I sneaked a glance. To my relief, the figure had his back turned to me and toward Victor's wall of painted saints. I dared to stare, hoping to spot an identifying feature, anything to tell a police sketch artist. Despite the dim light, I could tell that he was big and wore bulky clothes. Wiry, shoulder-length hair splayed into the glow of the flashlight. Massive hands reached out to touch one of the saints. I willed the police to arrive and catch him in the act.

Then he stopped, and for a long few seconds I didn't realize what was happening. His back remained turned, but squinty dark eyes stared straight into mine.

A mirror. I'd forgotten that Victor interspersed the saints with tin-framed mirrors. The suspicious eyes widened as we stared at each other. I'm sure my own eyes were as broad as pizza pans. I bolted upright, expecting him to lurch toward me. He did move, and fast, but not at me. He grabbed a small saint statue and ran toward the kitchen.

I crashed through the shrubbery, taking the shortest route to my car. When I got there, I fumbled with the door, half expecting the hulk to already be there, lurking in the backseat, knife in hand like a horror movie. No one rounded the corner or loomed in the car. I heard a door slam, followed by the sound of footsteps pounding down the stone pathway of the back garden.

The 911 operator's instructions sounded in my head. *Don't put yourself in harm's way.* I'd already put myself in danger. And the giant had seen me. Twice. He knew where I lived. Where my daughter lived. I had to know more about him. Clutching my tiny key-chain flashlight, I dashed into the darkness, following the sound of breaking willow branches and big feet splashing up the creek.

Chapter 20

I've had a lot of bad ideas. Marrying Manny the serial seducer ranks right up there, along with myriad missteps like attempting a carb-free raw diet and paying for the embarrassment of dance aerobics classes. Running after a giant prowler in the dark up a creek while wearing a party dress and ballet flats had to be among my top-ten worst moves.

The hulk moved quickly and I heard rather than saw him splash into the creek. Propelled by adrenaline, I followed. Branches slashed at my legs, ripping my tights. Tights could be replaced. My feet couldn't. Rocks jabbed into the bottoms of my flimsy shoes and the frigid water shot prickles of pain through my toes. To avoid the willow whips, I waded into the middle of the current, swirling my key-chain flashlight as I went. A few yards and rocky jabs later, the beam revealed footprints in the mud on the opposite bank. I turned to follow, but my party flats were not made for wading, and my foot slipped, sending my ankle into a sharp U-turn. Panicking, I flung my other foot forward. My body has never done splits, not now or twenty years ago. New pains ripped through my hamstrings and I fell, hands first, into the water. My end pose resembled a giraffe doing a poorly executed downward dog. I struggled upright and limped to the muddy bank, fighting off a wave of nausea as my ankle throbbed. By the time I reached the shore, I was shaking from pain and cold and frustration with myself.

How foolish could I be? I wasn't equipped for sprinting, let alone up waterways. And what if I'd actually caught up with the giant? Hadn't I chided myself about this last night and then only yelled at him? Peering into the dark woods, I shuddered. He could be feet away and I wouldn't see him. I couldn't hear him either, only the sounds of rustling leaves and the wind. Hopping over to a tree, I leaned against it and tested my ankle, which withstood tentative steps. Then I assessed the rest of me. My palm felt bruised from my tumble, but my ungainly yoga move had saved my phone, which was dry in my coat pocket. My keys, however, had taken a dunk, along with my arms up to my elbows. The little light on my key chain blinked weakly before giving up. I was literally in the dark, up a creek, and dripping wet.

My screaming ankle begged for rest, and I fantasized that help would magically appear. Prince Charming in a carriage would do. Or a taxi. I pictured Pacho's purple sedan bouncing through the forest and almost giggled. A cold breeze snapped me back to my senses. I thought of Linda. She'd worry that I had hypothermia, which brings on delusions and can strike, she claims, at any temperature under sixty degrees. According to Linda, the walk-in refrigerator at Tres Amigas is a hazard and should require a spotter. The temperature had definitely fallen below Linda's danger threshold. A few snowflakes floated in the air. Had I been warm, dry, and less injured and terrified, the woods might have seemed Christmas-card pretty. As it was, I couldn't sit around waiting for an icy death and/or a lurking giant.

I began my slow, cold limp across the stream, up the garden, and back home, where an array of red and blue lights lit up the driveway. I saw Manny first.

"Where's Celia?" he demanded. "Is she okay?"

Manny did have some good points, I thought, as I assured him that our daughter was safe at Flori's.

His next sentiments reminded me why I'd left him.

"God, Rita," he said, frowning at me. "What have you been doing? You look like a wet cat."

Manny hates cats. This should have tipped me off to our ultimate incompatibility, along with his refusal to eat most green vegetables or anything French. I'd have to watch for Jake's reactions to kittens, baguettes, and spinach. Not that I wanted to date him. No, I'd only be confirming whether he was the good man I presumed him to be.

I didn't want to deal with Manny. Telling him I needed to sit down, I limped toward the casita, hoping he'd go do something useful like collect evidence and solve crimes.

He didn't. "So where's this supposed burglar?" he said, stepping in front of me. "Is this another of your fantasies?"

I tried to keep my voice patient as I explained that the intruder had escaped up the creek, finishing with, "And that's why I'm all wet."

"You're all wet because you make rash decisions," Manny retorted. "You put yourself in danger, which is why Celia shouldn't be living with you. That was a low move, dragging her from my place last night."

Now was not the time for a parenting discussion or argument. I changed the subject, gesturing at Victor's house.

"Someone was in there. An intruder. He touched Victor's altar. He stole food. He could be the murderer."

Manny muttered about my vivid imagination. He probably would have said more except Bunny called his name from the house. She stood by the back door, framed by an icy mist glittering against the porch light.

"We'll resolve this later," Manny said.

I didn't know what we had to resolve. As far as I was concerned, Manny and I were done. The wind picked up. I yearned to hobble back to the casita and exchange the soggy dress and torn tights for warm flannel pj's. Then there was the ankle. It needed treatment, but what? Were you supposed to ice first or use heat? My medical knowledge focused on cooking hazards. I knew, for example, to never put butter on a burn or underestimate the danger of boiling caramel. I recalled Celia's sporting misadventures. Ice, I decided. Elevation and ice with some kind of nighttime pain reliever to knock myself out. Except for the pain pill, the treatments sounded like a lot more work than flannel, ice cream, and self-pity.

I watched Manny jog toward the main house. No, he wasn't jogging. He was practically bounding, jumping over decorative stones and skipping up steps, showing off the prowess of his fine, untwisted ankles. I wondered what Bunny had found. Had the intruder broken in a window? Kicked in the door? Left fingerprints or conveniently dropped an ID? The latter would be too much to ask.

Curiosity got the best of me, or maybe hypothermia overrode good sense. I followed Manny, taking the long way along a relatively flat flagstone path.

At the back door, I searched for signs of splintered wood, broken glass, or a picked lock, but found nothing. The laundry room also looked the same as always, neat and tidy with its terracotta walls sporting dozens of Victor's saints. It had to be one of the cutest laundry rooms around, and I really had no excuse for disliking laundry days.

Bunny leaned against the washing machine. "No one's home next door at the brother's house. Nothing seems amiss here, just unlocked doors, which is odd because I know these were locked when we left last time. Whoever was in here must have had a key or be an excellent lock picker."

"*If* someone was here," Manny said. "Rita has an active imagination."

I rubbed my forehead, tired of this line, which

had been Manny's favorite during our divorce. According to him, his extramarital pursuits were figments of my imagination, except that some of those imaginary women had confirmed the truth. A slurry of white face paint came off on my palm. I was a mess. He was right about that.

"I don't understand," I said, turning my smeared face to Bunny. "Someone was in here. I looked right at him. He saw me in the mirror and ran off. I chased him up the creek."

"Not a good idea, Rita," Bunny said, shaking her head.

Manny snorted. "You can say that again. Rita has a lot of bad ideas."

Yeah, like marrying you.

Bunny continued, her seriousness a sharp contrast to Manny's childish sniping. "Someone was here. We found fresh footprints outside and this jacket." She held up a padded camouflage coat with ragged cuffs and POW/MIA patches down one sleeve. A skull with flames was embroidered on the back. "Recognize this? Is it Victor's?"

"That is *not* Victor's," I said, thankful for some evidence of an intruder's presence. I described where I'd seen the hulk and tried to recall his features. "Small eyes," I said. "And frizzy hair, going all over the place. Some gray."

Manny's phone rang, and he went outside to take the call, to my relief.

Bunny scribbled in her notebook. "We need to clear this matter up," she said. "This break-in is suspicious. You have to know, though, Rita, it doesn't prove anything."

Blood pounded from my sore ankle straight

to my confused brain. "Doesn't prove anything about what?"

Bunny cocked her head. I interpreted this, and her thin smile, as an attempt to look sympathetic. "We're waiting for word from the medical examiner. There's still the possibility that your friend took his own life."

"But the break-in—"

"Could be pure coincidence. We get a lot of burglaries in this part of town. It's a thief's dreamland. Big walls, big-time art collections, absent owners, and it's no secret that this place is deserted."

Deserted. The word tugged at my heart. It sounded like Victor had simply walked away. Had he? Had he left this world on purpose? I refused to believe it. I bundled my coat around me, feeling clammy wetness instead of the warmth I craved. What's worse, I could almost buy Bunny's explanation about the coincidence of the intruder. Victor was gone and decay in the form of dirty cars and filthy thieves was taking over.

"We'll know more soon," Bunny said. "Probably by Monday the coroner will give us her report." She inspected the wall of saints behind the dryer. "You'd be surprised how easy people make it for thieves to break in. They give out keys to workmen and casual friends. They leave keys under flowerpots or under the doormat or those ridiculous fake rocks."

Her words reminded me of what Jay-Jay had told Broomer. According to her, Victor hid keys in obvious spots. "You have to see this," I told Bunny, unwrapping my coat to get to my phone. The phone, as usual, took its time waking up. As it did, I rushed through explanations of the Jay-Jay and Broomer sightings.

"Here," I said, when the photos finally appeared. "Look at this." I hadn't exactly expected an "aha" moment from Bunny, and I didn't get one.

She frowned at the shots. Her silence eventually ended in a perfectly reasonable, "This doesn't prove anything."

I explained again what we'd overheard from the party. "Victor's ex-wife was telling Broomer to find Victor's key. She wanted something in this house. She said the same thing you did, that Victor was silly about leaving spare keys in obvious places."

Bunny seemed overly hung up on a detail. "So you said you were in some Texan lady's pantry when you overheard this?" To her credit, she wasn't Manny. She didn't call me a fool or disparage my judgment or sleuthing. She did, however, look unimpressed. "We'll look into it," she said, in the rote way that I warn customers about hot burrito platters.

"You should have heard them," I protested. "They're up to something."

Bunny gave me the head-tilting sympathy look again. "Go home, Rita. Put your ankle up."

I felt my cheeks fire up, this time in anger. "I'm not going to sit around with my feet up eating bonbons when my friend's been murdered."

For one of the first times ever, I earned a genuine smile from Bunny. She nodded toward my ankle. "I meant, elevate that sprain. Put some ice on it too. Rest, ice, compression, elevation: RICE. I'll call you in the morning."

"To check on my ankle?"

"To get you in to look at mug shots. Your intruder might already be on our radar."

I shuffled home, thinking about Bunny's departing words. *Stay out of it, Rita,* she'd said. She must have known that I couldn't do that.

Chapter 21

"Rise and shine, Rita. The dead will be here at midnight!" Flori, a morning person, sounded extra perky this morning.

My eyelids felt heavy and my head fuzzy from the sleep-inducing pain pill I'd popped less than six hours earlier. I considered smothering the cell phone under my pillow.

"You there?" Flori demanded on the other end. "Wake up! You're like your daughter, sleeping the day away."

I wrenched an eyelid open and squinted at my digital alarm clock. In too-bright, too-red numbers it announced the time as 6:56. My mother had taught me to never call before nine. The only exception was an emergency like the call recipient's house actively burning down, in which case Mom would probably still start the conversation with "Sorry to bother you so early, but . . ." Flori considers any time after 6:00 A.M. fair game.

When I'd told her—jokingly yet pointedly—about Mom's 9:00 A.M. rule, she laughed and said that my mother worried as much as Linda. That was probably true.

"Didn't Bill Hoffman tell you about my late-night run-in with a burglar at Victor's?" I asked. I immediately felt guilty for sounding grumpy. Today was Halloween, which meant that the Day of the Dead and Flori's *pan de muerto* baking contest were tomorrow. In other words, this was like the day before Christmas for Flori.

The silence on the other end of the line heightened my guilt, as did Flori's next statement. "Sugar! Bill Hoffman got himself admitted to the hospital last night, the old fool. Of all the nights to abandon his scanner! Are you okay?"

I assured her that I was fine, except for feeling terrible about poor Bill.

"Oh, he's fine and dandy. His diverticulitis was flaring up again, that's all. We all tell him that he can't eat Indian takeout. He won't listen to anyone and can't resist chicken korma. Stubborn, that's what he is."

Flori was also stubborn, refusing my offers to come in and help her with her busy day and bread preparations.

"You stay in bed and recover," she commanded. "And since you're lying around, you can give me all the details. Tell me all about this intruder."

I gave her all the details that I could remember.

"Hold on," she said, midway through my description of his face. "What color were his eyes? I'm writing this down so I can ask around."

I described his eyes as dark and squinty, his

height as tall and looming. In my memory, he seemed more of a cartoon villain than a real person. I admitted to Flori that I might not recognize his photo in Bunny's book of mug shots.

Flori offered comforting assertions that I'd do fine. I suspected that she couldn't truly understand my concern. She can remember what she wore on her first day of kindergarten or what flavor pie she served to the then-mayor on a Thursday in 1971. I, on the other hand, am surely one of the world's worst witnesses. I'd stared right at the intruder and all I could remember were forms and feelings. "He was big," I said again, for lack of concrete details. "And scary."

"And suspicious," Flori added. I heard tapping on her side of the line. "This could move suspect number three up to first place in our list."

"Unknown intruder?" I asked, not trusting my memory of Flori's list.

"Exactly. Maybe he was looking to rob Victor and got scared off when Celia and Manny's Jeep girl arrived."

I shuddered, wracked with the sudden desire to hold Celia close. She was safer with Flori, I told myself. Safer away from the casita and the unknown prowler. I thanked Flori again for including Celia on her weekend activities.

"My pleasure. Bernard's going to get her and Rosa up soon for blueberry pancakes. Then we'll all be off to the Folk Art Museum. I'm betting we make big money this year, thanks to Celia's artistic talents."

In the background, Bernard's jolly rumble of a laugh was followed by a chant of "Big money."

"Okay," I said. "But if you need me . . ."

"Nope. I'll mix up my dough this afternoon and let it rest overnight. I don't need any help. I'm no cheater, like some people. You rest up. That's an order from your boss."

Normally I'd love a morning completely to myself with nothing to do except lie in bed. That's one of my favorite things about my new single life. On weekends I can read late into the night, unbothered and knowing that I can sleep in. Now I felt more rudderless than free. Besides, I sure could have used some blueberry pancakes.

I limped out to the kitchen and settled for old granola and aspirin, washed down with the strongest coffee I could make without Gloria Hendrix's Italian sports car of an espresso machine. Coffee made the day look better, as did wrapping my ankle in a stretchy compression wrap from Celia's closet of sports clutter. Outside, the bright sun and glittering frost of a late fall morning beckoned. I decided that I wouldn't sit around. I'd get out, enjoy some sun, and stretch my stiff ankle. I bundled up and swung the door open.

To my surprise, another car was parked in the driveway and it looked familiar. I walked up the driveway to check. Its owner was familiar too. However, when I called out Linda's name, she ducked behind a nearby conifer.

"Linda?" I called again. "Are you okay?"

She peeked out from behind the tree, her face red. "This is *not* what you think, Rita," she snapped.

I hadn't been thinking anything except to

wonder why she was hiding from me and what was in the picnic basket looped over her arm. Did she have something in there she didn't want to share? Now, however, my wondering took a different track. Linda, here at her old flame Gabriel's house, ducking behind an evergreen in the early hours of the morning. I rushed to assure her that I fully supported any romantic evening she may or may not have had.

"Good for you!" I concluded perkily, to which Linda's mouth twisted in frustration.

"No! You've been hanging around my mother too much! Gabriel came over to my house last night to talk and it was too dark for him to walk home. You know what a danger the roads are this time of year with all the Halloween craziness and drunk drivers. I insisted that he stay on my pull-out bed, which he did. The perfect gentleman. I merely drove him back this morning because it's so chilly out."

Throughout this rambling explanation, I'd been nodding vigorously. "Yes, of course," I said. "The roads are way too dangerous for pedestrians after dark. Especially this weekend and out here where there aren't any sidewalks."

Linda seemed mollified by my affirmation of her worries. She held out the basket. "I brought you these tamales. Green chile and cheese. I didn't want to knock since it's so early. I was thinking of leaving them on the door. Then I worried, what if a coyote or raccoon got to them first?"

Or a lurking prowler. Now I knew why Gabe hadn't been home last night. I'd have to warn him to get new locks or put bolts over Victor's laundry room door. I told Linda about my evening as we walked back to the casita.

"You chased the burglar? Rita, that's dangerous. What if you'd caught up with him? Do you know how many people carry guns nowadays? What if he'd turned on you or you'd fallen in the creek after hurting your ankle? You can drown in an inch of water, you know." She shuddered, thinking about the dire possibilities.

I'd thought some of the same things as I hobbled across the creek last night. Now, however, Linda's worries made me almost proud of my bravery/ foolishness.

"I need to find out who he is," I told her. "He knows where Celia and I live."

Linda, the mother of a daughter and a son, understood this worry. "So what are you going to do?" she asked.

"Right now? Eat some of your wonderful cheese and green chile tamales," I said. "Will you come in and have some with me? I could use some company and more coffee."

She hesitated on my doorstep. "Okay," she said after a moment. "But only if you let me come with you afterward."

"Come with me?" I was trying to play innocent. It wouldn't fly with a daughter of Flori's. Linda was too used to her mother's guises and exploits.

"You've definitely been around Mama too long," Linda said. "I know you're going back in that forest to look for clues and I'm not letting you go alone."

Emboldened by two more cups of coffee and a particularly fiery jalapeño in Linda's delectable tamales, I tugged a rubber boot over my shoe and puffy, wrapped ankle. Linda managed to squeeze into some of Celia's old waterproof snow boots.

"You should go to a doctor," she chastised. "An ankle and foot specialist." She'd said this several times already.

"It's okay. Just a little sprain. Exercise is good. I'm sure of it." I wasn't actually sure of this. In fact, I suspected that the exercise I had in mind— namely, fording the stream and tromping through the forest—was the last thing my abused ankle wanted. I'd rest it later, I vowed. Or become an aspirin addict.

Fully booted up, we set out down the back garden. Linda paused to look around. "I haven't been back here in decades. It used to be so plain. No rocks or art or anything. This is lovely."

"This is what Broomer wants to destroy," I said, raising my voice, hoping he was over there in his hot tub and could hear me. "It would be a sin to destroy something so lovely."

Linda agreed more quietly. "I feel something here. A spirit." She looked around some more. "Maybe it's Victor."

If Victor's spirit was here, I hoped all the more that Gabe could fend off his pushy neighbor. Linda and I followed a path made of mosaic bits of tile before going overland to the creek.

"Here," I said, pointing to the sandy mud. "Look at these footprints. These are mine and the big ones are the giant's."

Linda shuddered. "Why would he come this way? Why not take the road out front?"

I had a theory about that, but I wanted to get across the stream first.

"Are you okay?" Linda asked repeatedly. She had her purse swung around her chest and my arm in a vise grip for the entire crossing.

"I'm okay," I kept assuring her. Except for my arm. When we reached the other bank, I resisted the urge to rub away the pain where she'd squeezed. Instead, I pushed through some willows to show her my theory.

"I think he got onto the trail on this side of the creek. I didn't reach it last night, but look, it's right here." We emerged from the brush in a patch of forest. The trees here drank from the stream and grew tall. A path wove through them, leading to a small field of waving grasses and gnarled apple trees. I knew that if we followed this route farther up the gentle valley, we'd connect with the bird sanctuary and a web of hiking trails. If we climbed uphill and out of the floodplain, we'd find houses and a road leading back into town.

Linda pointed to steep stone steps camouflaged by lichens and wild grasses. The steps ended at a terraced patio and a coyote fence beyond. "When I was a kid, I knew a girl who lived in that house," she said. "I thought we were so far out in the country. We used to ride horses up there on Cerro Gordo Road. It's still a dirt road like I remember, but the neighborhood feels different now. Fancier."

I tried to make out the home of Linda's child-hood friend. Trees and the fence hid all but a few patches of tan adobe. I guessed the house was almost directly north of my casita. My feeling of being lost in a deep dark forest last night had been unfounded. I probably could have yelled and someone would have come to help me.

"Maybe he parked in the lot for the bird sanctuary and hiking trails," I postulated, turning in a circle to take in the thief's numerous escape options. "Then he could have driven down Cerro Gordo and wouldn't have crossed paths with the police coming up Upper Canyon Road."

"In any case, he'll be long gone," Linda said, sounding relieved.

She was right. A burglar wouldn't hang around, waiting for a decent hour to call on his next victim. The trail gave up no clues. It was well-trodden and the few fresh footsteps in the frosty leaves could have been those of an early-morning dog walker.

"Good, then," Linda said briskly. "No one's out here. We can go back and you can rest and put that foot up."

It wasn't a bad idea. Yet I lingered as Linda turned back toward the creek. "I'll be with you in a moment," I called to her. Wandering down the path into the forest, I came to an area blocked by a fallen tree. Gingerly, I stepped through its dry branches and over its trunk. Here I was, picking the most difficult route again. And for what purpose? To injure my other ankle? To try to affirm why I'd felt so scared last night? I looked around, seeing nothing but a tangle of braches, wild and unkempt. Except, I realized with a start, it wasn't all a natural mess. My heartbeat picked up as I tiptoed toward a tepee-shaped mass of branches.

It's probably a kid's playhouse, I told my jangling nerves. I'll find comic books and candy wrappers or old beer cans. The thought of beer cans reminded me of Celia and my recent vow to set a good example and not get myself into trouble. Trouble didn't seem imminent in the bright sun and clean air, with Linda only a few yards away. I'd peek in to confirm my theory of kids. I stopped tiptoeing. No normal kid would be up at this early hour on a Sunday. I approached the hut. This kid was a pretty good architect. The structure was cone shaped with a nifty triangular opening formed from bent willow branches.

"Rita, are you okay?" Linda's voice sounded far away, disappearing into the birdsong and branches.

I peered in the triangle. Beady eyes stared back at me, so intense that I barely noticed the giant hand reaching for my neck.

I was not okay.

Chapter 22

know you." His voice sounded like he'd smoked since kindergarten. His hands grabbed my elbows, yanking me into the dark hut. I filled my lungs to scream, but a rough hand clamped over my face, turning my yell to a whimper.

"Shhhh . . ." he said. "Hugo's sleeping. You'll scare him."

Hugo? I didn't care about waking him, whoever he was, unless he was another terrifying giant. Frantic, I tried to recall the moves Cass and I learned at a women's self-defense luncheon. As usual, I spent most of the time thinking about the food. Now I regretted it. My kicks landed in air, as did flailing attempts to scratch and gouge. Finally, I resorted to the meeting-a-bear-in-the-woods defense. I went limp.

"Hey, lady? You okay?"

Great, the giant was worried, probably concerned that I was fit enough to be murdered. That's what happened with psychos in movies. They wanted their victims alive and kicking. I maintained my play-dead pose. The hands released me, and after a moment I dared open an eye. The giant hunched in a corner making cooing noises. This was almost scarier than being manhandled. Images of every scary movie I'd ever foolishly watched flashed through my mind. Who was he talking to? His mummified mother? A murderous clown doll? His chain saw?

"Rita? Rita, where are you?" Linda's call sliced through my psycho images, giving me hope until I realized her voice was becoming fainter. She must have picked the logical way, the path not blocked by an entire tree. I had one chance. I had to make the best of it. Praying that my ankle would hold up to a sprint, I lunged for the opening. I almost made it.

"Hey! Where are you going? Don't you want to meet Hugo?"

The huge hand that reached out grabbed at my jacket and pulled me back in. I squirmed, desperate to extract myself from the coat. I was halfway out of it when the twisted mass wrapped around my neck and head, like a dressing-room nightmare. I gulped for air, feeling like I could faint or hyperventilate or both. Should I play dead again? No, I decided, clawing at the coat. I yelled with what felt like my last remaining air. "Linda! Help!"

Surprisingly, the hands released me. "Who needs help? Linda?"

I was free. I could have fled if the coat weren't stuck over my face, blinding me. I bellowed with all my might and had managed to free up my sight in one eye when Linda arrived, yelling. "Stop! Nine-one-one! Fire!" She grabbed my free arm, yanked the coat off my head, and pulled me outside.

Back in the daylight, the forest seemed startlingly sunny and friendly. Relief flooded over me until I realized that Linda and I together would be no match for the giant. All I'd done was put her in danger too. "Run," I urged her. I followed this up with a noble, breathless platitude. "Leave me, save yourself."

Then I noticed Linda's hands, or rather what was in them.

"Ack! Linda, is that a gun?!"

She had assumed the Robocop stance of Manny's fantasies, feet spread, knees slightly bent, elbows locked, hands gripping a pocketbook-sized pistol.

I can't say I was relieved. I don't like guns. I hated when Manny refused to take his off at the dinner table or left it lying around the bathroom with his dirty clothes. I got sweaty-palmed at simply the sight of a gun, any gun, even this one, which would presumably save us from a hulking psychopath. "Let's go," I urged Linda. "Quick. I'll call the police when we're safe."

It was too late. The giant was emerging from his cave.

"Any funny moves and I'll shoot!" Linda cautioned.

I marveled. This was not the Linda I knew, the timid Linda worried about fridge hypothermia or global warming bringing on prairie dog plagues. This was a hard, determined Linda. My eyes locked on her unwavering gun, so it took me a moment to register the figure before us.

"I know you," he said quietly, and my heart did a flip. In the darkness of Victor's house and the hut, the man had seemed like a terrifying giant. Now, in the sunny light, he was an old guy in a patchwork of ragged clothes. However, my interpretation may have been swayed by what he cupped in his hands. A tiny buff-colored kitten.

Dirty Harry Linda lowered her weapon and immediately turned back into the kind, worried person I knew. "Tops? Oh my goodness, Tops, you scared us nearly to death. You can't do that. Someone could get hurt."

The giant held the kitten closer. "Hugo," he said. "He's not mine."

Linda stuffed the gun back into her purse. "Tops, you terrified Rita here." She pointed to me, and I felt a prickle of irritation. Yeah, of course I'd been scared. Who wouldn't be?

Linda's questioning was hitting a nerve with the giant too. He hung his head as she shook a disapproving finger at him. "And what were you doing at Victor's last night and then running away?"

The old man turned his broad back to us. "I don't want to talk about that," he mumbled, and ducked back into the hut.

My heart, which had relaxed to a normal speed, started to race. What didn't he want to talk about? Burglary? Murder? Had I let my guard down prematurely, fooled by his age and the kitten?

"Linda," I whispered. "We have to go call the police."

I expected her to agree, to worry about getting

back across the creek and whether too much cell phone use would lead to head tumors. She didn't.

"Not yet," she said, disappearing into the hut.

I felt awful. Here I was, surely failing another friend test. A good person would have bounded right into the nice-old-man/psycho-killer's hut to support her friend, right? Or maybe she'd sensibly stay outside so that someone could get away and call the police. I held my phone, my finger poised to dial Bunny's number. The reception bars wavered between poor and zip. I could try to call Bunny. I *should* call her. Yet something held me back. Mainly, if Linda wasn't scared of this man, I shouldn't be either.

"Linda?" I stood at the opening to the hut, my emotions a mix of fear and vexation. The fear, I thought, was logical. So was the vexation, albeit somewhat selfish. Had Linda not noticed how this guy dragged me into his hut and terrorized me? What was she doing, going in there and leaving me alone in the forest? What about hypothermia and my bum ankle? I felt my inner teenager well up inside me. It would feel good to have a sulky Celia moment. Then I thought about Linda. Tromping into the forest had been my idea. She'd come along to back me up, and she had, bravely. I took a deep breath and stepped inside.

"Greetings!" the giant said. A gracious host, he spread his hands out in a welcome-to-my-castle gesture.

Now that I wasn't blinded by fear, I took in the place. The hut was actually pretty nice, with walls lined in blankets and a floor padded with outdoor chair cushions. I suspected that he'd stolen the cushions, but lawn theft was the least of the neighborhood's problems right now.

Linda stood to one side, holding the purring kitten. "Come on in, Rita. Tops and I know each other from the church." Her tone was cheerful yet firm, aimed to tell me that everything was okay.

"We eat soup together," Tops clarified. "By the Guadalupe lady. Mrs. Linda makes nice soup."

Now I understood how they knew each other. Linda volunteers at the soup kitchen at Our Lady of Guadalupe, where day laborers and the struggling gather to seek work, solace, and a hot meal.

"She makes really good soup," I agreed.

"Mr. Victor gave me soup too," he said, with a note of pride in his voice. "And bread. And the laundry machine."

"You have a key to the laundry room?" I asked. *Why didn't Victor tell me?* I pushed this thought back. Victor didn't have to tell me who he gave his keys to. I was his renter. However, I also considered myself a friend, and as someone who used the laundry room, I would have liked a heads-up.

"I see you there," Tops said, not directly answering the question about the key. "Sometimes. Sometimes I see you."

Sometimes would be about how often I did laundry. I'd do it even less now that I knew I was being watched. I shivered.

"Tops," Linda said, as if chastising a naughty

kindergartener. "It's not nice to spy. You'll scare people."

He shrugged. "Nothing wrong with watching. I only went in at night if it was really cold, to stay warm. Mr. Victor said I could." He held out his hands for the kitten. Linda handed Hugo over. The little bundle of soft beige fur mewed softly as he nestled against Tops's scraggly beard.

I was still feeling creeped out about being watched. For how long? And doing what? I didn't always shut my bedroom curtains at night, reasoning that there was no one in the dark backyard. Worse, if he'd watched me, he'd watched Celia too. I narrowed my eyes, holding back a protective mom instinct to lash out at Tops.

Linda, in her usual way, was managing to bustle around the small space. "Where is that nice feather quilt we gave you a few weeks ago, Tops?"

The big man shrugged and claimed not to remember.

"Did you remember to take your medicine?"

As Linda's list of questions went on, it became clear that memory was not one of Tops's strong points.

"Tops said that he'll come stay at the shelter when it's cold," Linda said, addressing me but really chiding Tops.

"I meant to," he mumbled.

Some of my anger had quelled. He was a forgetful old guy living out in the elements and caring—hopefully—for a little kitten. Victor had helped him. Kind, trusting Victor. Too trusting, possibly. I wondered what else Tops had seen.

I tried to keep my voice light. "Tops, were you over at Victor's two nights ago?"

"When's that?" He looked at me, small eyes squinting in confusion.

I tried a different approach. "You saw me in Victor's place. Who else did you see there recently?"

He hesitated. "You. And the pretty girl with ugly black hair."

"That's my daughter," I said, hardness creeping into my voice despite my best efforts.

He nodded. "I know. Mr. Victor introduced us. She's nice." His expression was one of pride. I felt like I'd been slapped in the face. Celia had encountered Broomer and his pot-smoking friends. She'd met Tops. She'd also met Ariel before I even knew about her. She hadn't mentioned any of these people to me.

"Who else?" Linda said, gently. "Who else did you see visiting Mr. Victor?"

"Mr. Gabriel lives next door. He doesn't see me. Victor says we shouldn't bother him."

"Okay," Linda said. "And who else."

"The gold lady and the mean man with the outdoor bathtub. He doesn't like me."

He hesitated, mumbling to the kitten, who purred loudly. "There was fighting," he said through a moan. "Yelling. Bang! I ran away. I ran. Ran, ran, ran."

"Why'd you run away, Tops?" Linda asked.

He moaned loudly and tugged at his hair. The kitten crawled down his leg and disappeared into a pile of pillows. "No!" Tops cried. He pawed through the pillows and I thought he was seeking the kitten. Instead he pulled out a newspaper.

I recognized the front page immediately. Victor, renowned artist, gone, the headline proclaimed.

"Tops, tell us what happened," I urged, but his muttering was rising to a bellow. "No!" he said over and over. "No, I did a bad thing! Bad, bad!" He threw the newspaper at the wall and reached for a pillow, which he tore mercilessly. Stuffing spilled out as nylon fabric ripped. I thought of those huge hands that had dragged me in and nearly suffocated me.

"Linda," I whispered. "It's time to go."

"We can't leave him alone like this," she said, but she was also backing away.

"We won't be leaving him alone. We're going to call in the police."

Chapter 23

Now it was Linda, trailing behind me, repeating the word "No."

"Linda, please," I begged as I limp-jogged up the back garden to the casita. I didn't care that my ankle felt like an angry blimp or that both of my supposedly waterproof boots carried more water than the not-so-mighty Santa Fe River. I wasn't stopping to rest, empty the boots, or debate about Tops.

"We *have* to call the police," I said again. "You know that. Tops may have witnessed Victor's murder." *He may* be *Victor's murderer,* I didn't add.

"He's confused and old, Rita," Linda said, catching up to me. "He has dementia and probably post-traumatic stress. He was in the Vietnam War. He's a vet with medals and everything. We've tried at the shelter to get him help. We contacted the VA, but he's too used to being on his own. Rita, if you call the police, something bad could happen. He gets agitated and lashes out. They might hurt him."

"You can tell the police all about him," I said, thinking about Tops lashing out. He might have already lashed out and hurt someone. Victor. "Linda, we owe it to Victor. And to Gabriel. He deserves to know what happened to his brother."

We'd made it to my door. She nodded now, glancing sadly at the main house. "I know. You're right."

Bunny answered her cell phone on the first ring and said they'd be right over. Stay inside and lock the doors, she added. Keep out of trouble and keep your phone line open.

This time I had no trouble obeying police orders. I draped a chenille blanket around my shoulders and attended to my puffy ankle, wrapping it in a pack of frozen peas and elevating it as I lay on the sofa. Munching goldfish crackers and flipping through the Italian cookbook, I tried to distract myself with lesser concerns, like my pasta maker languishing in Manny's garage. I imagined myself making homemade lemon-pepper pappardelle or ravioli. In my make-believe world, I was free of murder and prowlers and none of my raviolis broke apart. I sighed. My fantasy was just that. Still, freeing my kitchenware boxes seemed like an important step in realizing my new life.

I closed the cookbook and looked out the window. Linda was not obeying orders. Not only had she gone outside, she was also on her cell phone. I popped more goldfish and wondered who she'd called. Linda usually avoids her cell phone because of her brain tumor worries. She's also read way too many news stories about distracted cell phone users being run over by trains or cyclists. She didn't seem worried about those dangers now. She paced the driveway, talking animatedly. For her safety, I hoped that Manny wasn't leading the police brigade. He was a worse driver than Flori without her glasses on.

Reluctantly, I got up and cracked the door. "Linda, come inside! I have tea . . ."

It wasn't much of a lure. She put away the phone but didn't come in. "I'm going to go over and warn Gabe," she said. "He'll be terrified if he sees police cars again. If they get here before I come back, tell them to be careful around Tops. He's delicate."

He wasn't so delicate when he dragged me into his hut. On the other hand, she was right about giving Gabe a heads-up. What would he think if Manny roared in with sirens blaring? I watched as Linda hurried up the path, around the corner, and out of view. I was settling back on the couch when the doorbell rang. Linda, I thought. Gabe must have been out.

I got up, wrapped in the blanket and frozen peas, and swung the door open. In retrospect I should have checked to see who was there. Had I known, I would have smoothed my hair and ditched the peas. As it was, I could only hope that Jake was so thrown by my pea-padded ankle that he didn't notice my mouthful of goldfish crackers.

"Is this a bad time?" he asked.

All times seemed bad for me lately. "Please come in," I said, after clearing the lump of crackers from my throat. "I was waiting for the police." As I said this, I realized it probably wasn't a classic welcome of the gracious hostess. I tried to cover. "Would you like some tea? Goldfish crackers?"

He smiled and my heart did that annoying flip-flop. "A goldfish cracker while we wait for the police sounds lovely."

My brain was slow because of how good he looked. Jeans and cowboy boots along with a fall-toned flannel shirt that would be so perfect to snuggle up to under my blanket. I mentally slapped myself. Remember the moratorium! *And what had he said?* "Wait . . . you're waiting for the police too? How did you know? I don't need a lawyer, do I?"

He was still smiling and, like a true Santa Fean, assessing the architecture. "Lovely place. Fabulous ceiling. I love the fireplace. But, no, I hope you don't need a lawyer or I'll be double-booked. I'm here for Joseph Topsman. You might know him as Tops. Linda called me. Did you say you have tea?"

That explained who Linda called. Manny would be furious to find his suspect already lawyered up. It didn't explain why she had called Jake, though. Tops surely didn't have the money to pay Jake the Strong Defender's fees. Neither did Linda.

"But why did she call *you*?" I asked, again putting my hostess foot in my mouth.

Jake put on a wounded puppy dog look. "Why not me?"

I didn't have time to launch into another poorly worded reply. Tires skidded in the driveway.

"Rain check on the tea and crackers?" Jake said, halfway out the door.

Manny had to hop to the ground to exit Ariel's jacked-up Jeep. He surely wouldn't like how the Jeep accentuated his shortness. He also wouldn't like being called in on his time off. But what would really get to him was the presence of a lawyer, and not just any lawyer, my "hot lawyer," as Flori put it.

"Where's the suspect?" he snapped.

"Key witness, I think you mean," Jake said, stepping off my porch.

I watched the two men hold each other's gazes. Jake looked serene as Manny's cheeks turned pink with irritation.

From the Jeep, Ariel interrupted the face-off. "Hey, hon," she called out, lowering her window. "If you're tied up, I'm going over to the mall with the girls."

Manny responded with a gruff "Fine" and waved her off. Get used to his I'm-too-busy-for-you attitude, I was tempted to tell her. She frowned, gave me a little wave, and then spun the Jeep into a bold backup maneuver that spit a cloud of dust on Manny. Ariel could take care of herself.

Bunny arrived in a police cruiser before the dust had settled. "Two minutes until backup," she announced.

Manny fingered his gun belt and I suddenly felt protective of Tops. "He's an old man," I said, directing this information at Bunny. "He's confused. He *could* be a witness. There's no need to rush in with an army."

"A witness who breaks into a victim's house?" Manny said. With a suspect in easy apprehension reach, he seemed to have relented on his suicide theory. Or he simply wanted to contradict me. I wished I'd brought the goldfish crackers. Manny-induced stress gave me carb cravings. In fact, since freeing myself of Manny, I'd lost about five pounds. Thinking of this added benefit to divorce, I smiled at my ex, which seemed to throw him off.

He frowned at me, then at Jake, who was leaning against a porch beam. "What is he doing here?"

"I'm here for my client, Mr. Topsman," Jake said calmly. "Whom I'll be advising to remain silent."

"Your client?" Manny said. "A guy who lives in a tent? What's he pay you with, old cans?"

"It's more of a twig yurt," I clarified over Manny's grumbles about defense lawyers.

Bunny, meanwhile, held up her cell phone. "Records came in, Manny. Seems Mr. Strong here has already worked with our person of interest."

"Potential witness," Jake corrected amiably.

"Got him off from a few disorderlies, did you, Mr. Strong?" Bunny said, reading from the phone's screen. "Oh and look at this. Manslaughter. Seems he's innocent of that too?"

Manslaughter? I recalled my terror when Tops dragged me inside his hut and I lay on his floor playing dead. I'd felt a little silly afterward, seeing him as a dottery old man. Had my first instincts been right? Maybe I'd talked myself into misjudging Tops. I glanced at Jake, who was looking cowboy-casual and darned good.

To my irritation, Manny gave voice to my nagging worry. "Well if you're his lawyer, Strong, we know one thing. He's guilty as sin."

Gabe and Linda joined me as the police and Jake drove off, taking the dry route to the other side of the stream. We stood at the top of the back garden, forbidden to follow the search party.

"I told him." Gabe stuffed his hands deep into his pockets and rocked on his loafers. "I said to Victor, 'You're too trusting.' He never wanted to listen to his little brother."

Linda patted his arm. "Tops is like a big kitten. He puffs up and hisses, but he wouldn't have hurt Victor. He might know who did, though."

Gabe sank onto a bench overlooking the garden, running his hands over the colorful tile mosaic created by his brother. Nearby, two magpies hopped onto a birdbath featuring a similar design. The bath was empty. A feeling of failure swept over me. I'd fill the bath, but who would keep up Victor's garden? Who would protect it from Broomer?

Gabe also watched the big black and white birds. Then he turned to Linda. "I'm sorry, Linda. I'm having such a hard time processing all of this. As much as I hate it, I still think that Victor killed himself. And what can this homeless man tell us anyway? You said yourself that he's not right in the head."

"It did seem like Tops saw something that night," I said, thinking out loud. "When we asked him, he became really agitated."

Linda agreed. "Your neighbor, Broomer, that's who Tops was talking about when he got so upset."

Gabriel stared out over the garden. "If you're right about someone hurting Vic, maybe this Tops

guy did it, then. Maybe that's why he's so upset.
You said he committed manslaughter."

"He was acquitted." I said this without much
conviction. We all knew that a certain fancy
lawyer could manipulate the line between innocent and guilty.

"Victor was always taking on lost causes," Gabriel said, tracing the broken tiles making up the
bench mosaic. "Some of those kids he worked
with had criminal records, you know. He got
robbed once, right outside work by the very kids
he was helping.

"He was a good man," Linda said.

"Too good for his own good," his younger
brother contended. "How did this Tops get in Victor's side of the house anyway?"

It was a question neither Linda nor I could
answer. We should have quizzed Tops more.
Did he have a key on him or merely know where
Victor hid a spare? In either case, I wanted that
key. And if he knew where it was, maybe others
did too, like Jay-Jay and Broomer.

Silence stretched over the garden for a moment.
The magpies turned their attention from the dry
bath to glittering wind chimes made of mirrored
glass. They circled below the chimes, hopping
up in failed efforts to pull away the shiny objects
with their beaks. The pretty scene, in other circumstances, would have been relaxing. Instead, I
had the feeling of waiting for a root canal. Dreading it but wanting the agony over as soon as possible.

The silence was broken by Manny's voice booming over a bullhorn. The sound echoed across the little valley and the magpies flew to the trees. "Come out with your hands up! This is the police! You're surrounded."

Manny and his TV-cop lines. He loved the posturing and blustering and accolades of police work. It was the actual detecting he had little time for.

More threats by Manny filtered through the trees. Tops must be resisting, hiding. What about Hugo? I feared for the tiny kitten, as well as for the hulking old man. When my leg buzzed, I thought my anxieties were taking over my limbs, until I realized it was my phone. I found a text from Jake. *No one here.*

I know some adults who can text faster than any teenager. I'm not one of them. I tapped with my right index finger as quickly as I could. *Look for kitten. Buff.*

The reply took some time. I wondered if Jake had gotten the message. What if he was like Manny and didn't care about felines? That would be a sign I'd listen to this time. My thigh buzzed again. *No kitten. Will search. Stay inside. Lock your door!*

So much for believing in the innocence of his clients. I herded Linda and Gabe into the casita, where I bolted the door behind us.

Chapter 24

Gabe, Linda, and I stood in my living room making small talk about my casita and its pretty features. We'd begun extolling the Mexican tile work when Linda turned to me.

"Rita, I want you to borrow my gun. Unless you don't know how to shoot, in which case I'll stay here with you."

It was quite a switch of subject. I managed some words of thanks, followed by firm assurances that I could do without the gun or a gun-toting body-guard. I was still shocked that safety-worrying Linda owned a gun. Gabe was surprised too, although with the opposite reaction.

"A woman on her own should have some protection," he said, his expression one of admiration. He went on to compliment Linda on her resourcefulness and bravery.

"It was Santos's gun," she said, her eyes cast down at her knees. "I never liked it. After he passed, I found it in a drawer. I wanted to toss it, but then my neighbor got robbed walking home from church. That's when I took lessons. Mama says I'll shoot my own foot if I ever have to use it." She smiled. "She's such a worrier."

I had to smile at that. Calling Flori a worrier was like calling me a dancer. Sure, it happened once in a while, but only under extreme and exceptional circumstances. I also couldn't help thinking of another surprising gun owner. Victor.

"You're right," Gabe said, in response to my wondering aloud where the gun came from and why Victor had it. "Vic sure wasn't a gun fan. He only kept that old Remington because it was our dad's." He paused, his chin drooping. "And because of me."

I felt awful for pressing him, but I had to know. "You?" I asked, as gently as possible.

He stood by my fireplace, running his hands over the colorful tiles on the mantel. They featured intricate patterns of orange, blue, and yellow and had been a much nicer topic of conversation. Gabe kept his gaze on the fireplace when he responded. "I like to target shoot. That's how I relaxed back when I worked in the emergency room. Victor, he'd sometimes go with me. Brother time, we called it. I'm the one who wanted to go last week, to work off some stress. We hadn't gone in ages. Maybe it's because of me that he got thinking about the gun."

Linda moved to Gabe's side. "We shouldn't talk about this." She shot me a frown of disapproval.

I knew I was poking at a hurtful topic. I also knew that the gun was crucial to the question of suicide versus murder. "Where did Victor keep this gun?" I persisted. "If someone broke in, would they be able to find it right away?"

Gabe clutched Linda's hand, both of them scowling at me. I deserved the scowls. I was being a horrible hostess. Not only had I brought up the worst subject imaginable, I hadn't offered tea or snacks. I considered dragging out the cheese crackers or my box of emergency Girl Scout cookies stashed in the freezer. Not even a frosty Thin Mint would sugarcoat this conversation, though. I kept going.

"Please, Gabe. I'm trying to understand. Flori and I believe that someone killed Victor. We have to help him and his spirit."

"Spirits," Gabe sputtered, and I saw his knuckles go white against Linda's. "You don't believe all that talk of ghosts too, do you?"

When I didn't respond, he sighed. "Okay, you want to know where he kept that gun? In the wardrobe in his bedroom, that's where. That's all my fault too. I told him to keep it there in case someone broke in at night." He sniffled loudly and went to the front door. Linda followed.

Gabe didn't seem to hold a grudge. Reaching out, he grasped my hands in both of his. "Rita, I know that you and Flori want to do what's right. The best that any of us can do now is to let Victor rest. Rest in peace."

I stood on the porch and watched Gabe and Linda drive off in her car. They were going to lunch at

Tune-Up Café, one of my favorite places. Linda, ever polite, had invited me along. My manners knew enough to decline, overriding my rumbling belly, which craved yummy Santa Fe classics with a Central American flair. I knew just what I'd order too. The *pupusa* special, a Salvadoran corn cake filled with cheese and chiles and served with salty-sweet pan-fried plantains, pretty purple cabbage slaw, and savory black beans. The dish was at once exotic and comfortingly homey.

I sighed, wistful and wishing that Jake would reappear with an invitation for lunch. I'd accept, moratorium or not. I craved comfort in food and company. Linda's tamales would have to do. I was about to go inside and reheat some when a friendly "Yoo-hoo" stopped me.

Dalia Crawford, neighbor and unlikely suspect number twenty-eight on Flori's list, stood at the top of the driveway waving a gift bag. Seeing my hobbling, she hurried down the driveway to meet me.

"What's going on?" she demanded, tension raising her voice to a squeak. She waved her hands toward my ankle and the neighborhood in general. "I saw police cars again, so toxic for our local aura. And what's happened to you? You're hurt? I should have sensed it. How did I miss it?"

"You're here, right?" I said, trying to make her feel better. "You must have felt the need to come over."

Strands of hair splayed from Dalia's braid. She smoothed them back and took a deep breath. "Thanks," she said. "You're right, but my chi is thrown off balance by all of this."

Tell me about it. I'm sure she'd read my chi as a wobbly disaster. I told her about my sprained ankle and the encounter with Tops. Dalia expressed concern for my ankle and promised to give me the name of her hot-hands healer. Like Linda, however, she was even more concerned about the not-so-gentle giant who'd terrified me.

"Oh, that poor old man living rough in the woods this time of year. Do you think I should leave out some jelly and sprouted wheat bread for him? I have an extra massage table he could sleep on."

I told her what Jake had told me, that it was best to lock her doors and call the police if she saw Tops. "He could be dangerous," I said. "He's either a prime witness or a prime suspect in Victor's murder."

Dalia's hands, clutching the gift bag, flew to her chest. "Murder," she murmured. "I heard that from the mailman and the neighbors two doors up and some people at the natural foods co-op. Everyone's saying it."

"Yes, I'm ninety-nine percent certain of it," I said stoutly. "My friend Flori is too. Victor would never commit suicide. Not now. Not ever."

I expected her to agree. Instead, she thrust the bag at me. "Oh Rita, I hate to say this, since you seem so certain." She scrunched her face into a sad/sorry expression. "It's like I told the co-op cashier this morning. Honey, I'm sorry, it wasn't murder."

She sounded so certain that my shoulders slumped under the weight of doubt. Maybe Flori and I *were* wrong. Maybe we only wanted to see evidence of murder because we couldn't admit that our dear friend took his own life. I thought about Gabe's depressing revelations. Victor knew how to shoot. He kept the gun in his bedroom. Spirits sagging, I delayed any reply by peeking in the gift bag. My belly betrayed me, rumbling loudly at the sight of brownies and blondies.

"I know, I know," Dalia said sympathetically. "Phillip and I loved Victor so much. He was different these last few months, though. Kind of off. I should have done more. I should have seen the signs. There were signs. I see them now."

What had I missed? Feeling bad, I reached for a brownie. Huge semisweet chunks studded the rich and gooey chocolate treats. I held out the bag to Dalia but she declined to indulge, citing a gluten-free weekend.

Gluten wasn't about to stop me. Nor were sugar, butter, and chocolate. "What signs?" I asked, after fortifying myself with half of a delicious brownie.

My neighbor shrugged. "Lots. Like I knew it was his birthday last month so I checked the stars. I got really bad indications regarding his spirit."

I won't say that this lifted my spirits, but I did feel a bit better. Dalia was rehashing what she'd told me before, only focusing on the stars instead of the tarot cards. Neither, in my opinion, was on the suspect list. I'd moved on to munching a caramel- and butter-rich blondie, zoning out as Dalia fretted about Libras with type-A blood, when she dropped her closing zinger.

"Then there was the will," she said, as if this was the least of her concerns.

I nearly spit out a butterscotch chunk. "What? A will? You saw a will?"

Dalia bemoaned the ominous position of Venus before getting to the point. "Phillip and I told him it was the wrong star phase for such things, but Victor said he needed two witnesses, so we went ahead and did it. Signed on the dotted line, as they say. I did a sage smudge of the house and garden after he was gone. It reminded me of death. Well, it was a will, after all."

I got Dalia to translate star dates into actual calendar dates. She estimated that Victor brought the will by about three months ago. "About the time he and Gabe started having all that fence trouble with Mr. Broomer. Now, he has bad chi, that man. I'd like to take some sage to his place."

I wished that smoky sage was enough to cure Broomer's toxic nature. I also wished I'd paid more attention three months ago. I'd been in the last stages of my divorce around that time. Wrapped up in my own troubles, and worrying about Celia, I clearly hadn't paid enough attention to Victor.

"What did the will say?" I asked.

"Phillip and I didn't *read* it." Dalia sounded rather offended. "It was nice looking, I can tell you that much. Pretty and artistic, like everything Victor did." At my further quizzing, she recalled that the document was two sheets of thick cotton paper, handwritten in elegant cursive done with an ink pen.

"And did Victor say anything? Anything at all about who he was leaving his estate to or why he was making a new will?"

Dalia tugged her long ponytail into a faux mustache. "No . . . I don't think so. I can't remember."

"Think," I said, in what I hoped was a hypnotic voice. "Think back. Victor's at your door, he's explaining why he's come by—"

"Actually, he came to the garden. He saw me out planting herbs in the rock wall. Oh, that reminds me, can I dig up some of Victor's tarragon? Word is, it came from Ghost Ranch, grown by Georgia O'Keeffe herself."

"Sure," I said, becoming frustrated by Dalia's lack of focus. "It's not my place to say, but I'm sure Gabe won't mind. But think back to the will . . . anything you can remember . . ."

Dalia indulged my hypnosis attempt, shutting her eyes and pressing her palms together. "Yes, I can see him. He's there," she murmured. "In the garden. He asks us to sign his will. He's brought a nice ink pen and says he's getting paperwork in order. Has to set things right, he says. Has to make sure things are set right."

She opened her eyes abruptly. "And that's when I told him about the unfavorable celestial alignment, but he wouldn't listen, and he refused a card reading too." Her brow furrowed in vexation, which cleared rapidly. "Now, let's poke around and look for that tarragon. It should be dormant right now, so no worries about anything dying."

I shuddered at her words. The death of a pedigreed tarragon wasn't what I was worried about. What had Victor meant about setting things straight? And where was this will?

Dalia made her way to the herb garden under Victor's kitchen window. I followed. The raised beds, bordered by punched tin flashing, had over-flowed with herbs and sugar-sweet cherry toma-toes in summer. Now, frost had withered most of the plants. Only a hardy, curly parsley stood up to the cold.

"Did you tell anyone else about this?" I asked.

Dalia, on her hands and knees, sniffed at frost-killed leaves. "I'm not one to gossip," she said. She produced a spade from her pocket and aimed it at the earth. Herb pillaging, I suspected, had been her intent all along.

"Not gossip, but did you tell the police? Did anyone else see you signing the will?"

"Smell this," Dalia said, holding up a clump of dried leaves in my direction. "Does that smell like oregano to you?"

I agreed that it did, and she rewarded me with a response. "I told the police, of course, when they came by. I thought they should know. It was that nice, fit policewoman and her sour little male partner. She said they'd search his place."

Her description of Manny made me smile. I was also relieved that Bunny would be on the lookout for Victor's will.

Dalia rummaged through some dead leaves. "Ah! There you are," she said, addressing a leaf-less woody skeleton. "Don't worry, my darling, I'll take this little babe here . . ." She plunged her spade into the soil. "Perfect," she said, holding up a twiggy stalk. "Now what were you asking me again?"

"Who else you told . . ."

Dalia flushed. "Okay, I confess, I came over here yesterday afternoon. I wanted to say a prayer to

Victor's aura. You and Gabriel were both out and I remembered the herb garden and started to look around. Well, it would be wrong to let his plants go unloved." She had the grace to look sheepish. "That's when I met Victor's widow. Can you call an ex-wife that? I had no idea who she was at first. She came around from the back of the house with that yellow hair of hers and for a second I thought she was a spirit."

If Jay-Jay was a spirit, she wasn't a benevolent one. "She was in the house? In Victor's house?"

Dalia shook her head in the negative. "That's what she was after, Victor's key. She said that this was her house now and she needed to get in. She waved some typewritten document at me, claiming it was Victor's will. I'll tell you, it made me break my anger-avoidance vow. I said that it wasn't the will I witnessed and she shouldn't be trespassing." Dalia's cheeks flared red. "I suppose I was trespassing too. Do you think I did the right thing?"

Had she done the right thing?

After Dalia left with the tarragon, I polished off two more brownies and chewed over the new information. Dalia had told me she thought Jay-Jay was surprised and angered by the news of another will. But where was the will? I had to find it before Jay-Jay did.

Buzzing from sugar and my spinning thoughts, I couldn't stay locked in the cottage. I yearned to hug my daughter and share my new information with Flori and Cass, and I knew right where to find them all: Museum Hill, surrounded by skulls.

Chapter 25

I found Cass first. She stood at her display table in the museum foyer, demonstrating her amazing skill with a jeweler's saw. In her hands, a tiny-toothed blade, barely half the width of angel-hair pasta, sliced through copper sheeting.

"See," she said, holding out the resulting skull form to two admiring women. "Loose but firm grip, that's the key. Let the saw do the work. Now, you pierce the interior with a drill to make the eyes and saw out the lines of the nose and cheek-bones. Then buff the piece with the six grades of polishing I mentioned before. Forge it with a ball-peen hammer for a little texture, anneal with your torch, form some more for dimensionality, solder on a silver pin back, apply color with liver of sulfur or ammonium, wax, polish again, repeat the wax, buff . . ." Before she finished her list, both ladies were selecting premade pins to purchase.

"Good strategy," I said after the women moved on.

"It's all those DIY shows on TV," Cass said, grinning at me. "People see a handmade item and think they can go ahead and make it themselves. Not that they can't, of course. This skull pin is a few easy steps, like I told those ladies. Want to try?" She held out the saw.

The one time I attempted to use her tiny saw, I snapped three blades before moving it an inch. "Well . . ." I said, gamely taking the lightweight tool from her. What I wanted was to blurt out my new information. My silence gave me away.

Cass narrowed her eyes. "Something's up, isn't it? You're not here for sawing demos and skulls. You look ready to burst." Her expression turned to concern as I limped to her side of the table. "What happened?" she asked, pulling out a chair and demanding I sit in it. "You weren't limping last night. Did you get hurt driving home? Did that man Broomer attack you? Parties are danger-ous. We should never have gone. I knew it!"

Before Cass escalated her party-blaming, I broke in, starting with my first encounter with Tops and the ankle-spraining incident.

"You should have called," my friend chastised, after I recounted twisting my ankle in the dark forest and the return trip with Linda. "And then you went looking for this creep again? You defi-nitely should have called me." She gripped a mallet in her hand, looking ready to defend me from the holiday shoppers.

"I had Linda as backup," I said. "Did you know she carries a gun?"

Cass shuddered. "Hit the ground if she starts shooting. She and her sisters attended one of my soldering workshops once. Linda was so jumpy with the torch, she set a lamp on fire. A chandelier. To this day, I don't know how she jumped that high."

Cass's torches could send me jumping for the ceiling, I thought, thinking also of Linda and her gun. She'd seemed pretty darned steady-handed back in the forest.

I was about to tell Cass about Victor's will when a dozen ladies in red hats and purple shawls approached her table. They swarmed her ring display, gushing about the special skull rings and pendants she'd created for the event. I couldn't keep her from her business.

"There's more," I promised. "A tip that Victor made a new will just a few months ago. Can you take a break for lunch?"

She looked at her watch. "I'm swapping lunch breaks with the lady at the next table. Maybe in an hour?"

"You pick the place."

"Somewhere quiet, with no crowds or skeletons," she requested.

Bones and crowds were unavoidable at the museum event. I went outside to the patio, where I spotted Celia holding a skull. Beside her stood Flori, bundled in her red coat, scarf, and hat. My daughter flashed me a smile as I approached. It was wonderful to see her happy, surrounded by art and appreciative buyers chipping away at her traffic ticket. Celia was busy talking up sugar skulls to a customer so I turned to Flori.

"Let me take over," I said. "You can go inside and warm up."

The fluffy scarf was wrapped over her nose, causing her glasses to fog. Although the temperature hovered in the high fifties, in high, dry Santa Fe under a sparkling sky, it felt much warmer. That doesn't matter to Flori. Once a weatherman utters a number below seventy degrees, she dresses for the Arctic.

"What are you doing here?" she demanded in a snappy tone I interpreted as concern. "I told you to stay home and rest." Behind the foggy lenses, her dark eyes squinted into suspicion.

If Flori hadn't heard about the police search for Tops, I thought, Mr. Hoffman must still be in the hospital. Only after Flori confirmed that her elderly friend was merely stuck in limbo waiting for a discharge doctor did I debrief her on my morning with Linda.

"Very interesting," she said.

"Interesting?" I felt rather let down. Interesting was her array of painted sugar skulls or the neighboring booth's skeleton dolls playing chess. The little food cart advertising chile-spiked chocolates was definitely interesting. I thought my adventure would count as "daring," "brave," or "exciting."

"Very, very interesting," Flori said, pressing her gloved fingertips together. "We may have a new prime suspect. Or a key witness, if your ex can manage to find him."

I felt a bit more affirmed. "That's not all." I nodded for her to follow me to an unpopulated spot. I didn't want anyone to overhear us talking about Victor's will.

When I was done, she clapped her hands in relief. "Thank goodness. Victor surely came to his senses and got his priorities straight. This Dalton woman, she's sure it was a will?"

"Dalia," I corrected. Flori has the memory of an elephant for everything but names. "Yep, it was most certainly a will, witnessed about three months ago." A new worry struck me. "I wonder if it's valid? She said it was handwritten."

Flori had her back to me and was looking out over a dry arroyo dotted with puffy pines and silvery sage. Somewhere in the hills to the north was Gloria's mansion. Was Armida mixing up their bread of the dead dough right now? It was a wonder that Flori didn't have her binoculars out.

"You get to be my age, you know the answer to that one," she said. "Handwritten's fine for a personal will, as long as witnesses see you sign it."

"Jay-Jay must be worried," I said.

Flori agreed. "From what I hear, she's running around town saying she's the heir to Victor's estate. She's waving around that old will too, saying she's going to file it as soon as the probate courts open tomorrow. It would be her lifeline. Word is, she's deep in the hole. Her house is up for sale and her business isn't doing well either."

"So, if there's a new will, the old one wouldn't be valid, right?"

Flori turned to me and pushed up her glasses. "Probably, but the new one has to be found first. We have to get into Victor's place."

She started talking about her lock-picking set,

and I knew I had to come up with a new plan. Fortunately, I had a perfectly reasonable one, as I tried to explain to her. After lunch, I'd simply call Gabe and ask him to let us in. "Or you call Linda and ask her to ask him," I said when Flori didn't respond to my reasonableness.

In lieu of an answer, she elbowed me, not at all reasonably or gently. "Look at that!"

"Ouch! Look at what?" I looked around, seeing shoppers delighting in skulls and other death-themed art and trinkets.

"Over there, at our table. Look who Celia's helping."

My daughter was gesturing to the skulls like a *Wheel of Fortune* hostess turning over letters. Although the customer's back was to me, I recognized the slim figure, the wispy strawberry-blond hair, and the air of arrogance. "Broomer!" I exclaimed. He turned sideways and, to my maternal eyes, looked more interested in Celia than the skulls. "That's it! I'm going over there and run him off."

"Wait!" Flori held me back. "Now this is interesting. Look who's come to chat him up. Gloria the Cheater."

Flori was right about the chatting-up. Gloria leaned on the edge of Flori's table, her tight-skirted derriere perilously close to a stack of mini-skulls. Her arms were tucked in close to her sides, bolstering her balance and her cleavage. Broomer said something and she threw back her head and laughed. Celia scowled from behind the table. That's my girl, I thought, proudly. She can spot fakery when she sees it.

"She's worse than Jay-Jay," I muttered.

"Worse for me," Flori agreed. "Rita, this is an emergency, what do you have on under that coat?"

I had on a sweater with a widening hole in the left armpit. If I took off my coat, my plan was to keep that arm down. This seemed a whole lot safer than doing the laundry to obtain a clean, non-holey sweater, and easier than darning the sweater.

I informed Flori that I was wearing my orange chenille sweater.

"That one with the hole in it?"

Clearly I'd overworn the sweater and forgotten to keep my arm down.

"That won't work," Flori declared. "What do you have on under it? Anything in the sexy lacy top category?"

"No." I didn't like where this was heading. "Why?"

"One of us needs to go outflirt Gloria," Flori said. "Or trip her."

Gloria was obnoxious, I agreed, but I told her I didn't see why a flirty intervention was needed.

Flori pushed back her hood. "I'll tell you why. According to my sister-in-law's cousin's niece, Mimi Davis got kicked off the Day of the Dead committee until she's off probation for fixing parking tickets. Laurence Broomer is her interim replacement."

I struggled to make sense of the sister-in-law's cousin's family branches and how one fixed parking tickets. Most of all, I couldn't see why this would involve me flirting with a slimy murder suspect. Then I realized. "Wait, that's the committee that judges the food contests, right?"

Flori glared at Broomer and Gloria. "That's the one, and I know someone who'll be awfully happy about this." She assessed me again. "Too bad about that sweater. Is that what you had on when Jake showed up at your door this morning?"

"Yes. Along with sweatpants and a bag of frozen peas wrapped on my ankle." I said this with defiance.

Flori chuckled. "You're as stubborn as Linda when it comes to batting your eyelashes at handsome men, Rita. At least Linda's being friendly to Gabe." She grabbed my arm. "Come on. We have to do something about this."

Gloria smiled when she saw us approaching.

"Rita, how nice to see you! You all ran off last night before the raffle. I put names in a hat and seven lucky winners got to taste my famous *pan de muerto.* I was telling Laurence that he was one of the lucky winners."

"You're not bribing a judge, are you?" Flori demanded, scowling behind her spectacles.

Gloria, towering in high-heeled boots, looked down at Flori. For her sake, I hoped she didn't do anything foolish, like pat Flori on her pointed red hood. Flori has an elbow jab that goes straight for the gut.

"Now, Ms. Flori, there are no rules against sharing goodies with friends," she drawled. "Especially those as discerning as Mr. Broomer."

Broomer had spent this discussion glaring at me. I yearned to have an assertive drawl like Gloria's. *Manners*, I'd tell him. *Watch your staring and stop your glaring.* I didn't have Texan confidence or an accent, but that didn't mean I'd let him intimidate me.

"So you left the party early last night, Mr. Broomer?" I asked. "Didn't you notice all the police cars at Victor's place last night?"

He snorted. "I noticed them. I noticed them this morning too when I was trying to meditate. You people are a nuisance. When I tear down that ugly coyote fence, I'm going to build a concrete wall to block out your noise."

My heart clenched. "I won't let you do that!"

"You, eh? You sound like Gabriel. What are you going to do? Tie yourself to a tree? My bulldozer guy can work around that. He likes a challenge." He leaned in so close I could feel the heat of his breath. Remembering the night in the kitchen when he stalked by me, I shuddered. Throngs of people milled around, yet I felt vulnerable and alone.

Broomer leaned even closer, his lips at my ear. "You want to help? I won't budge on the fence, but come by and visit my hot tub tonight and maybe I'll put in a good word for your old friend's bread."

I froze, squeezed between Broomer and the table. No one else knew what he was saying. Gloria was yammering on to Flori about her cupcake prizes. Celia was plugged into her earphones. The latter was a relief. I certainly didn't want her hearing him. What would someone like Gloria do in this situation? I wondered. She'd flirt right back, I thought, or throw a drink in his face. Tough Texan socialites probably carried around drinks specifically for throwing in lecherous men's faces.

When I didn't say anything, Broomer continued, a coyote's grin on his face. "Interested, are
you? Divorced ladies always are."

Just then, red splattered across his face. For
a horrible moment I thought he'd been shot. I
tensed, ready to spring across the table and throw
Celia to the ground.

My daughter looked up and said in a deadpan
voice, "Ooops. Sorry dude, guess I squeezed this
pastry bag too hard. My bad."

Bright red icing oozed from the bag in her hand.
Broomer wiped a hand across his face, smearing
the icing. It clung to his wispy hair and stained his
tan jacket all the way down to his pants. "Stupid
kid! Watch what you're doing," he fumed, and
stomped off toward the museum.

As he disappeared, I caught Celia's eye and the
faintest hint of a conspiratorial smile.

Chapter 26

Cass declared our lunch venue perfect. "Lovely," she said as I relocked the front door of Tres Amigas.

It was lovely. Rays of sunlight glowed across the Saltillo tile floor and the air smelled intriguingly of baked goods.

Cass chose the bench seat by the fireplace and removed her leather boots. Stretching out her socked feet, she said, "I love it in here when no one's around."

I did too, although I also loved to see the restaurant bustling with satisfied eaters. "We didn't escape bones," I said, glancing up at the colorful body parts strung from the ceiling.

"That's okay," Cass said. "You can't avoid them this time of year. It's still awfully relaxing here."

I agreed. Only one thing had me concerned. Addie, or rather her unexpected presence at the closed restaurant. I'd heard her singing when we reached the porch and had called loudly to alert her to our arrival. After bouncing out to greet us, she insisted that we both sit. Now she hovered by our table. "Cheers, me loves, what'll it be? Scones and tea and clotted cream? The house plough-man?" She adjusted her beehive wig and patted down her frilly apron featuring Union Jacks, corgis, and the Queen. As far as I knew—and I should know since I was a co-chef, the second *amiga*—the café didn't serve scones or clotted cream unless you counted sour cream. We could, I supposed, manage a cheese and pickle sand-wich to approximate a ploughman, but the pickle would be a dill spear or a jalapeño.

When I'd suggested Tres Amigas, I'd promised Cass there would be leftover green chile stew. That's what I wanted, and I wanted it extra spicy to burn away the bad taste of Laurence Broomer. I hadn't expected Addie to be here offering up Brit-ish treats.

"A scone and tea sounds wonderful," Cass said, ignoring my under-the-table kicks.

"I'm going to heat us some green chile stew," I said, and then registered the disappointment on Addie's face. "Plus a scone with the works for des-sert," I added with forced enthusiasm.

"Smashing!" Addie exclaimed. "I'll get the stew for you, dearie, and the scone. This is my first batch of scones ever, don't you know? Miss Flori left me with some recipes to practice. You'll be like my . . . mmm . . . what's an English version of a guinea pig?"

"Hedgehog?" Cass said helpfully.

"Right-o! Hedgehogs!" Addie skipped off to the kitchen in a swirl of red, white, and royals.

Cass smiled. "I'm with Flori on this one. Far-fetched dreams need a little support. Look at me. My mom could have considered me a budding arsonist when I asked for a torch one Christmas. Instead, she got me a tank of butane and soldering lessons."

"I'm all for dreams," I assured her, grateful that Celia painted mopey fairies and wasn't requesting vats of flammable gas. I lowered my voice to a whisper. "It's Addie's baking skills you have to worry about." The scent of charred fruit wafted from the kitchen. Pans crashed. A few minutes later Addie emerged, carrying a steaming bowl of green chile and a plate of smoking scones.

"Nice and well-done," she declared. "Like we like 'em in Brighton." With a chipper "Ta" and "Cheers," she flounced back to the other room.

Cass gamely picked at the top, less-burned portion of her scone, slathering it with butter and what appeared to be deflated whipped cream or watery sour cream. "It's not the worst," she said, generously, "but what's this English dream of hers, again? It's not cooking, is it?"

I was pleased with my spicy stew, even if it was microwaved to molten on the outside and chilly in the middle. "Singing," I said, to which Cass mouthed *Thank goodness*.

"Not so fast," I cautioned. "She went down to Albuquerque recently and saw an English tea/dance theater act. She wants to do dance, song, and food performance. Flori, of course, thinks it's a grand idea."

Cass chuckled. "I think it's grand too, although not with these scones." She grabbed a spoon from another table and stole a bite of my chile stew.

She made happy sounds and was even more delighted when I told her about Victor's new will. "Good. Setting things in order, your neighbor said? Surely he cut out that awful Jay-Jay. I can see how he might have felt guilty after their divorce, but he must have seen how she exploited artists."

Cass was apparently so happy that she could stomach Addie's cooking. She polished off the scone she'd begun, all except the black bottom.

"Does it put Jay-Jay lower or higher on our list, though?" I asked. I'd been pondering this and couldn't decide. Flori said that Jay-Jay was hurting for money. Maybe she remembered the will and decided to call it in early. On the other hand, would she go as far as murder? And wouldn't she check to make sure Victor hadn't disinherited her?

Cass took some time to ponder these questions. "She's ruthless and slimy, but undercutting art deals are a long way from cold-blooded murder. And it seems like she and Victor were civil after the divorce. They must have been, right? I mean, who goes to the trouble of making a new will to include his ex?"

That bothered me too. Not all divorced couples were like me and Manny, I told myself. Some exspouses stayed friends. I thought about what Flori said about Victor feeling guilty. What was that about? Something personal? Something criminal? Perhaps that was why he needed Jake's legal help. I asked Cass, who didn't have an answer. She did, however, have a suspect higher than Jay-Jay on her list.

"I still like Broomer for it," she said, bravely helping herself to another scone.

Bile rose in my throat. Broomer was slimy, that was for sure, and he had a motive, although more against Gabe than Victor. Maybe he got the brothers mixed up. Or maybe I had it all mixed up. Tops's jumbled words kept rolling through my head. Out loud, I tried to recall what he'd said.

"Back up," Cass said midway through my recitation. "He said 'golden lady'?"

"Golden someone. Lady, I think, but he could have said woman."

"Oh, well there you have it. Who were we just talking about who has a tacky gold wardrobe?"

"Of course! Jay-Jay."

"Exactly," Cass said. "You weren't here years ago when she was first starting out. She had a gallery downtown and hokey TV commercials in which she'd wear all gold pantsuits. I think she may have called herself the 'gold lady' with the 'golden touch,' but I've tried to block those out of my memory." Cass took a big bite of scone and chewed resolutely.

Addie had arrived with a tray of cups and a teapot. Momentarily, she dropped her English accent and became local-girl Adelina again. "I know who you're talking about. I saw her this morning. She looks the same as ever." Addie scowled. Then she put back on her British accent and patted her bouffant. "Horrid hair. A real cow, if you don't mind me saying."

"Where'd you see her?" Cass asked. If I knew Cass, she was asking to avoid crossing paths with Jay-Jay again.

"Somewhere where she shouldn't be," Addie said. "Down at the arts center. Victor's center, you know? I stopped by to pick up me wee cousin, and there she was, acting like she owned the place. She was kicking the kids and Victor's workers out." Addie set the tea down hard. Liquid the color of watered-down coffee sloshed out, soaking a scone. She didn't seem to notice. Her face was turning the color of her cherry-red lipstick. "She was yelling at one of the staff members, saying that she owned the building and would sell it if she wanted to. That can't be, can it? She *can't* shut down the arts center!"

The fire alarm chirped in the kitchen, and Addie rushed off. Cass and I groaned.

"It's okay, there's the new will," I said, feeling not at all okay.

Cass shook her head. "If she gets her hands on that building, she'll have a fortune in real estate."

"And a motive," I said. "A big one."

Cass insisted on driving, brushing off my protests that the Railyard District was only a few blocks away.

"I *can* walk," I said, feeling slightly guilty yet also pleased. I had the seat reclined and a bag of ice cubes wrapped around my ankle. Forced relaxation was just what I needed.

"Nonsense," Cass said. "You should stay off that ankle. Anyway, we need the car to make a quick escape from Jay-Jay if necessary."

From my prone position I watched a moving

picture of puffy clouds and adobe stovepipes set against a shockingly blue New Mexico sky. It was nice. I may have even dozed off.

"Here we are," Cass said. I sat up to a view of the Railyard, a hip part of town with industrial lofts and sleek art galleries. The Farmer's Market building was next door, and I yearned to go there instead. How nice it would be to shop for fresh cheese or winter squashes instead of tracking down Jay-Jay.

"Doesn't look like much, does it?" Cass said. We stood by the tracks across from Victor's warehouse building, waiting for the Rail Runner to pass. The roadrunner-emblazoned commuter train blew its whistle as it chugged off toward Albuquerque.

Victor's warehouse resembled a giant tin can cut in half, from its shape to the corrugated metal exterior. However, the land alone had to be worth a fortune. Cass led the way to a red door, not stopping to knock.

Inside, the tin can was a jewel, as fanciful as Victor's home. Canvas hung from the walls, painted in murals ranging in styles from urban graffiti to old Spanish primitive. To my surprise, one featured morose fairies, Celia's signature subject. The loss to her and all the kids Victor helped stabbed at my heart. So did the thought of Jay-Jay selling this wonderful space.

"We're closed!" The snippy voice came from behind a paneled wall.

Beside me, Cass bristled. "It's her," she hissed. "The nerve of that woman!"

I'm not good with conflict, although I keep finding myself in the midst of it. I gripped Cass's elbow, hoping to calm her down. "We're just here to get clues," I said.

After a moment Cass sighed. "You're right. We'll trip her up with kindness."

"Jay-Jay," she trilled. "Is that you? It's Cass and Rita."

I spotted the yellow hair first, then an unnaturally orange furry boot. "Cass Sathers!" The full gold-glittery form of Jay-Jay emerged and she trotted over to greet us. "You're just the woman I wanted to see, Cass. Oh, and Victor's neighbor. I was hoping to find you!"

I bet she was, hoping that I'd let her in Victor's place. As she air-kissed Cass, I slipped around to peek at the other side of the panel. Papers covered the floor and spewed from file folders.

"Don't mind the mess. I'm trying to organize Victor's files. What a dear but scattered man he was." She took me by the elbow and pulled me back into the main room.

"Are you looking for something in particular in the files?" Cass asked, her tone one of complete innocence. I envied her skill at sounding so calm.

Jay-Jay hesitated. "Oh, you know," she said. When Cass and I didn't say anything, she continued. "Getting his paperwork sorted out, that's all. When I take over this place, I'll need things in order."

"So you can sell?" Cass asked. This time her voice had a hard edge. She stared down Jay-Jay, who didn't blink.

"Yes, possibly. I can't very well make any money from a nonprofit can I?"

Anger burbled up inside me, erupting as a

jumble of words. "The kids. Look at these paint-ings. How can you take away their art center? You can't. You won't. You won't inherit this building."

Cass backed me up. "Exactly. We know that you heard about Victor's new will. Until that's found and probated, you're trespassing. We'll call the police if you don't leave right now."

"And a lawyer. We'll call Victor's lawyer." I was thinking of Jake and how nice it would be for him to come to the rescue. I imagined him hauling Jay-Jay off to prison, like the cowboy lawman hero of old Westerns.

Jay-Jay shook her yellow-haired head as if dis-appointed in us. "Why, I already spoke to Victor's lawyer. He's the one who gave me the key to this place."

"What?" Cass and I said in unison.

Jay-Jay walked to a table covered in little kids' paintings, the kind featuring trees and stick fig-ures and giant suns. She ran her hand over a stick family. "Roy Hernandez," she said. "He's been Victor's lawyer since I don't know when. He has Victor's will on file too. The will that leaves this all to me. He's going to file it for me tomorrow and then, as you say, we'll sort this all out."

I had to practically pull Cass out the door. She wanted to drag Jay-Jay with us.

"We can't," I said to her as the red door clicked, locking behind us. Cass turned to glare at it. I tried to reason with her. I grabbed her fist before she could pound on it. "What can we do? Jay-Jay says that the lawyer gave her the key and permis-sion."

"I know what *you* can do," Cass said. "Chummy

up to Jake. We need legal help. Jay-Jay might be mean and hurting for cash, but she has influence around here. If she gets that will approved, this center and Victor's home are goners."

For once I didn't chide her for encouraging me to call Jake. The trouble was, without the new will, I wasn't sure how he could help.

Chapter 27

Cass wasn't the only one pushing me to call Jake. "It's Halloween dinner!" Flori insisted, making it sound like I was refusing to invite a lonely pilgrim to Thanksgiving.

"It's Sunday night and a workday tomorrow," I protested. "And a school night."

Celia, who was playing a game of chess with Bernard, gave me a classic *Whatever, Mom* look. I didn't care. I continued with my good-reason lecture.

"We all need to get to bed early tonight. You too, Flori, especially if we're going to keep the café open regular hours and do the bread contest tomorrow.

Flori's look approximated Celia's, only with eighty years of wrinkles. "It's inconvenient having that contest on a Monday night," she said. "I know, it's the actual day and the spirits and businesses will appreciate it. But so will those idle types who don't have to work like you know who."

"May her name never be mentioned," Bernard called out merrily from the living room.

Flori's house, like a lot of old adobes around town, is a basic box shape. You enter through a rounded door to a combined living room/dining room/kitchen, all facing a pretty kiva fireplace and a hallway leading to three cozy bedrooms. The ceiling beams are dark with age and slightly sagging. The floor is wooden planks, worn soft by over a century of use. A little island covered in colorful Mexican tiles demarcates the kitchen. Flori's home is a warm, happy place, and I'd readily agreed to let Celia stay another night. She'd argued that she could walk to school, and truth be told, I didn't want her back at the casita if Tops was still around, finding keys and letting himself in. I didn't know if the locks on our casita had been changed ever. Thinking about the wobbly lock and elderly doorknob, I doubted they had.

My thoughts lingered on doors and locks when Flori's front door flung open and bashed into my nonsprained ankle.

"Ooops," Gabe said. "Sorry."

I couldn't very well fuss to a man in mourning, not to mention my new landlord. At least, I hoped he was my new landlord, and not Jay-Jay. I made a mental note to ask Gabe to change all of our locks.

Linda followed close behind, carrying a tray of enchiladas.

"One side's cheese and the other's chicken," she said, placing the long earthenware casserole dish on the table. "Aunt Aida's favorite."

"She'll be with us by midnight," Bernard said, as Celia crowed, "Checkmate!"

Gabe went to sit with them, sinking into a puffy armchair. Linda joined me and Flori in the little kitchen. "I hope you don't mind that I invited Gabe," she whispered. "He'd be all alone otherwise and I can't stand the thought of him in that big old house, waiting for trick-or-treaters who won't come by. I wouldn't let *my* kids or grandkids go to a murder house. Oh, but what if teens come by for a thrill? He shouldn't be there." She checked herself, looking embarrassed and worried. Mostly worried.

"I'd be disappointed if you hadn't invited him," Flori assured her daughter, while shooting me a look that implied that I should call a certain handsome lawyer.

"I'm sure that Jake has plans," I said. What those plans would be, I couldn't imagine. Single adults without little kids didn't dress up and go trick-or-treating. Maybe he stayed home with his bulldog and handed out candy. Or maybe he was on a date with someone who didn't spend her free time chasing criminals or have all sorts of rules about not dating. Or maybe he was like Cass, who had plans to turn off all her lights, lock her doors, and avoid any calls from would-be dates who wanted to invite her to haunted houses.

"Imagine how horrible," she'd told me earlier, recounting an invitation to a haunted house. "This guy, who I'd only met once before, wanted to go to someplace claiming it was haunted by a demented clown family. As if I'd want to see that. I'll be screening calls, though, so if you get lost in the forest again, promise you'll call and I'll come get you. Promise me, Rita!"

I'd promised. I had no plans to get lost in the forest or chase after Tops or any other potential murderers. As I assured Cass, I would help Flori hand out Halloween candy to cute children. Then I'd head home, secure my own locks, and be in bed by nine.

I lifted the tinfoil from Linda's casserole dish, letting the warm cheesy scents waft up to me. Who needs expensive spa treatments when you have steaming enchiladas and a vat of posole? Flori dished out the stew, rich with tender chicken and puffed hominy bathed in a smoky red chile broth. For decoration and flavor, she topped each bowl with fresh cilantro, pickled radishes, a dollop of sour cream, and a lime wedge on the side. My mouth watered in anticipation.

"I invited Addie too," she said, handing me a bowl. "But she has a full singing schedule tonight. That girl is going places, I tell you. How were her scones?"

"Ah . . . well . . . they were really thoroughly done," I said, trying to avoid adjectives that implied burned doorstops. The land of flakey soft baked goods was not where Addie was headed.

"Overbaked them, did she?" Flori shook her head. "She's not a natural cook, not like you. Even if you didn't have your fancy cooking certificates, you're a born chef, Rita."

I basked in Flori's praise and in the carefree meal that followed, which was happily interrupted every few minutes by trick-or-treaters, ranging from babies to teens taller than me. Celia and Flori joked with the little ones, pretending to be terrified by tiny pirates, ghosts, and witches. No one spoke directly of the dead.

By nine I was stuffed to the gills. Two helpings of *tres leches* cake hadn't helped, but I couldn't resist the soft white cake soaked in milk and cream. My eyelids sagged and I remembered my vow to be in bed by now.

Flori urged me to stay. "You shouldn't be driving in your state," she scolded.

I hadn't had more than a tablespoon of Bernard's homemade pear liquor, and as far as I could tell, Flori hadn't spiked the cake. I could drive. Gabe, on the other hand, had drunk several glasses of beer and as many pear nightcaps. "We're going to the same place," I said, dangling my keys and confiscating his. "I'll drive, Gabriel, if you keep a lookout for trick-or-treaters."

He didn't put up a fight. He sat in the front seat, leaning back contentedly. I drove like a little old lady should—as in, the opposite of Flori. I scanned the road for darting kids. I turned on my brights on dark stretches and barely pushed the speedometer over thirty the entire way.

"Thank you for the peaceful ride," Gabriel said, gentlemanly, when we finally arrived.

"Bolt your doors," I said, sounding like a worried mother and Linda.

"Wouldn't want you terrorizing me in my sleep again, now would I," he said with a slight smile. I smiled too. It was good to see him forget his sorrow for a moment.

I settled into bed after double-checking that all doors, windows, and curtains were battened down. My eyes were sagging over my bedtime reading when I heard footsteps crunching on the gravel driveway and approaching my porch. I froze, fighting back the irrational urge to hide under the covers.

The footsteps stopped at my door, as I dreaded they would. A trick-or-treater, I told myself. A big one, who doesn't know what time it is. I didn't believe that, especially when the pounding on the door shook the house. I reached for my phone, ready to call Bunny's direct line. But what would I tell her? Someone was knocking at my door? I could imagine Manny's scoffing if the visitor was a trick-or-treater looking for candy or directions.

I padded barefoot over the tile floors, grateful that the tile, although frigid, didn't squeak like old wood. The antique door didn't have a peephole. It did, however, have a little window the size of a postcard, covered by a tiny curtain. Through it, from the darkness of the living room, I could barely make out the shape illuminated under the motion detector light. It wasn't Tops, unless he'd shrunk. It wasn't some overenthusiastic trick-or-treater in a ghost costume either. I risked being spotted and flicked the curtain aside. Two eyes looked straight back at mine, separated only by glass. I yelped and jerked my head back. On the other side of the door, I heard another yelp.

"Rita, it's me, Gabriel!"

I was so busy with apologies when I opened the door that I forgot I was wearing a flannel nightshirt with plaid moose all over it.

"I'm so sorry. You were in bed already," Gabe

said, after I ushered him in and shut the door against the cold, dark night. "I was reluctant to come over, but I had to check that you were okay."

My heart sped up again. "Okay? Why? What's wrong?"

He slumped onto one arm of my couch, his face sagging as much as his shoulders. "My house— someone came in and made a mess of my kitchen. Looks like it was that homeless guy. Probably has a key to Victor's." He shuffled his feet. "I should have changed all the locks, like you said."

"We'll call the police," I assured him, shivering, and not from the cold.

'm really tired of coming out here," Manny griped.

I was tired of seeing him. More than that, I was tired of living in a crime scene. I had quickly put on jeans and hidden my nighttime moose attire under a long coat. Now I stood by Gabe's French wonder stove, running a finger over its shiny blue enamel. The rest of the kitchen was not looking as sleek as the last time I saw it. Tomato sauce was spewed across the floor, just one of the casualties of the trashed fridge and pillaged pantry.

"Why make such a mess?" Gabe muttered.

Why indeed? Gabe might not have noticed a few missing items if Tops had simply sneaked in and taken a few nonperishables. I surveyed the mess. "What's missing?" I asked Gabe.

"What, you're looking to make a midnight

snack, Rita?" Manny asked. "Want me to put an APB out for chocolate cake?"

I ignored him.

Bunny shot Manny a frown. "Ms. Lafitte asks a good question," she said tersely. "Sir, please inspect your refrigerator and cupboards and tell if anything has been taken." She gestured for an underling officer to come and take notes.

Gabe wearily obeyed. "Milk," he said. "But it was almost out of date, since I haven't wanted to shop. Who'd want old milk?" He continued listing, making his way through tuna fish and granola bars and canned chicken broth.

Through it all, Bunny nodded. "We may need the bloodhounds," I overheard her telling Manny.

"Tomorrow," he said. "A tuna robbery for some mangy stray cat can wait until morning. We have enough to worry about with Halloween. Anyway, I have a date."

My eye had developed a thumping tick, surely a symptom of too much late-night exposure to Manny and stress and crime scenes. I needed some air. Slipping by a police photographer snapping shots of spilled rice, I wandered down the hallway to Gabe's serene foyer of art. The Indian woman in the gilt frame seemed to gaze at the door to Victor's wing. I imagined that she was guiding me, like a sign from one of Dalia's readings. I was thinking about Dalia having her head in the stars when I noticed that the door was open a crack.

I mentally apologized to Dalia and thanked the Indian woman on the wall. This was definitely a sign, a path I should follow.

Making my way down the hallway, I steeled myself to enter the living room. I hadn't been in this part of the house since Victor's death. I expected the wave of sadness that struck me, yet I felt something else too, something good. Was it Victor's comforting spirit? The lingering scent of spiced cookies?

Flipping on a small table lamp, I scanned the room, trying to determine if anything was missing. In a house so laden with artwork, I had little chance of spotting a missing ornament or saint. The only obvious gap was the glaringly clear spot where Victor's life had ended. A cleaning crew had bleached and scrubbed, but the emptiness might as well have had a chalk body outline on it. I forced my eyes up to the altar. There were Victor's dad, mom, great-uncle, and a bunch of people I didn't recognize. The unlit candles made me sad. Would the spirits Victor cared for find their way here? Even if they did, there was no one to greet them.

I was staring at a mosaic of fading color snapshots encircled by skulls when a finger tapped me on the shoulder. I imagined a skeleton beckoning or Tops about to grab my neck and drag me off. My knees buckled and I let out a scream to wake the dead.

Chapter 28

S hhhh . . ." My presumed attacker wore a red-
hooded coat and smelled of freshly baked
pan de muerto. "With all that yelling, you'll
summon the spirits and the police, Rita."

"Flori!" I thumped my hand on my pounding
heart. She didn't take the hint that she'd terrorized
me. Her eyes were squinting at Victor's altar.

"Mmm . . ." she said, sounding grumpy. "Too
bad his recipe box isn't here. Let's go search the
kitchen."

I managed to grab her Little Red Riding Hood
hood before she made it past the kitchen threshold.

"Hold on. How did you get in here?"

She turned to grin at me. "Through the front
door, of course. I saw that the police were occupied
in the kitchen, so I guessed you were over here.
Now let's get a move on. We won't have a chance
to look around if your ex, Detective Spoiled Sport,
gets wind of us."

"Bill Hoffman's out of the hospital, I take it?"

"Right as rain and back at his police scanner. I called that Indian restaurant and told them to re-route any of his chicken korma orders straight to me. That oughta keep him safe for a little while, and I do love korma."

I followed Flori toward the kitchen. "And how did you get the Indian place to agree to that?"

"Free meal at the café anytime they foil him. The code word is Bombay Bill."

"I'll remember that," I said, rolling my eyes, a gesture that Flori also missed. She was pulling on knitted gloves and talking about finding Victor's will and recipe collection. While she peeked in drawers, I scanned the room, my nerves overriding my helpfulness. The police would soon check on Victor's place. I imagined Manny bursting in, gun drawn. Or Bunny's disapproving scowl. Worse yet, what would Gabriel think about us, snooping in his brother's sacred kitchen?

"Hurry," I urged Flori, now regretting that I'd started this snoop. To calm myself, I studied Victor's colorful tile countertop and admired his paintings of San Pasqual. In Victor's renderings, the kitchen saint wore the brown robes of a monk and sported a monk's haircut, bald on top with a bowl-shaped cut below. His peaceful, benevolent expression reminded me of Victor. So did the pies, cookies, and strings of red chiles the saint stood beside.

"Woo hoo!" Flori followed this whoop with the announcement that she'd found the recipe box. She hefted a tin the size of a loaf of bread down from an open shelf crowded with carved saints.

"Aha!" she exclaimed, lifting the lid. "I see several *bizcochito* recipes here. Ooo, and his nana's peach pie. She won a contest in Pie Town with that one."

She had the box on the kitchen table and was leafing through the recipes, some on yellowed recipe cards, others written out in Victor's scrawled script on folded sheets of drawing paper.

Snooping in Victor's house had already felt wrong. Pawing through his secret recipes seemed way too personal, worse than rifling through his underwear drawer or medicine cabinet. I reached for the box and gently closed the punched-tin lid. "We should look at the recipes later," I said, keeping my hand on the lid. "After we get permission from Gabe."

Flori made a huffy sound.

I held firm, both to the lid and my principles. "These are Victor's secrets, Flori."

She didn't look convinced until I added, "And we have to get going before the police notice we're in here."

Flori tore her eyes from the box. "Fine. Then I have a surprise for you. Turn around and don't look until I tell you."

I wasn't in the mood for surprises but turned around anyway. The happier she was, I decided, the sooner we could leave.

"Bingo!" she cried and told me I could turn back.

I twisted around to see her half engulfed by the fireplace. My cries of alarm brought happy, echoing laughing from the chimney.

"Don't worry," she said, scooting out. "It's not that dirty. Victor never used this chimney. There are swallows' nests up at the top and he told me that he couldn't bear to disrupt them." Her cheeks were rosy and her nose sported a black smudge, like a Christmas elf burglar.

"Why the 'bingo'?" I asked.

She opened a grimy hand to reveal an old-fashioned key. "Now we look for what this opens."

I wondered aloud how she'd known to search a chimney. Maybe she really did have a sixth sense. Who sticks their head up a birdy, sooty chimney and comes out with a secret key?

The answer wasn't quite so impressive. "Victor told me," she explained as we hurried around the house, trying the key in any trunk, door, or desk with a keyhole. "Well, he didn't actually tell me, but it was easy enough to guess. See, I was telling him that I keep my safe deposit key frozen in a tamale, and—"

The absurdity of this was enough for me to momentarily forget my nerves. "Wait. You have a key frozen in a tamale? What if someone eats it?" I added a Lindalike worry for emphasis: "Bernard could choke."

She tapped her forehead in a *good thinking* kind of way. "That's why I label the tamale 'Ida Green's vegan.' No one in their right mind would eat it, see? Not even Bernard."

Ida Green ran a notoriously awful restaurant and bail bonds business out by the police station. Only the desperate would eat her cooking or pay her bond fees. As far as I knew, she'd never embraced the vegan trend, as meat was said to be her only saving culinary grace.

Flori continued with her story. "And that's when Victor told me that he keeps his secret key where only St. Nick would find it. See? Too easy."

We checked a china cabinet and writing desk before finding the key's proper place.

Flori slid it into the keyhole of an old metal-framed steamer chest and twisted the lock open. "Prepare yourself for the truth," she said dramatically.

I couldn't help it. I held my breath as she opened the lid. The result was kind of a letdown, not as bad as Al Capone's empty vault, but not an instant revelation either.

Flori removed a patchwork quilt and some lace doilies.

"This is good," she said, stubborn in her conviction that we were on to something. "Look, here, paperwork. See what's in this folder while I keep digging."

She handed me an accordion folder marked *Important Papers*. This was the kind of filing system I used, namely throw everything in a folder and hide it away. I dug out insurance policies for the house and for Victor himself. "Life insurance," I reported. "But it's an old term-life policy."

"Who's the beneficiary?" she asked from neck deep in the trunk.

My heart sank when I found the right page. "Jay-Jay." Hopefully, the policy had expired. I kept looking and in the very last accordion fold found a manila envelope marked *Will*.

I told Flori, and she watched as I opened the envelope with trembling hands. As soon as I saw the typewritten words, I knew what they would say.

Flori took the paper from me and sighed. "Jay-Jay. Don't worry, Rita. We'll find the right one. These look like his old files anyway."

"Yeah," I said, not feeling consoled. I stuffed the folder back in the trunk and leaned against the wall. It was then that I registered the squawk of a police radio, a sound that seemed to be coming closer.

"Flori," I whispered. "Did you hear that radio? We have to put this stuff back. If Manny finds us snooping in here . . ."

Flori was sitting on the floor holding a shoe box of old snapshots on her lap. "Just a minute more," she said, flipping through photos. She held up one. "These bring back memories. Look, this is the boys and Linda and their gang of friends." She smiled. "Inner tubing on the Pecos, picnicking on Mount Baldy."

My fear of discovery was reaching panic levels when she grunted in disgust and snapped the shoe box closed.

"You're right, Rita. Let's get out of here." She held out a hand and I helped her up, noting the limp in her knee as she tottered down the hall.

Manny's voice boomed across the house. "Police! Who's in here? Identify yourself!"

"Quick, to the kitchen," Flori said, glancing back at me. "We'll tell him that we came in to look for recipes."

This was partially the truth, and a good idea too. Manny would write off recipe snooping as typical behavior by Flori and me. I told Flori that I'd be right behind her. I would be too, but not before I peeked in the shoe box. The color photos had faded to chartreuse and yellows, but I easily recognized a young Linda, standing by a river with a boy. He looked somewhat familiar. Had I seen his photo elsewhere? His arm was around her waist and they were both smiling. *Linda and David, '68*, read Victor's slanted scrawl on the back of the photo. No wonder Flori had been upset. That smiling, redheaded boy would soon break Linda's heart. I shut him back in the shoe box, closed the trunk, and ran to join Flori.

"Freeze!" Manny bellowed. His supercop aspirations were ruined by Flori throwing up her arms and releasing a shower of recipes onto his shoes. To her chest, she clasped the tin box. Manny hopped back, cursing.

"Stop yelling," she chided him, as if he was a misbehaving child. "Look what you made me do."

Bunny and a policeman barely older than Celia jammed through the doorway, with Bunny demanding to know what was going on.

"Your partner nearly scared me into a heart attack, that's what's going on," Flori said in her most indignant voice. "No respect for the elderly."

"I have no respect for snooping old women," Manny sputtered.

"Don't call me old!" Flori waved her finger at him. "Rita and I have half a mind to call her hot lawyer and have you cited for harassment."

Manny's face was turning the color of San Pasqual's wreath of chile peppers.

Turning to Bunny, I told her, truthfully, that we'd been drawn into the kitchen out of sentiment and nostalgia. I neglected to mention the sleuthing.

Bunny shook her head as if extremely disappointed. "Please leave this to us," she said. "Please. We have enough trouble already."

"Absolutely," Flori said agreeably. "We'll leave as soon as we clean up this mess your partner caused." She pointed to the recipes. Manny stalked off, followed by the patrolman and Bunny, who instructed us to turn off the lights and leave the door as we'd found it.

When they were gone, Flori gave me a sly look. "We're lucky they left. Now we can take these. I can stuff the box under my coat."

I helped her pick up cards and shove them back into the overflowing recipe tin. Despite myself, I glanced at some. Recipes for sour-cream apple pie, red-pork tamales, Miguel's secret mole, and Navajo lamb stew tempted my resolve, until my midwestern rule-following guilt kicked in.

"We can't . . ." I said, as much to myself as to Flori. "We can't steal these."

"It's not stealing," Flori reasoned. "We're saving. Gabriel doesn't cook and that awful Jay-Jay wouldn't know a treasure like this if she fell on it. They might throw these old recipes away. That would be wrong. A tragedy."

She cradled the box as if it were a baby. "If it makes you feel better, Rita, I'll promise on my mother's grave and Our Lady of Peace that we won't open this box again until we get Gabe's permission. I'll ask him tomorrow and offer him some code words for free meals. How about that?"

When I nodded, she tucked the box under her coat. "Now, let's go," she said. "We'll take my car."

I didn't want to go anywhere except to bed. How did Flori get so much energy? I apologized and said that I had to get some sleep.

"Oh, you will sleep, dear," she said, looping her hand around my elbow. "At my place. It's not safe here, not with people breaking in, and I don't mean us."

Chapter 29

There are a lot of things to love about sleeping overnight at Flori's. Her guest bed, for instance, is like a fairy-tale princess's bed. Filmy lace cascades from the antique four-poster frame, which is seemingly from a time of giants. I need a stepping stool to heft myself up to its heights. Flori would need a ladder. The reward is worth it, though. I nestled into the pillowy mattress topped with heavy patchwork quilts and masses of fluffy pillows. Best of all, Flori's big cat Zozo slept at my side, lulling me to sleep with his purrs.

A negative, however, had been encountering Celia in the hallway when we returned. She'd looked pointedly at an imaginary watch on her wrist.

"Dad texted," she'd said, turning heel toward the bathroom. "In case I was worried about you getting in trouble for breaking and entering or whatever."

I'd figured that "whatever" about covered the night, kissed my daughter's frowning forehead, and told her to sleep tight. The other drawback of sleeping at Flori's was her version of a wake-up call.

"Rise and shine!" she bellowed before even a hint of sunrise peeked through the shutters. Zozo shot off the bed, seventeen pounds of fur and claws, motivated by breakfast. Flori switched on the overhead light and handed me a cup of coffee. The coffee almost made up for being rousted in the wee hours. So did Flori's enthusiasm.

"Today's the big day! Gloria and Armida, meet your match! Now we have to get going if we're going to get the breakfast and lunch prep done and have time to scope out the setup down at the *pan de muerto* contest."

Eyes half open, I carefully made my way off the pedestal bed. I wished I could bathe in coffee. Instead, I gulped the first cup, reluctantly replaced a borrowed nightshirt with my same clothes from yesterday, and followed Flori out the door and into the darkness. She lived close enough to Tres Amigas that we could walk.

"Nothing like beating the blackbirds up," she said as we waited to cross the street. I hugged my arms around my chest and wished I had Flori's wool coat and hat instead of a light fall jacket. A single car rolled past. Most houses sat quiet and dark, except for porch lights that sensed us as we walked by.

To my surprise, light glowed in the café and smoke curled from its chimney. Linda greeted us at the door, wearing a cactus-print apron and an expression of concern.

"I heard what happened over at Victor and Gabe's place last night," she said after hugging us both. "I couldn't sleep for all the worry so I came in early to cook."

When I worry, I eat, especially salty crunchy snacks. During the height of divorce stress, I'd taken down entire tubes of Pringles and family-sized bags of Fritos, with and without chile and cheese toppings. Taking Linda's approach, I could have had breakfast preps done hours in advance and been several pounds lighter.

Linda was listing the items she'd finished. Salsas, done. Chiles, charred and peeled. Cheese, grated. Enchiladas, filled, wrapped, and ready for baking. Green chile stew, simmering. Even Flori looked at a loss about what to do next.

"I can't think of anything you missed," she told her daughter, who was folding napkins around sets of silverware and looking fretful.

"Your breads," Linda said. "That's what you need to focus on, Mama." She turned her worried frown toward several Ziploc bags in which Flori's dough sat, seemingly stagnant. "Why aren't they rising? Are they okay? Should we make another batch in case?"

"No need to worry," Flori said stoutly. "The yeast is chilly from resting in the fridge. It's the slow rise that gives them the extra flavor. They'll warm up and rise and then we can bake them by early afternoon so they'll have time to cool to the perfect slicing temperature." She sounded confident. She looked confident. Until Linda went out to the dining room to fill flower vases with sprigs of Chinese lanterns.

"We could be cooked," Flori whispered to me.

For a second I thought she meant the soup of the day, a chicken tortilla soup that I was making. I was about to say that it had barely begun to simmer when I saw her face and the wrinkle lines creased deeper than Linda's. "Oh," was all I could say.

Flori confessed to doubts. "What if that Gloria has something up her sleeve? What if she's bought a judge? I've heard some rumors. She sure has the money to do it."

I began to protest, then stopped. Broomer wouldn't think twice about being bought off. He'd practically offered me an edge for Flori if I joined him in his hot tub. I could feel my blush rising, this time out of anger. Flori and the other competitors deserved a fair contest.

Flori poked her dough, testing it by its dimples. "I'm not giving up. Those other judges will know honest bread when they taste it. They'll know the real winner."

In the lull between breakfast and lunch, she and I went to inspect the contest venue, leaving the café in the hands of Linda, Addie, and Juan. Flori insisted that we take the route past Jake's office.

"It's out of our way," I protested, to no avail.

"Well you're not going to catch his attention by hiding out. Besides, you look good today." She looked me up and down, probably realizing that I was wearing yesterday's clothes and not looking all that good. Finally, she said, "You're not wearing frozen peas, that's good."

It was good, although I continued to walk like a peg-legged pirate. To avoid peas, which aren't practical for work, I'd wrapped the ankle in menthol-coated tape I found in the café's medicine cabinet. Consequently, the ankle stumped along, unbendable and emitting a minty scent that seemed irresistible to canines. A basset hound waiting outside the café had coated my shoe in drool, and a small herd of Chihuahuas had nearly pulled their owner over to get to me. If any coyotes roamed the streets, I'd be a goner.

I didn't want Jake to see me in rumpled yesterday's clothes, menthol patches, and dog slobber. I also didn't need to be attracting anyone, I reminded myself. Luckily for my image and dating moratorium, Jake's office was closed. A sign on the door read: CLOSED FOR DÍA DE LOS MUERTOS. Flori was thrilled.

"That's the way it should be," she said. "I would have closed the café, but we can't let our customers go hungry on such an important day. Jake Strong is a good, fine man. You should—"

"I know, I know," I sighed. "I should show some interest."

"Exactly!"

The bread contest was being held on the Plaza, along with an arts and crafts fair and music. The artists were already set up. I lagged behind Flori, distracted by beautiful bobbles of silver and chunks of turquoise. Native American artists sat along the ancient Palace of the Governors Museum, where they had a special reserved spot throughout the year. On blankets laid out in front of them, they showcased gorgeous squash-blossom-style necklaces, ornate bolo ties, and black pottery buffed to gleam like obsidian. The scene of the covered walkway, adobe walls, and sellers with their wares might have been from centuries ago.

I recognized familiar faces too, including café regulars and, to my surprise, Gabe. He squatted in front of a vendor near the end of the row and seemed to be inspecting a covered pottery jar. Or maybe it was an urn. The thought turned my stomach. Linda had told us that the medical examiner was releasing Victor's body. Gabe was arranging for a closed-casket visitation at a funeral home, followed by a cremation and a service at their family plot. Was he buying Victor's final resting place, his brother's last piece of art? Part of me wanted to go to him. The wimpy other part of me rationalized that if that was Gabe's mission, he'd want his privacy.

To avoid disturbing him, I crossed to the Plaza, where other local vendors had rows of stands. In between a lady selling wind chimes and a tin artist, I spotted Cass.

"The holidays will never end," she said glumly. "They're just getting started and I can barely stand all the crowds and social obligations." She lowered her voice and leaned in. "And these wind chimes are about to drive me batty! Ding, ding, ding." After a deep breath, she stretched and smiled. "Sorry, had to get that off my chest."

Poor Cass. She was getting business, though. A group of ladies stopped at her stand, and we both put on beaming smiles until they left.

"I heard about your night," she said after the ladies moved on, each sporting new silver rings. "You should have called."

"Flori took me to her house," I said. A yawn overtook me as I explained how late it had been.

Cass's brow was as wrinkled as Linda's in full worry. "Rita, I didn't want to bring this up before because I know you like your new place, but maybe you should think about moving."

As she courted more potential customers, I considered this advice. I'd had the same conflicted thoughts. Although I loved the casita, would it ever be the same without Victor? Could I afford to move, and find a place right before the holidays? It all seemed like too much to think about. I gave Cass a quick hug good-bye and left her to a group of Chinese tourists. My most immediate task was helping Flori scope out the bread contest. I found her in front of the bandstand, studying a row of tables.

"This is it," she said without looking up. Sometimes I swear she does have a sixth sense. Either that or her bifocals allow her to see behind her.

"Nice," I said, patting the folding table. Farther down the row of tables, a worker set out sugar skulls, while another hung paper banners featuring grinning skeletons.

"High noon's at five tonight, y'all."

I didn't need Flori's magic bifocals to guess who'd come up behind us. Gloria's drawl, and the wave of perfume that preceded her, set my nerves on edge. Her perfume couldn't mask the menthol stench of my ankle, however. I looked down to see a white poodle in a pink coat snarling at my wounded limb. I jumped back, nearly toppling the contest tables. The poodle snapped and missed.

"Twinkle Belle! You naughty girl, don't you love-bite the nice lady." Gloria scooped the growling poodle up into her arms, making cooing sounds. To me, she said, "I can't imagine what got into her. She never bites."

Flori stood eye-to-eye with the reluctantly snuggled pooch. "That's not what we heard," she muttered.

Gloria laughed. It sounded forced, as did her overly chipper voice. "Oh, that silly little mix-up. You were innocent of those awful charges, weren't you my pookie pookie poo. We got you the nicest lawyer, yes we did. Nice Mr. Strong."

I hadn't had enough sleep to listen to Gloria baby-talk her ankle-biting pooch. And I certainly wasn't going to stay around and let my scented ankle become poodle bait if Twinkle Belle became mobile again.

I turned pointedly to Flori. "Well, we should be getting back to Tres Amigas, shouldn't we, Flori."

I expected her to take this bait. She didn't budge. "Where's your helper, Armida?" she demanded.

Gloria's expression and wave of her hand implied that she couldn't be bothered to care. "Cleaning, I suppose. Or running errands. Housework. Don't you all dread housework?"

She chuckled like we were sharing a moment, as if Flori and I had housecleaners to take care of our tedious errands and housework and bread baking.

Flori fixed her eyes on Gloria. "Is that so? I supposed that she was busy baking. Your bread!"

Saying exactly what was on her mind was one

of Flori's traits that I aspired to but doubted I'd ever acquire. Gloria didn't blush. She didn't giggle or protest. She fixed her uplifted eyes on Flori and upped her drawl. "Now why would I need her to do that? I'm the reigning bread champion and I am setting to win again. I already have a judge who'll tell you that too."

Flori bristled. "I knew it!"

Gloria merely smiled before plunking down Twinkle Ankle-Biter and turning on her high-heeled boots. The poodle lunged at my leg. Stumbling backward, I planted my butt on the table and raised my ankle high. I prayed that Jake wouldn't come by, catching me in yet another embarrassing configuration. Happily, no one seemed to notice. Gloria was strutting off, dragging the growling Twinkle-Biter behind her. Flori was talking to a good-looking man in a leather jacket. He was about Linda's age, and I wondered if Flori was trying to play matchmaker again. No, I decided. They were shaking their heads disapprovingly. They had to be talking about Gloria and her blatant hint of a judge in her pocket.

"Dirty cheat," I said, joining the conversation.

Flori corrected my faulty interpretation. "Rita, this is Reese Hoffman, my friend Bill's son. He's telling me something upsetting. Your neighbor Dalia called the police, reporting trespassing and destruction of property in progress at Victor's place."

"Dad doesn't know what's being destroyed," Reese said. "He heard the report on his police scanner and tried to call you, Flori, but that British girl at the café said you were here. He knew I was down here so he called and told me to look out for you ladies. And look at this, here you are."

I could guess the target of destruction. Victor's fence and garden. "I have to go!" I took off running before I realized that my left leg wasn't following.

Reese caught up with me easily. "This way," he said, motioning in the opposite direction. "I'll take you on my bike."

Chapter 30

At the mention of a bike, my mind went straight to old-fashioned single-speeds. I imagined us chuffing up Canyon Road on a bicycle made for two or me balanced precariously on the front handlebars.

"Here, you take the helmet." The World War II–era helmet Reese thrust at me dispelled any foot-powered notions. So did the antique motorcycle that sputtered to life in eruptions of smoke and noise.

"What is this?" I yelled, coughing as the machine blasted out another cloud of fumes.

"Nineteen thirty-eight Harley-Davidson Knuck-lehead," he yelled back. "Hang on!"

As if he needed to tell me that. I clung to his back for dear life as we spun out and into the path of a hotel shuttle. The shuttle blasted its horn, as did a behemoth SUV coming the other way.

"Like the bike in that photo of O'Keeffe," he

screamed as we skidded around a corner, barely missing a pack of mothers and strollers.

I wouldn't have picked this moment for an art history lesson, but I knew what he was talking about. Georgia O'Keeffe, hitching a ride on the back of a friend's motorcycle. Georgia looked happy and mischievous, like Flori would if she were about to roar across the desert with a handsome younger man. I, on the other hand, was likely a picture of terror, a look interrupted only by overwhelming urges to cough up smoke and plug my ears. The ear plugging wouldn't be happening. I had a death grip on this stranger barreling through town. Dust stung my face as we bumped over a construction zone. I shielded my eyes by hiding behind Reese's shoulder blades. Occasionally, I dared to sneak peeks at oncoming traffic, curves, and road hazards. It was during one of these glimpses, as Reese spun across traffic to reach Canyon Road, that I spotted a chiseled face shaded by a cowboy hat.

Jake was walking a panting, broad-shouldered bulldog. They were about to step off the curb when the aptly named Knucklehead plowed up the street. Jake tugged back his dog and appeared to have a flash of recognition. Forgetting my terror, I raised my hand to wave.

"Hang on!" my driver bellowed. We sped past in a gassy, sputtering roar. I risked a look back and saw irritation on Jake's face. Once again I'd failed on the good-image front.

We arrived at the house in a cloud of dust and skidding of tires.

"Woooo!" Reese yelled, which might have been

annoying if it hadn't been drowned out by the roar of his bike. "Call me anytime if you need a ride," he yelled before spinning out and roaring away.

I didn't care about helmet hair or the grime on my face or the twinges of pain in my ankle. I raced toward the back garden and another mechanical roar. I was intercepted midway by Dalia, her hair flying wild and her arms overloaded with dirt-dripping plants.

"Rita, thank goodness!" She hurried toward me. "I have to get these babies some water. They're wounded. They're heirlooms!"

Beyond her I could see the cause of the heirloom injury. A yellow bulldozer, armed with a toothy scoop, gouged into Victor's garden.

"We have to stop him!" I yelled to Dalia, but she was already halfway up the driveway.

"I tried!" she yelled back. "I have to leave. I can't watch this anymore. Save whatever plants you can!"

I'd do more than that. I ran to the backyard. "Stop!" I yelled, waving my arms and stepping in front of the machine. Its blade was raised, as if cheering its own destructive powers. Before it, a section of the coyote fence between Victor's and Broomer's gardens lay twisted and broken. Deep gashes slashed into the earth and what had been the setting of a peaceful birdbath. The ceramic bath lay in pieces, as did a toppled wooden carving of St. Francis, the peaceful patron saint of animals. "Stop! Stop this right now!" I yelled.

I didn't recognize the man driving the bulldozer. He waved his hand to shoo me out of the way. Then he raised the blade, preparing for more destruction.

I've always admired those protesters who stand up to tanks, risking their lives for the greater good. Admiration is one thing. Getting crushed by several tons of metal is another. The driver had an amused look on his face that bordered on psychotic. He probably won every game of chicken he ever played. Staring steadily at me, he began to lower the blade. The engine churned and massive tires started moving, right toward me.

In the movies I would have clamored up the machine and taken out the driver with a few well-placed and well-deserved kicks. This was not the movies. I yelled as the blade dipped into the earth and began tearing up rocks and shrubs. "Police!" I screamed, pointing in the direction of downtown. I tried miming, channeling the image of Bunny reaching for her badge and gun. None of it did any good. The driver grinned and mimed back, playfully cupping his ear and shrugging with exaggerated incomprehension.

I backed away as the destruction inched closer. Were the police really coming? Bill Hoffman had heard the notification on police radio, but what if Manny took the call and dragged his feet about coming out here again? I kicked myself for leaving my cell phone and purse back at the café. Did I hear sirens? The clash of metal against rock, earth, wood, and tile drowned out all other sounds. I made up my mind. If I couldn't get to the driver, I'd get to his boss. As the driver took aim at a wobbling bit of fence, I dashed around the other side of the machine and into Broomer's garden.

In contrast to the destruction at Victor's, the Zen garden was untouched. Steam wafted from the soaking pool, where I half expected to find Broomer, smugly sipping a cocktail. I peeked into the bamboo grove, finding the bath empty. Just as well. I'd seen all of his pale body I ever wanted to see. Continuing up to the main house, I took in the beauty that seemed so incongruent with Broomer's character. The house was an elegant adobe that formed a U-shape in the back, protecting a serene patio. With its massive outdoor fireplace and crisscrossing strings of lights, the patio would be a lovely place to sit and listen to the river and birds. It was also a perfectly fine spot to meditate, I thought angrily. Broomer could sit here all he wanted without any need to destroy Victor's garden.

I suspected that he was inside, close to the destruction yet not getting his own hands dirty. Pounding on his back door, I yelled, "Broomer! The police are coming! Cease and desist immediately!"

When his pale, smug face failed to appear, I circled around the back of the house, stopping occasionally to rap on windows and peek inside. Buddha statues gazed back at me, unemotional. The décor was a mix of old Santa Fe and Asia, an admittedly gorgeous blend of wood beams and calligraphy scrolls. I supposed that even jerks could have good taste. And where was the resident jerk? I was beginning to revise my theory. Maybe Mr. Meditation didn't like the noise and had fled to his gallery.

I didn't have time to waste. I hurried from

window to window, glancing in quickly. That's how I almost missed the foot.

A foot? A bare foot? Had I really seen that? I stepped back up to a side window and looked in again, expecting to see the foot attached to a lounging Buddha statue. It was attached and its owner was laid out, but not in a peaceful way. By wedging my face at the very edge of the window, I could see a leg in khaki pants twisted at the knee.

"Broomer! Laurence! Get up!" I yelled, pounding on the glass. The figure didn't move, and the more I stared at the twisted limbs, the more I realized that he might never move. I turned and ran.

The bulldozer driver didn't see me at first. He was busy uprooting shrubs and overturning a bench. When he did spot me, he made exaggerated shrugs, implying that he couldn't possibly interpret my waving arms. He did put on the brakes when I got up the nerve to jump on the machine's side steps and pounded on the window of his cab.

He rolled down the window. "Lady, listen. I've got a work order to take down this fence and clear four feet of land. If you don't like it, take it up with Mr. Broomer. This here is his property. I've got that paperwork too."

My voice came out as a high squeak. "Broomer," I said, gulping for breath. "He's hurt! I think he could be dead."

The driver's expression morphed from irritated to startled and then back to irritated. "Dead?" He cursed and smacked his control panel. "I talked to him last night. You're saying I'm doing this job for a dead guy? You sure?"

I felt like I knew a thing about emergencies after the last few days. "Dead or really badly hurt. Look, I don't have a phone with me. You have to call 911!"

He shut off the engine and pulled out his phone. Before he dialed, however, he cocked his head in the direction of a low wail. "Sounds like someone already did."

Kitchen door: kicked in. Lock: broken. Cabinets: pilfered. Refrigerator: open and contents scattered." Bunny stood by Broomer's gleaming stainless steel stove, talking into a tiny tape recorder. Beside her, a crime scene photographer captured the scene in staccato flashes. The photographer had already shot the other room, focusing on Broomer's dead body.

Bunny paused her tape recorder and directed the photographer to pay special attention to a bit of camouflage cloth stuck to the broken door window.

I knew who wore camo. If only the police, instead of me, had discovered Tops in his forest hut the other morning. If only Victor hadn't been so nice to him. If only—

Bunny's voice interrupted what could have been an endless string of *if only*s.

"Rita Lafitte, neighbor, reports arriving at her home address at . . ." She looked at me expectantly. I checked my watch.

"About twenty minutes ago?" I said, before correcting myself in the face of Bunny's scowl. "Approximately 10:45."

Bunny nodded, seemingly satisfied, and turned her back to me, speaking softly. "The neighbor—or possible POI—confronted a bulldozer driver before trespassing onto the victim's property—"

"Hey! I'm not a person of interest!" I cried.

Bunny assessed me before answering. "I suppose not, but you have been present at two bludgeoning deaths and several break-ins."

I was about to protest, then registered what she'd said. "Two bludgeonings? What do you mean?"

"Your landlord's death. There was evidence of blunt-force trauma to the back of Victor's skull, inconsistent with a gunshot wound. The coroner can't be sure that the trauma killed him, but it's suspicious. You were right, it doesn't look like suicide. Don't leave town without letting us know."

Bunny's cell phone rang and she strode outside to answer it. I wanted to follow and pepper her with questions, but the two deputies guarding the kitchen had instructions to keep me where I was. However, they couldn't stop my eyes from roving.

Broomer's kitchen was a showcase, one that I doubted saw much cooking. No stray dishes littered the sink, and the cabinets held plates and glasses as artfully arranged as a catalog backdrop. The pantry was a mess, but that was the fault of the intruder. The same with the open fridge, which contained take-out boxes and containers of soup from a fancy food truck. I sighed, depressed at the unloved kitchen, but most of all for the cruel disdain for life. Poor Victor. Poor Broomer too. He might have been a major jerk, but he didn't deserve this. I craned my neck to watch white-suited men covering his body with a sheet.

"Another body, Rita? You're turning into a menace to society." Manny strode in, his smile overly bright in the gloomy scene.

I held back the urge to bristle. I wouldn't stoop to his level. Instead, I informed him that I had to go. "I have to get back to work."

"What, you're on your coffee break, so you come home to bludgeon your neighbor?"

"I did not bludgeon anyone. Even *you* can't think that."

"How do I know what you'd do, Rita? You sprung that divorce out of nowhere, remember that?"

He put on a pouty face, like he was completely blameless. When I didn't answer, he flashed his sharky whites again. "But I have Ariel now. And you, wait here until one of the deputies can take you in and get a statement."

"I'm not waiting, Manny. I told you, I have to get back to work. It's Día de los Muertos. We're very busy."

He made a scoffing sound. "Look at you, trying to talk like a local. You'll wait here until we tell you that you can go."

"My client can leave whenever she wishes." The deputies by my side parted at the sight of Jake Strong. Manny snorted and rested a hand on his holster. I wanted to hug Jake, but is hugging allowed between a client and lawyer? Is dating? I doubted it. I'd likely maneuvered myself from romantic prospect to prospective client, although given my finances, I wouldn't be an attractive client either.

Manny held his ground, making me out to be Santa Fe's most notorious material witness and/or potential perpetrator.

Jake looped a suit-coated arm around my shoulder. I couldn't help myself. I leaned in.

"Ms. Lafitte has done enough of your job already by uncovering this crime and responding to the destruction-of-property call. We're leaving. You can make an appointment for her statement by calling my office." He handed Manny a business card and guided me out of the kitchen.

"You do lead an exciting life," he said once we were outside. "I'd like to offer you a ride, unless you want to call your biker friend."

"No!" I said, and then quickly clarified that yes, I would like a ride, and no, I didn't want to call any bikers. I got into Jake's car. When he reached an intersection, I thought to ask where we were going.

"To the café. Flori's so worried that she was about to abandon her breads." He looked at his watch. "In fact, I'm under a deadline. If you're not back in ten minutes, she'll come looking for us."

"Gun it," I said, attempting a joke.

"Hang on," he replied, unknowingly echoing Reese. This time, however, I felt like I wasn't rushing into danger, but instead to safety.

Chapter 31

At the café, Linda and Addie offered me pot-loads of tea.

"Lovely chamomile mint, pip, pip," Addie chirped perkily, although I could tell that she was rattled. As Linda kept saying, things like this—things like multiple murders—simply didn't happen in Santa Fe.

Linda accepted an ominously dark-colored scone from Addie and took a seat across from me. Most of the lunch crowd had left, helped along by Flori erasing the entire specials menu and turning the door sign to Closed. The scent of scorched scones provided added incentive to flee.

"I worry about Gabe," Linda said. "I wish he hadn't insisted on going back to the house." She took a bite of scone, frowned, and then dropped it back on the plate. It landed with a thud.

I'd stuck to chicken soup, a comfort dish from

my childhood. This, however, was not my mother's chicken soup. It was better, although I'd never tell Mom that. The chicken tortilla soup at Tres Amigas features succulent chicken in a vibrant broth of tomatoes and chiles. The best part is the toppings. Lime wedges, radish slices, chopped cilantro, a dollop of sour cream, and crushed tortilla chips make the soup tangy, savory, crunchy, and salty all in one, but I wasn't in the mood to eat. Like Linda, I was worrying about someone.

"Jake said that Tops was spotted down by the train tracks," I said, trying to ease her worries about Gabe. "There's a tip that he might be heading to Albuquerque. Someone will find him soon and this will be over."

Linda shuddered. "I misjudged Tops. If I'd known, if any of us at the shelter had suspected he was so dangerous . . ." She paused to gulp tea. Then she gave voice to the worry I'd been keeping silent. "I wish Jake hadn't gone looking for Tops. What if he finds him? What if Tops hurts him too?"

My worries exactly, although I kept chiding myself for thinking them. Jake Strong was a full-grown lawyer who dealt with criminals every day. He could take care of himself. I was only concerned for the safety of a friend, I rationalized. He was a nice person who helped me out. A hero who rescued me from the scene of a crime and then rushed off into danger for the sake of justice. *Good grief.* I rubbed my temple. "I think I'm losing it," I said to Linda.

Cass would have laughed this statement off in a girlfriendly way and offered to buy me a drink.

Linda cast grave eyes on me. "Stress is dangerous to your health. Deadly even."

Great, now I was killing myself. I did feel like a physical and mental mess. I desperately needed a hot spring weekend. Ten Thousand Waves, a Japanese-themed spa a few miles outside town, would certainly work. So would Ojo Caliente, a mineral spring nestled under red-rock cliffs. I could imagine the stress melting away in the hot waters. Except stress sprang straight back when I thought about the time and money I'd need for a relaxing soak. I didn't have enough of either, especially if I decided to move.

I reached for a scone, only to have my hand batted away.

Flori snatched away the scone plate and hid it under a napkin. "Shhh . . . we won't tell Addie, but even the raccoons shouldn't eat these." She looked over her shoulder. "She's working on a second batch. I'm going to watch that she doesn't burn this round."

"Good luck," I said, my mood as dark as the scones.

Flori plunked down at the table. "I know. What a day. Addie and her scones are keeping me occupied, but I can barely stand the waiting. I hate not knowing. I want that awful man caught!"

I squeezed her hand sympathetically. If this mess of unknowing was bad for me, I knew it had to be ten times worse for Flori, who couldn't take suspense in any form.

At a nearby table, protected by DO *NOT* TOUCH OR EAT signs, her Day of the Dead bread cooled on wire racks. She'd outdone herself. The breads featured cranial curves and bulging teeth. An egg wash had turned them golden and glossy, and the sweet scents of anise, orange zest, and butter triumphed over the odor of burned scones.

"They're winners," I said, smiling at my elderly friend.

She pushed up her glasses and shrugged. "If they hold the contest."

"What?" Linda and I demanded in unison. Then it hit me. With Broomer's death, the judging committee was down a member.

"Misty Gonzales, the organizer, is supposed to get back to all of us contestants," Flori said. "They're debating whether it would be unseemly to continue without Broomer."

"I'm sure that he would have wanted you to go on," Linda said.

Flori wasn't buying the trite words of comfort. "I'm sure that he was in it for the publicity and bribes, dear. But we mustn't speak ill of the dead. Not on Día de los Muertos, especially." She turned to me. "You should get some rest. And a shower." The wrinkling of her nose made me suddenly conscious of my appearance. I reached up and felt grime in my hair and forehead. My clothes were crumpled, and although I'd removed the menthol patches from my ankle, a gummy, minty residue remained.

"I'll be back by the time of the judging," I promised. "They'll hold the contest."

"Whatever," Flori said, sounding like my teenage daughter, with a similar fake nonchalance. "If Gabe lets me keep Victor's recipe box, I'll enter the Christmas cookie contest in Victor's name."

As I got ready to go, she tried to convince me to shower at her place. I declined, citing a lack of clean clothes. "Besides, Tops is long gone by now," I said. I wondered about his kitten, Hugo. Was he too on the lam? I hoped that Manny wouldn't be the one to apprehend Tops. Not only would his ego inflate, but he also wouldn't bother to save the tiny kitten.

Linda gave me a ride but declined to stop in. "I don't want to give Gabe the wrong idea that I'm hanging around to see him," she fretted. "We can be friends, but never teenagers again."

She dropped me off at the mailbox, leaving me in the awkward situation of hobbling down the driveway and encountering Gabe, forlornly removing a swath of police tape caught in the apple tree.

"Was that Linda?" he asked.

For his sake, I fibbed and said that she needed to help Flori with the bread contest.

He nodded. "Things will get better now that it's almost over." A few wrinkled apples fell from the tree as he yanked. When he'd wadded up the tape, he turned to me. "Thank you again for helping me, and Victor too."

"I don't want to move!" I blurted. I didn't know where this burst came from. Maybe I was under some psychedelic influence of Addie's charred scone smoke. Or Linda's deadly stress. "I mean, unless you want me and Celia to move or you'll be moving or—"

Gabe didn't miss a beat. "I don't want to move either," he said. "Don't worry. We'll start fresh around here. It'll be okay again."

Later, I stood in the shower a long while, letting scalding water pelt my skull. A new life was what I kept saying I'd create for myself. I wished I knew what that would be.

After the shower, I faced a more short-term dilemma of what to do. I had a few hours to spare before the bread contest, if it happened at all. Celia was at school, followed by an after-school art program. Out the back window, I could see the destroyed fence. I yearned to push the rubble onto Broomer's side, but the property line was strewn with yellow police tape. Manny's doing, I bet. He loved to go overboard with caution tape, just like his version of home repair involved wads of duct tape.

I drew the curtain and tried not to think about the garden destruction. The best way I knew to do that was to read a good book. Foot elevated, a bag of pretzels by my side, I lay on the couch, savoring a British cottage mystery with an elderly sleuth who would have made Flori proud.

I was caught up in a critical scene when a sound distracted me. I put the book down and listened. There was silence and then a high-pitched chirp, like a baby bird or a coyote pup singing for its mother. I pulled a throw blanket around my shoulder and tried to concentrate on my book.

I couldn't. The cry sounded increasingly plaintive. I'd feel reassured to discover a lonely cowbird, I told myself, and padded to the front door in my slippers.

Outside, a few crows congregated in the trees, hunching and dipping their heads. If it was a baby bird, the little creature would be in trou-

ble. I scanned the mosaic of earth tones. Golden
grasses waved against apache plume, an ethereal
shrub topped with feathery puffs. Smooth rocks
lined a cactus patch, and old orchard trees stood
amidst carpets of dark leaves and wrinkling fruit.
I was about to go back inside when I heard the cry
again. I refocused my eyes farther in the distance
and that's when I saw the bit of buff-colored fluff.

"Hugo? Kitty?" At the sound of my calls, the
little creature turned and waddled forward a few
steps, only to stumble over a branch. He seemed
stuck and was meowing louder. Still in my slippers, I rushed out, gushing kitten talk as I went.
"It's okay, sweet baby boy. You're okay."

The kitten purred as loudly as a food processor
when I reached him. "It's okay," I told him again,
rubbing his fuzzy head. "Let's get you unstuck."
He wore a thick collar with dog bones printed on
it. The collar had looped around a branch and was
keeping him pinned in place. Gently, I cupped the
kitten's belly.

"Poor guy. What's this?" The kitten responded
with more high-pitched mews as I removed the
collar and the plastic sandwich bag stuck to it.
Inside, the bag held a scrap of paper with the
scrawled words, *Please take care of Hugo. He's yours.*
Hugo purred.

For a moment I forgot my bad feelings toward
Tops. He loved his kitten and turned him loose to
find a better home. That, if only that, was kind of
him. I cuddled the vibrating fur ball close to my
neck, vowing that I wouldn't let infatuation over-
power reason. Celia and I would have to discuss
finances and the long-term commitment of a cat.

Hugo's tiny paw reached out for my chin. *Who was I kidding?* I was already smitten with him.

I carried him inside, taking him immediately to the blanket on the couch and mentally listing the accessories he'd need. Litter box, food, toys, a new collar, a catnip plant.

"He likes milk. Lactose-free, only 'cause he's a cat."

My shriek sent Hugo's claws into my neck. The pricks of pain were the least of my worries. A hulking figure stood in my entryway. Tops shut the door, locking us both inside.

Chapter 32

Okay," I said. "Lactose-free. Got it. Thanks, Tops, we'll be fine now." Electric jolts prickled through my head as I tried to remember where I'd left my phone. The kitchen, or possibly the bedroom or lodged in my messy purse.

"Okay, 'bye now," I said shakily, earning a scowl from my uninvited guest. His back was against the doorknob and there was no other door. He didn't look ready to go.

"He doesn't like dog food," Tops said. "He's not a dog. And he won't eat hot dogs or chile. If you can nab a rotisserie chicken, he loves that." His eyes darted from side to side. Twigs stuck in his beard and he wore several sets of clothes. When he moved, I caught sight of a knife handle on his belt.

I nodded so he wouldn't hear the quaver hovering in my throat. I was afraid that if I opened my mouth, I'd bleat like the stranded kitten.

"He likes you. I knew he would." Tops took a giant step forward. I took several faltering steps backward and ended up knocking myself down onto the couch. Hugo crawled off my shoulder and onto the top cushion, where he scampered around happily.

Tops stood over me, his hand on the carved blade of the knife. He smelled of wood smoke and tobacco and was becoming more agitated, talking about helicopters and surveillance. I squished back into the couch as his voice turned to an angry monotone. I had to bring him back to reality, or something more calming.

"Tuna fish!" I exclaimed.

He stopped mid-rant and frowned at me.

"Tuna," I said again, more calmly. "I have some in the kitchen. I bet Hugo loves tuna."

I forced myself to move slowly off the couch and to the kitchen. Every molecule in my body told me to sprint for the door, but in the confined space, I doubted my chances. Maybe, just maybe, I'd left my phone in the kitchen.

Tops claimed not to know about Hugo's feelings for tuna. I bet he knew full well, unless he hadn't yet opened the can he stole from Gabe. I forced myself to maintain happy chatter about kitten-friendly foods as I searched the crammed pantry, terrified that we'd run out of tuna. "Turkey, I bet he loves that. We'll have a nice Thanksgiving turkey in a few weeks, won't we, Hugo?"

The little guy wove around our feet, purring and mewing. I hauled cans from the broom closet that served as my pantry. When I got to cartons of premade mac-and-cheese, Celia's favorite, Tops perked up.

"I like those."

"Take them!" I practically shouted. Lowering my voice, I said, "Ah, tuna. You'll love this, Hugo. I'll get a bowl, and Tops if you'll open the can . . ." I held it out to Tops and plopped the opener by the sink. In my ideal scheme, he'd take the can to the sink, whereupon I would bolt for the door and run to summon help. I prayed that I could run fast enough and that Gabe was home and not napping with his ear plugs and white noise machine.

My hopes were soon dashed. Tops leaned against the kitchen door and produced a can opener from one of his many pockets. After a few cranks, he removed the lid and then offered the entire can to Hugo.

"Here you go, little buddy," he said. His voice was softer now and he sounded like the elderly man that he was. "You like that don't you?" He grinned at me, lines creasing his weathered face. "You'll be all right together. I gotta go. People have seen me. They're watchin' me."

I agreed heartily with this plan. "Yes, you should go. Right now. Fast. I'll take the very best care of Hugo."

He patted the kitten, his big hand covering its entire body. "I've gotta go, buddy," he said again, in such a sad voice that it tugged at my heart. I followed him to the front door, ready to bolt it as soon as he crossed the threshold.

He stopped in the door frame, giving the sky a suspicious scan. "Looks clear."

"Yep, looks good. Good time to go." I wanted to give him a good firm push. He was looking in the direction of Victor's house. "What's that?" He turned to me, face aflame with rage. "Look at that! Spies! They're back!"

Through the sliver of space not blocked by Tops, I spotted a flash of gold near Victor's back door. "It's probably his brother," I said, then added, "or the police." I hoped Tops would take this as his cue to flee.

"No. It's *her*!" Tops practically spat out the words. "She did a bad thing! She's a spy. They're after Victor!" He took off with surprising speed toward the main house.

I'd been counting the seconds until I could lock myself in and call the cops. Now his words stopped me. *Spies after Victor? A bad thing?* What did he mean? I couldn't help myself. I too hurried toward Victor's house.

A woman's scream spurred me from a limping shuffle to a full-out run. Jay-Jay stood by the back door, brandishing a potted cactus, thorny side pointed outward. Other pots were upturned and saints that had been hanging by the doorway lay on the flagstone.

Tops was backing Jay-Jay into a corner, literally. By the time I reached them, she was wedged in the door frame with only the spiny cactus separating her from Tops.

"Help me!" she yelled when she saw me. "This maniac is attacking me!"

Tops turned to me, his eyes as wild as his hair. "She stole. She stole Victor's key." He extended a baseball-mitt-sized hand toward Jay-Jay's throat. "Give it back," he growled.

Jay-Jay waved the cactus and screamed for me to do something. "Call the police! Don't just stand there!"

Standing here was about all I could do, unless I ran back to the casita to find my phone. It was a tempting move, but I couldn't leave Jay-Jay. I remembered the strength of Tops's hands around my neck, and he hadn't even been mad then, only worried that I'd wake a kitten.

I summoned the last crumbs of my inner courage and jumped between Tops and the cactus. A spine poked my shoulder blade. "No!" I commanded. Tops's eyes flashed with anger as he looked down at me. I fought to sound calm. "No," I repeated, in the best normal voice I could muster. "Hugo will be worried, Tops. Leave the nice lady alone."

Confusion replaced rage on his face, if only for a moment. "She's not nice. Not nice. Not like you."

I supposed I should have felt flattered. I was terrified. "It's okay, Tops," I said. "This woman is Victor's ex-wife."

"No, no!" he stuttered.

I knew how he felt. How Victor could ever have married Jay-Jay was incomprehensible to me too.

"That's right!" Jay-Jay crowed from behind me, scraping more spines across my back. "And I'll inherit this house so this key is mine!"

Tops wobbled in confusion. Not for long, though. His bellow echoed across the little valley as he pushed me aside, reached through the cactus and tore something from Jay-Jay's hand. He yelled again as he raised his fist. A few spines stuck to his knuckles. He plucked them off as he backed away, and then he took off again, running up the driveway to the road.

Jay-Jay cursed. "You let him get away! He stole my key!"

Talk about gratitude. Here I'd saved her from possible strangulation, and she was complaining about the strangler getting away? I informed Jay-Jay that I was calling the police and then stormed back to my house, slamming the door behind me. Hugo jumped off the couch, his tiny tail poofed and a ridge rising on his back.

"Oh, I'm sorry, baby," I told him, cuddling his warm body up against my heart as I searched the house for the phone. As I did, I replayed Tops's muddled words. *She did a bad thing.* Did Tops witness the crime? What if Jay-Jay was the actual killer? I found the phone under the pile of yesterday's clothes and punched in numbers with trembling fingers. I was certain that I'd been in the presence of a murderer. I just didn't know if it was Jay-Jay or Tops, or both.

I did know who I wanted to call first, however.

Jake answered on the first ring. I sped through an explanation without stopping for breath.

"I'm at Kewa Station," he said, naming the train station at the former Santo Domingo Pueblo, now known by its original name, Kewa. "I heard that Tops had hit the rails. Guess that was wrong. I'll be there in half an hour."

"Be careful!" I said, before thinking how overly concerned this might sound.

"You be careful too," he said. "Watch out for Jay-Jay. Don't let anyone in until the police arrive."

Young patrolmen I didn't know arrived first, for which I was grateful. Bunny came a few minutes later. "They'll find him," she said, standing in my living room and making the room seem smaller. The eerie bays of bloodhounds floated down the creek. "The dogs are just a little confused right now because his scent's all over this place."

I shuddered at the thought. Hugo was even more upset. His tail poofed with each canine howl and he climbed up into my hair. I supposed that I looked a little like a crazy cat lady when Jake arrived.

"Is that a tail over your ear?" he asked.

I explained how I came by Hugo, who resisted any attempts to extract him for introductions.

"Cute," Jake said, reaching up to pet Hugo's haunches before turning back to lawyer mode with Bunny. "My client has special needs," he said. "He suffers from dementia. You are right to try to locate him, but you'll find that he's an innocent man, a valuable witness who can help you with your case."

Bunny made a sniffing sound, suggesting cat allergies or skepticism. "He's a suspect." She turned her attention to her radio. "Got him?" she said. "Got it. Be there in two minutes."

"But wait," I said, stepping in front of the door, Tops-style. "What about Jay-Jay? She was trespassing again. She tried to steal Victor's key and Tops said that she did something bad."

Bunny almost looked sympathetic. Or maybe she was simply too tired to look stern. "From what you've told us, Tops also imagines black helicopters and steals food. Ms. Jantrell does have a will establishing her as a potential inheritor, pending probate and any other newer, valid wills." She paused for a moment. "However, we will continue to search for the recent will that your neighbor Dalia and her husband witnessed and signed. And Ms. Jantrell's been warned not to enter the property until probate clears. That will be some time. In the meantime, Rita, you might want to make plans to move. Just in case."

With that, she strode off, Jake following as keen as a well-dressed bloodhound behind her.

I stewed over Bunny's words. I didn't want to move, but maybe I would if Jay-Jay took over the property. Maybe she'd kick me out, regardless of what I wanted. We had to find Victor's new will.

Flori would know what to do. Then it struck me. In all the chaos, I'd forgotten about her bread contest. I managed to extract Hugo from my hair. He cried and scampered after me when I put him on the couch in a nest of blankets. "Okay," I said, swaddling him firmly in a scarf against my chest. "You can come, but you're sticking close to me." He purred with a contentment I wished I felt.

Chapter 33

After a stressful search for a parking spot, I arrived at the Plaza just as the winners of the fry bread contest were being read out. The *pan de muerto* results would be announced last. I hadn't missed Flori's moment. I breathed a sigh of relief and took in the pretty scene. Autumn scents of roasting chiles, grilled corn, and piñon smoke perfumed the air. Red chile-shaped string lights ringed the bandstand, where Flori stood behind her bread. She was bundled up in her red coat and scarf, a contrast to Gloria's shapely shearling jacket and cowgirl hat sparkling with a tiara. The loudspeaker voice announced that the bread contest was next. Gloria waved like a beauty queen to the crowd, palm cupped, smile plastered on her face. I waved too, effusively and in Flori's direction. She saw me and smiled, nodding toward the judge's box. In place of Broomer sat another interim judge, Jeb Parsons, an actual judge and a Tres Amigas regular.

Flori mouthed something that I couldn't make out. A person diagonally in front of me could. Armida turned to a woman standing next to her. "Hot stuff?" she demanded loudly. "What does she mean?"

I knew what she meant. I nodded my understanding to Flori. Gloria and Armida wouldn't have the advantage here. "Hot stuff" was the code that Flori had given Judge Parsons years ago, allowing him unlimited, free hot drinks. He tended to go for hot chocolate, extra chocolaty.

I held my breath and cradled Hugo closer. The announcer was doing an annoying drawn-out lead-in. "And now, the category that we've all been waiting for. The most coveted award of the Day of the Dead culinary contest. The bread that will lure the ancestors back for this day and this day only."

"We get it, we get it . . ." I muttered to Hugo, who purred happily inside my coat. Beside me, other spectators shared my restlessness and muttered about technicalities, like *technically*, the dead traveled back for several days. *Technically*, the spirits had broken through the worldly barrier at midnight last night.

"And in this corner, the reigning champion, Gloria Hendrix." Good grief, I thought, as the announcer strung us on. What was this, a boxing match? It was a battle, one without physical blows. Yet. Armida and a group around her started to cheer and pump their fists in the air. The rest of the crowd clapped politely.

The announcer blathered on. "She holds blue ribbons from the Cowpoke Cupcake Contest of Amarillo, Texas." Armida and posse continued to whoop and clap. The mention of Texas drew a mix of boos and woos from the rest of the crowd.

"And in this corner, our very own native daughter, hailing from Tres Amigas Café, Mrs. Flori Fitzgerald—" The rest of the announcement was drowned out in cheers, including my own, although I tempered my enthusiasm when I felt Hugo vibrate with nerves. I whispered comforting words to him and he started to purr again. Three other competitors were announced, long shots who received polite applause. The crowd knew its bread.

"Fingers crossed!" Cass squeezed in next to me and gave me a little hug. Then she frowned, staring at my chest. "What's in there? Some kind of hot water bottle? You didn't sprain your chest too, did you?"

I didn't have time to explain Hugo or my most recent run-in with Tops. The announcer was finally about to say something useful. I heard Gloria's name, given in grand tones, and my heart sank. Then I realized that her name was being followed by glorious words, "First runner-up." I tucked my coat protectively around Hugo to shield his kitten ears from the roar when Flori was announced winner.

Cass and I high-fived and waved to Flori. Gloria looked stunned, as did Armida and crew, who pushed their way out of the crowd. My last glimpse of Armida that evening was of her being bundled into the car by two other women. The women pushed her into the backseat as she flashed middle fingers at the festival.

Later, with Addie on the stage belting out her Adele songs, Flori joined me and Cass. She held a trophy nearly half her size, gold like a bowling trophy except topped with a grinning skull. "Pretty sweet," she said with a grin. "Plus, Judge Parsons didn't know which bread was mine or Gloria's. He was out of town all week and came in straight from the airport on the train. No one can say that I'm a cheater."

As she received congratulations from her many fans, I checked my cell phone, seeing that Celia had texted. In text speak, my daughter conveyed that she'd be done with her school activity at seven-twenty. The implication was that I could come pick her up at the specified time, no sooner, no later.

"See, she's making the effort," Cass said. "And look, she sent a photo. I love that painting, and of course the handsome kid next to it."

We admired the photo with maternal pride. In it, Sky held a metal crow and pointed to one of Celia's paintings. He grinned widely. And was it my imagination, or did Celia's morose fairies look a little less down?

Cass was right. A nonsnippy text from my daughter, with information not dragged out under intense questioning, was something to celebrate.

My phone vibrated again. I would have ignored it, but I thought it was Celia amending her pickup instructions. It wasn't. I stopped walking and read the text slowly.

Cass watched me, looking concerned. "Everything okay with Celia?"

I nodded. "It's Jake." I read out the text word for word to Cass. " 'Tops caught. In custody. Police say he confessed.' "

"There it is," Cass said, brushing her hands together to imply case closed. "The easiest answer was right all along. It's like metal. The less you mess with it, the better it looks."

I wasn't sure what she meant about metal or that I agreed. I dialed Bunny's direct number. She sighed as a way of salutation.

"Yes," she said, after I reported my information from Jake. "The suspect confessed. I'm only telling you this so that you can go home and stop worrying. And stop investigating."

"Did he have his lawyer present when he confessed?" I demanded. "Are you absolutely sure he confessed and didn't mean something else? He can be confusing and confused."

More sighing was followed by, "He said, 'I did it. It's my fault Victor's dead.' Seems pretty lucid and obvious to us."

I wanted it to be obvious. Cass was right. Clean and simple was better. Yet doubts bounced around in my head. "What if he meant that metaphorically?"

"Rita," Bunny sighed. "You're sounding like your lawyer boyfriend. Leave this to us. Go home."

"He's not my boyfriend—" The other end of the line went dead. Bunny had hung up. She was right about one thing, though. Celia and I should go home tonight. We could have a normal, safe night in our cozy casita.

"I don't know how I feel," I said to Cass and Flori.

We were making our way back to Tres Amigas. Above us, the stars sparkled and the moon glowed over the adobe city. It was a good night for the spirits to be home.

"But what if he's *not* guilty?" I persisted. "What if the police misunderstood and Jay-Jay's been pulling the strings this whole time to get at Victor's art and property?"

Flori waved at a passing supporter who beeped from his car. "It's possible," she said. "If Jay-Jay finds his new will and destroys it, that old one will be hard to contest, unless Gabe does, and he doesn't have much fight in him these days."

"I suspected her all along," Cass grumbled. She cradled Flori's trophy in her arms, raising it whenever a supporter waved or beeped.

When we reached Tres Amigas, I unlocked the door and we entered to the aromas of buttery bread and burned scone. "Even if Jay-Jay's not the killer," I said, "she's up to slimy business, trying to take over Victor's art center and his house too. We have to keep at it and find that new will."

My *dos amigas* agreed.

"Absolutely," Flori reiterated. "Now tell us why your chest is meowing."

At the appointed time, I drove to meet Celia in front of her school. When she got in the car, Hugo immediately hopped from my lap to hers.

"A kitten! Oh my God, he's so cute." My daughter forgot her sullen facade. "Where did you get him, Mom?"

I explained briefly, glossing over the terror part of acquiring him.

"Poor Tops," Celia said, after hearing that he was arrested. "Victor said he was a kind man, only with problems. You know he helped make that carved wooden bench down in the garden."

I hadn't known that, and I realized Celia didn't know about Broomer's death or the garden destruction. I filled her in, adding assurances for both our sakes.

"We're safe now," I said. "And the garden isn't completely ruined. Gabe told me that he's going to have the fence repaired as soon as the police tape is gone." Then I steeled myself and asked, "Do you want to move?"

Celia frowned, sporting a buff-colored mustache formed by Hugo's tail. "Why should we move? We have to stay and help fix Victor's garden." Her tone was surly and defiant again, but this time I felt the same way. No one was going to scare us away from our home.

I didn't feel quite as bold when we returned to the dark casita with our haul of feline accessories. I checked the house for prowlers, telling Celia I was scoping out the best place for Hugo's new litter box. She suggested the bathroom closet, offering to move all her shampoos, hair gel, and boxes of black hair dye. I wished I could move the dye out of the house. I also wished that a falling roll of toilet paper hadn't startled me into bumping my head on a shelf.

"Chill, Mom, geez," Celia said, but then proceeded to clean out the closet without any grumbles.

Hugo padded between our rooms throughout the night. His tiny clawed feet weren't the reason for my lack of sleep. My mind kept spinning, thinking of Tops, missing wills, and Jay-Jay brandishing cactuses. But most of all, I thought of Victor's spirit. Was he satisfied, at rest? Or were we still missing something?

I must have fallen asleep at one point because the ringing phone startled me upright. "Flori?" As usual, my early morning thoughts flew to bad news.

"I'm calling to tell you to sleep in," she said.

I flopped back onto my pillow and counted to ten before answering.

"Thanks," I replied, not entirely keeping the sarcasm out of my voice. "You really didn't have to call to tell me that."

"Well it's nearly six. Your alarm will be going off any moment. Stay in bed. My daughters are rewarding my win by doing all the breakfast prep so I can go to the early All Souls' Day mass. You go back to sleep."

With that she hung up, and I lay in bed wide-awake, feeling grumpy. Sure, I would have been up by now, had I remembered to set my alarm. I tried closing my eyes but they kept springing open.

I consoled myself that I had a few free hours. I

could have a leisurely cup of coffee. Heck, I could have the entire pot before Celia got up. Then I would drive her to school and order would be restored, at least in our car-sharing arrangement.

Hugo gobbled kitten chow and galloped down the hall to Celia's room. I took my cup outside to enjoy the crystal clear morning. Tucking my phone in my pocket, I vowed to snap some pictures and e-mail them to my mother and sister, both of whom had sent petulant notes wondering why they hadn't heard from me. I would send some pretty, placating shots and then later—a lot later—tell them a highly abridged version of what happened.

Birds warbled in the cottonwoods and the frosted leaves glittered. It should have been peaceful, even amidst the police tape, except it wasn't. Someone was in the backyard, and this time it wasn't Tops.

Chapter 34

Standing at the top of the garden, I reassured myself that the confessed killer was in custody. To be on the safe side, I clutched my cell phone in one hand and the cinnamon-scented porch broom in the other, although I doubted I'd need either. How much harm could an obviously drunk Jay-Jay Jantrell do to me? She wobbled along the garden paths, muttering.

"Hi Jay-Jay," I called out, venturing down the steps to the lower garden. "What are you doing out here so early?" I said in the perky, high-pitched tone I'd use if approaching a snarling wolf.

She cursed to the world in general and then seemed to focus on me. Her eyes and nose were red and her gold spandex leggings were snagged. Bits of apache plume flowers stuck to her fur jacket, and even from a distance she reeked of alcohol. My immediate repulsion and fear were replaced by cautious sympathy. From her drunken mumblings, I gathered that she was mourning the death of Broomer.

"Such a go-getter," she slurred, lurching in my direction. "And that hot tub, ahhh . . ."

"Okay, let's sit down." I dropped my broom and caught her mid-lurch. With difficulty, I maneuvered her toward a bench that had managed to elude the bulldozer. My sympathy may have come too soon. She wrenched herself out of my grasp, fury focusing in her eyes. "This is mine!" she yelled. "Mine!"

I backed away, holding my phone but leery of looking down to dial. Would that set her off more? She tried to yank a garden saint off its tree-mounted pedestal. When the saint wouldn't budge, she tromped through the churned-up dirt in her furry fashion boots.

"Okay," I repeated, firmly. "We'll sort this out." And by "we" I meant the police. I was starting to dial when Jay-Jay screamed, ran to me, and grabbed the phone from my hands.

"Ha!" she yelled. "Ha! Now I know! That's why he was so upset! Divorce me, will you?" This was followed by maniacal laughter that made me abandon thoughts of snatching back my phone. What had set her off? I glanced at the pile of dirt. A wooden St. Francis statue lay on the ground. His hand and the sparrow it held were broken off. Distressing, but easily fixed with some glue. I went to pick up the statue. That's when I saw what Jay-Jay was raving about.

Bone, white and fleshless, poked out of the earth.

And not the remains of an unfortunate deer or a dog's lost chew toy. This was a skull and it was human.

"Oh my God, Jay-Jay, call the police!" She was messing with my phone, which has a fickle power button.

"Police? I'm not calling the police. I'm calling my lawyer! This place is mine! Victor left it to me! I deserve it."

She sounded out of her mind. I stepped away, ready to dash for help, until I saw that help was already coming. Gabe ran down the garden, dressed in polka-dot pajamas.

He blanched when I pointed to the skull, but immediately took charge. "Dear God, what did Victor do? I'll get Jay-Jay inside and call the police. Rita, you go back to your casita and lock yourself in."

Jay-Jay was still cackling as Gabe pulled her up the garden. "Rita, go, please!" he yelled back. "Go inside and stay there until I knock."

He half dragged, half shoved Jay-Jay up the pathway. I automatically began to follow his instructions. Then I stopped, feeling dizzy, thinking of Gabe's words. Victor? Could sweet Victor be responsible for this horror? Is that why he had surrounded the spot with benevolent saints? Feeling repulsed yet drawn in, I returned to the bones.

The forensics team wouldn't want me digging around in there. However, it wasn't like the killer had left fresh tracks. The bones jutting from the marred earth had clearly been there a long time. Plus, they were already unearthed. Broomer's bulldozer started the process and coyotes had apparently continued it. Canine prints dotted the dirt, and to my horror, I realized that some bones were scattered around. A few lay by a fallen log, others near the upturned birdbath.

Poor person, whoever you were. I stepped over to a spot dotted in coyote tracks. They'd dug up the area, exposing bone and what appeared to be trash. I squatted down to check it out. What I'd initially taken to be junk was a wallet, brittle and dirty but well-preserved in the dry New Mexican earth.

Using a tissue from my pocket, I opened the wallet to find cash, an insurance card, and a driver's license. The year on the insurance was 1971, and the cards were issued to one David Donaldson. Recognition took a moment, but when it did, a fresh chill ran down my limbs. Davy, the man who had seemingly abandoned Linda. All this time, he'd been here.

Shaking, I stood and reached for my phone. I patted my pockets twice before remembering that Jay-Jay had it. No matter. Gabe was going to call. I heard his screen door bang shut and waited by a bench until he came strolling down the path.

He carried a garbage bag in one hand. It seemed an odd time to tidy up, but maybe he meant to cover the bones out of respect.

"Gabe," I said, anxious to tell him of my discovery. "I found this wallet. I know who this is."

He shook his head, and I registered a sad expression on his face, mixed with something darker. "I know who it is too," he said.

Horror and a sickening realization struck seconds before he reached into the bag and pulled out a gun.

"No, Gabe, no," I repeated as he and the gun came closer. Should I risk running? I thought of the garden behind me, picturing any boulders I could leap behind. There were a few on the other side of the property, if I made it that far. We were so close that he'd have to be the world's worst shot to miss me. Reasoning with him also seemed unlikely to work. His eyes were dark pits of madness.

"I'm sorry," he said, his voice wooden. "If you'd only left this alone . . ."

I had my hands out in front of me, as if that would stop a bullet. Above us, crows cawed angrily. "I *can* leave it alone," I lied. "No one has to know. I'll move out and no one will know that these bones are here."

His gun wavered. "It's too late for that. You shouldn't feel responsible. It's Victor's fault. Him and his crazy spirits. He was going to tell. After all these years, he couldn't let it be. Now I'll live. Now it'll be like it was before."

I inched backward until I saw his finger move onto the trigger. "Gabe, please, I have . . ." I was about to say I had a daughter, but I didn't want to remind him of Celia, sleeping a few hundred feet away. I prayed that she wouldn't wake up and come outside.

"You have to go," he said, finishing my sentence in a way I didn't like. He raised the scope to eye level, but was momentarily distracted by a crow, flying low in front of him.

I took this as my chance and sprinted toward a grove of trees, wishing they were giant sequoias instead of gnarly oaks stunted by drought.

A boom sent me flailing to the ground. Pebbles raked my face and twigs rained down on me. I didn't care, as long as I was alive.

"Gabe, no!" I cried. "Stop!" Frantic, I scanned the garden for my next place to run. If I could make it to the creek, I could run upstream and hide in the thick willows. Not for long, though. Nothing would stop Gabe from following, whereas a fresh twist of my bum ankle could stop me in my tracks forever.

"Don't make this difficult," Gabe said from the garden. His voice was eerily reasonable. "I have things to do," he continued. "Linda is coming over to pick me up, and we're going to Tres Amigas for breakfast. Her sisters are there. They'll be happy to see me again."

I thought of Tres Amigas and wished I was there. I'd happily deal with fussy customers. I'd let them edit the menu and request extra whipped cream and vegetarian meat dishes. I squeezed my eyes shut and listened as methodical footsteps came closer.

"Gabe? Hello? Anyone home?" Linda's voice sounded far away.

"Linda!" I screamed. "Help! Run! Call the police!" I scrambled to my feet, hugging a spindly oak in front of me. Gabe let his gun drop as he turned toward the house.

"Linda, don't come down here, honey," he called out. "Stupid," he fumed in my direction. "Shut up. You'll ruin everything."

"Call the police! Help!" I screamed, letting go of the oak to scramble deeper into the thicket. Branches slashed my face and my ankle burned.

"What's going on down here?"

I stopped long enough to see Linda, hurrying yet careful to stay on the winding path. As usual, she looked worried. This time, that look was justified.

"It's nothing," Gabe said. "There's a coyote out here, that's all. Rita was scared." Did he really think I'd shut up and let him keep up his charade until Linda left? A new and worse thought struck me. What if my yelling had lured Linda to her death too? Would he kill her to keep his secret?

From where I stood, I could see he had an arm draped protectively over her shoulder.

Her voice trembled as she looked around, her gaze stopping at the bones before fixing on me. "Rita, what's going on here?"

I chose my words carefully. "We found bones, Linda. Davy Donaldson's bones." There, it was out. I'd told her. I hoped I hadn't doomed her.

She twisted out of Gabe's grasp and stumbled toward the disturbed grave. He followed close behind, yelling her name, shouting, "He never loved you. Not like me."

I yearned to run away, to flee toward my daughter and safety. But I couldn't desert Linda with this maniac. Leaving the relative safety of the grove, I inched toward the two of them. Linda stood over the grave, her hands dancing through the sign of the cross. Gabe, beside her, frantically kicked earth back over the white bones. The gun dangled from his hand. I said my own prayer and rushed at him, linebacker style.

My initial impact knocked Gabe off balance and allowed me to grab the butt end of the gun. He righted himself and struggled to regain control of it. We held the weapon between us, its barrel raised to the sky. I knew I wasn't as strong as Gabe. The barrel inched downward. Soon it would be aimed straight at me. My life didn't flash before me. Instead, my list-making lobe took over, absurdly nagging me about all the little things I'd never do, like getting Celia to school on time or taking Hugo to the vet for a checkup or making it to the café by the lunch rush. Linda would tell Flori that I'd be late, I told myself, before recognizing the ridiculousness of that thought. And where was Linda? Why wasn't she helping me? The metal barrel slipped in my sweaty hands, and my arms shook and ached with the effort of tugging against him.

Then suddenly there was no effort. I stumbled backward as Gabe slumped to the ground. Linda stood above him holding a large rock.

Chapter 35

A few days later we gathered at the café to remember two kind souls. Flori set out photos of Victor and Davy and surrounded them with their favorite foods, marigold wreaths, votive candles, and of course *pan de muerto*, baked fresh from her award-winning recipe.

"Davy loved your almond cookies too," Linda said, looking fondly at the snapshot I now realized I'd seen on Victor's altar. Her days of tears had turned to fond remembrances of both men, although we were all still shaken by the truth revealed by the bones. And by the contents of Victor's recipe tin.

Flori had found the will first, and then the confession, carefully folded and placed as the bottom liner of the recipe box. For today's event, she'd placed the pretty, punched-tin container in a prominent spot by Victor's portrait.

I went to look at it again, flipping through the

worn index cards and thinking of Victor making the recipes.

"Pretty clever to hide his will where the right people would find it." Jake's subtle cologne, smelling of pine and cloves, reached me before he did. Instead of his usual lawyer wear, he had on jeans and a flannel shirt the color of Hugo. He looked temptingly cuddly.

"He must have felt so guilty." I stopped flipping through the cards, and Jake took over, pausing over recipes for green chile stew, caramel flan, and Jemez enchiladas. "He hid his brother's secret all those years. I still don't know how or *why* he did it."

Jake shrugged. "I can tell you, guilty people do a lot of rationalizing with themselves. Of course, I'm not saying I know many guilty people." He smiled.

"Of course," I said, smiling back.

Jake rocked on the heels of his cowboy boots. "Like Victor said in that letter he left. He didn't learn that Gabe had killed Davy until months after the fact. I understand feeling protective about one's little brother. And turning him in would have killed their mother, what with her already fighting cancer and in such a fragile state."

"So proud of Gabe the med student," I mused. How wrong her maternal pride had been. How wrong we'd all been. I turned again to Davy's photo. In it, he was young and smiling.

Flori, aghast that she'd thought so poorly of an innocent man, had told me his story. He was an orphan, a wanderer. No one would have missed him except Linda, and Gabe had convinced Victor that she'd be better off not knowing the truth. From Victor's handwritten message, we learned that he had kept Gabe's secret out of love and guilt and eventually habit. Broomer, however, had churned up the issue by threatening to uproot the fence, and with it the shallow grave. Rather than move and rebury the bones, or throw them in a remote landfill as Gabe wanted, Victor told his brother that they should come clean. His commitment had only strengthened as the Day of the Dead approached.

"In any case," Jake said, carefully closing the tin lid, "it seems like Victor did the best he could. He did a lot of good in the world and forbade Gabe from seeing Linda. That was harsh punishment for Gabe for sure."

"Too much punishment, in the end," I said. Victor had been punished too, and terribly so. All his good deeds with the kids, all his devotions to the saints, they never could have alleviated the guilt of Davy's spirit in turmoil. Gabriel, recovering in a prison hospital, had pretty much said the same thing. Unlike his brother, Gabe seemed to feel no guilt, only anger that Victor had kept him from Linda. With Victor gone, he'd seen a chance to relive his youth. Killing Broomer had been spontaneous after the stubborn neighbor refused to give up his plans to take down the fence. Tops had provided the perfect scapegoat for both killings. Gabe faked the food burglary at his own house and left evidence implicating Tops in Broomer's murder.

The other person recovering from a head thumping was Jay-Jay. After Gabe had pulled Jay-Jay out of the garden, he'd knocked her out and stuffed her in his car trunk. She'd be okay, although her plans were also thwarted by Victor. His new will had cut her out entirely. Victor left all his art and property to his sister, Teresa, on the condition that she use any profits to support his nonprofit art facility for kids. The earlier will, Flori reasoned, likely reflected Victor's guilt. Hiding Gabe's secret would have put a toll on any marriage. Only later did he realize that Jay-Jay would not do justice to his art and good works.

Flori squeezed in between us, brandishing a plate of cookies. "You lucky people are the first to taste-test these. Well, other than me, of course, and Linda and Addie and Bernard and Celia and Sky over there."

I took one of the deceivingly common-looking *bizcochitos*. I knew it would taste anything but common. Indeed, the cookie melted into warm spices and evoked cozy feelings of Victor's wonderful home. His secret recipe had come back to life in Flori's kitchen.

"You're a shoe-in for the Christmas *bizcochito* contest," Jake told her.

She nodded gravely. "I am, but I'm entering in Victor's name. I owe it to him." She thrust the cookie plate toward me.

Despite my assurances, Flori kept apologizing for removing Gabe's name from her suspect list. "Sentiment and nostalgia blinded my senses," she'd told me, ruefully, when she showed up minutes after the police, dusty from a ride on the back of Reese Hoffman's antique motorcycle.

"Sometimes the guilty fool us all," Jake said,

smiling down at Flori. "But the honorable will win the day. Speaking of which, can I take one more of these cookies? I'm meeting Tops at the train station soon. He said that he wants to go to Texas and find some family there. I got him a ticket."

Flori insisted that Jake take an entire bag of cookies to the wrongly accused man.

Jake went to get his coat and returned with a paper bag. "I almost forgot, Rita. Tops wanted you, Celia, and Hugo to have this."

He handed me a small wooden plaque. On one side was a painting of St. Francis, protector of the animals. The saint held a smiling yellow cat. I would have recognized it as Victor's work even without the signature.

"Victor gave this to Tops," Jake explained. "Look on the back."

On the back was a drawing done in pen in a truly primitive but heartfelt style. It featured a round cat, peacefully sleeping on a bed. "Tops did this. He wants you and Celia to have it as a good luck piece for Hugo."

Tears prickled at my eyes. "Tell Tops that we're honored. We'll take good care of Hugo."

Jake hugged Flori, then me, his cheek lingering next to mine. "I'll call you?" he said.

In between blushing outrageously, I managed to whisper "Yes."

As he left, weaving through the crowd, Flori elbowed me in the side. "Now that's a fine, hot man with a good-looking tush."

I knew what was coming.

"You should show some interest!"

I didn't contradict her. Nor did I protest about

my moratorium or finding a new me. Looking out over the crowded café, I realized that I liked the regular old me, even if that came with some chaos and sleuthing. I had wonderful friends and family and a job that I loved, not to mention a kitten crawling up my pant leg.

Recipes for a Day of the Dead Feast

Jake's Favorite Carne Adovada

Serves 6-8 (leftovers freeze well, if you manage to keep any)

Red chile is the star of this classic New Mexican dish. For the best and most authentic flavor, use chile from New Mexico. A few mail-order suppliers are listed at the end of the recipe section. Other possible sources of chile powder in bulk include spice shops, well-stocked supermarkets, Mexican grocery stores, and some natural foods stores. Plan to start a day ahead of your feast so you can marinate the meat overnight.

INGREDIENTS

- 3 lbs. pork shoulder or butt. You can also use other stew meat, beef brisket, beef or pork shanks, or chicken.
- 4 c chicken or vegetable broth or water
- 12 T (about ¾ c) red chile powder. Note: sometimes even medium New Mexican chile powder can be pretty hot. Start with mild if you have any doubt about spiciness levels.
- 3-4 garlic cloves, crushed, peeled, and minced
- 4 T olive oil
- 4 T flour

2 t cumin
2 t dried oregano
1 t red wine vinegar
½ t salt, plus more to taste

DIRECTIONS

Prepare the red chile sauce. Add oil and minced garlic to a large, heavy-bottomed saucepan. Sauté for a few minutes over medium heat. Sprinkle in the flour and stir for a few minutes. Add water or stock and then whisk in the remaining ingredients. Simmer, stirring occasionally, for about 20 minutes. Taste for salt and other seasonings. Let the sauce cool to room temperature.

Cut the meat into 1- to 2-inch cubes. You could also leave the meat in large pieces and cut or shred after cooking. Arrange in a nonreactive bowl or casserole dish. Pour the sauce over the meat. Turn the meat to cover all sides with sauce. Cover tightly with tin foil or plastic wrap and put in the refrigerator. Marinate overnight or for up to a day or two (for longer marinades, stir occasionally).

Let the mixture come to about room temperature before cooking. You have a few options for cooking. This is a great recipe for a slow cooker. Transfer the sauce and meat to the slow cooker and cook on low for 4 to 6 hours. For oven braising, transfer the mixture in an oven-safe, lidded pot or nonreactive Dutch oven. Preheat the oven to 325° F. Bring the mixture to a simmer on the stovetop and then transfer to the preheated oven. Braise, covered and at a simmer, for about 3 hours or until the meat is fork tender, stirring occasionally. When stirring,

check that the sauce isn't getting too low or thick.
Add water or stock as necessary.

Serve *carne adovada* as a main dish with beans, rice,
salsa, and guacamole. It's also fabulous as a taco or
burrito filling. When reheating, add stock or water
to thin the sauce.

Note: the red chile sauce in this recipe can be used
in all sorts of New Mexican dishes, such as a topping for eggs, burritos, and enchiladas.

Roasted Tomato Salsa

Makes about 1½ cups

INGREDIENTS

3 ripe globe tomatoes cut in half with cores and
tops removed

½ medium onion, diced

2 garlic cloves, smashed and peeled

½ jalapeño or serrano chile, top and seeds removed. Chop coarsely, using gloves and care
when handling hot peppers.

1 t kosher salt, plus more for extra seasoning if
desired

2-3 T chopped cilantro

½-1 T fresh lime juice

cumin, to taste (optional; start with about ½ t,
adding more as desired)

DIRECTIONS

Arrange oven rack in top third of oven. Heat broiler.

Place tomatoes, skin side up, on a sheet pan. Scat-
ter onion, garlic, and peppers around the tomatoes.

Broil until the tomato skins start to blister, about
10 minutes depending on your broiler (check that
the vegetables aren't getting too browned after
about 5 minutes).

Transfer all vegetables to a blender or food processor. Add salt and blend briefly. Pour into a heatproof
bowl and let cool to room temperature. Stir in lime
and cilantro. Add extra salt and cumin, to taste.

Serve with tortilla chips or as a side for *carne adovada*, rice, and beans.

Rita's Guacamole

INGREDIENTS
2-3 medium, ripe avocados
1 small tomato, seeded and diced
¼ sweet onion, finely diced (about 2 T)
½ jalapeño pepper, seeded and minced
1-2 T fresh lime juice (to taste)
1-2 T chopped cilantro
1 clove garlic, minced
½ t kosher salt (or to taste)
½ t ground cumin (optional)

DIRECTIONS
Cut avocados in half. Using a large knife, carefully strike each pit and remove. Scoop flesh into a large bowl. Sprinkle with lime juice and stir to coat. Add salt and cumin and mash lightly with a fork or pastry blender. Stir in onions, jalapeño, tomatoes, cilantro, and garlic. Taste, checking whether more lime or salt is needed. Mash more if a smoother texture is preferred. If refrigerating, press plastic wrap directly onto the surface of the guacamole to avoid browning.

Serve at room temperature with tortilla chips or as a condiment for main dishes.

Perfect Pinto Beans

Serves 4-6

Sometimes the most basic dishes can evoke the strongest opinions. Beans are such a dish. To soak or not to soak? Salt or no salt in the simmering pot? These questions fuel bean debates, but pretty much everyone can agree that home-cooked beans are simple, tasty, economical, and nutritious. All you need is time . . . and patience.

INGREDIENTS
　　1½ c pinto beans, washed
　　½ onion, chopped
　　1 bay leaf and a few sprigs fresh parsley (op-
　　　　tional) for flavoring the simmering water
　　½ t each salt, cumin powder, New Mexican red
　　　　chile powder (mild or medium)

DIRECTIONS
Step 1: Soaking. Bean tradition long held that salting during soaking and cooking toughens the beans. However, recent bean research suggests that a brine soak can result in softer, creamier beans. This recipe uses a hybrid approach of a salty soak followed by a salt-free simmer.

Wash the beans and remove any debris. Place the beans in a bowl and soak overnight in about 4 cups of water and 1 t of salt.

Step 2: Simmering. Drain the soaked beans and add to a heavy pot. Cover with about 5 cups of unsalted water so that the water level is a few inches above the beans. Add chopped onions, bay leaf, and parsley (if using), but do *not* add any acidic ingredients such as tomatoes at this time. Acids inhibit beans from softening.

Bring to a simmer, uncovered, over low heat. You want a gentle simmer, not a rolling boil that could break apart the beans. Check the water level occasionally. Add more water as necessary to keep the level about an inch above the beans.

How long to simmer? Count on approximately 2 to several hours. The time will depend on the type of bean and its age. Older beans that have languished in the pantry will take longer than a new crop of dried beans. High altitude can also inhibit bean cooking. At Santa Fe's seven-thousand-foot altitude, beans require patience. At higher altitudes you might want to reach for canned beans or a pressure cooker.

Step 3: Seasoning. This is the fun and creative step. When the beans have just turned soft and creamy in texture, add more seasonings. The water level should be slightly above the beans (drain a bit if your water is several inches above the beans). Start with about ½ t each of salt, powdered cumin, and red chile powder. You could also add diced tomatoes at this time or some of the tomato sauce left over from making Spanish rice. Simmer for 30 minutes more or until the beans are creamy and the sauce is thick and flavorful. Adjust salt and other seasonings to taste.

Serve with Spanish rice and *carne adovada*. Top with sour cream, crumbled Mexican or fresh farmer's cheese, and/or red chile sauce. Enjoy!

Don't have time to soak and simmer? Drain

and rinse a can or two of whole pinto beans. Sauté chopped onion and minced garlic until soft. Add beans, some broth or water, and salt, cumin, and red chile powder. Simmer for about 15 minutes until the beans are saucy. Taste for seasoning and serve.

Fluffy and Flavorful Spanish Rice

Approximately 6 servings

INGREDIENTS

- 1 c long-grained rice, such as Jasmine rice
- 1 can (14.5 oz.) diced tomatoes drained (reserve liquid for other uses)
- 1 c broth (low-sodium chicken or vegetable) or water
- ½ large onion, diced
- 2 New Mexican roasted green chiles, deseeded and diced, or 2-3 T canned green chiles or diced bell pepper
- 2 T olive oil or any flavorless oil
- 2 garlic cloves, peeled and minced
- 1 t salt

DIRECTIONS

Spanish rice can sometimes become gummy. In this recipe, rinsing, sautéing, and baking the rice in a pilaf style produces a wonderfully fluffy and flavorful dish.

Preheat your oven to 350° F. Set out a 9 x 9-inch casserole dish.

Prepare vegetables and drain the canned tomatoes, reserving liquid for flavoring other dishes such as pinto beans.

Place rice in a fine-mesh colander and rinse and drain thoroughly. Add the oil to a large skillet or heavy-bottomed saucepan and heat over medium heat. When the oil is hot, add the rice, being careful to avoid splatters. Stir the rice over medium heat until it turns translucent and golden, about 7-10 minutes.

When the rice is golden, add onions and garlic. Sauté for a minute or two. Then add the drained tomatoes, diced peppers, broth, and salt. Stir and cook for about 2 minutes.

Transfer the rice mixture to the casserole dish and cover tightly with tin foil.

Bake for 15 minutes. Stir. Recover and bake another 20 minutes. Remove from oven and fluff the rice again. Check for tenderness. If the rice needs more time, cover tightly and return to the oven, testing after another 5 or 10 minutes.

Flori's Award-Winning Pan de Muerto

Makes two loaves

Don't be intimidated by yeast bread. The heavenly scent alone is worth the effort and the taste of fresh-baked bread is even better. And, although this recipe takes some time, most of it is spent waiting for the yeast to work its magic. Start in the morning, and you can enjoy warm bread with hot chocolate for afternoon tea.

INGREDIENTS

- 4-5 c all-purpose flour, plus more for dusting the work surface
- 8 T unsalted butter
- 4 large eggs
- 1 egg yolk beaten with 2 teaspoons water (for the glaze)
- ½ c granulated sugar, plus more for sprinkling
- ½ c whole milk
- ½ c warm water
- ½ oz. (2 packets) active dry yeast
- 1 T orange zest (from about 1 large orange, preferably organic)
- 1 t anise seed
- ½ t fine salt

DIRECTIONS

In a small bowl, add the yeast to ½ cup of warm water (about 90° F). Add a pinch of sugar for the yeast to munch on and then whisk gently. Soon, the yeast should start to bubble and froth. If nothing happens after about 15 minutes, your yeast might be dead. In that case, start over with a new batch of yeast.

While the yeast proofs, warm the milk and butter in a small saucepan just until the butter melts. Do not boil. Transfer to large mixing bowl. Add the orange zest and anise seed and let the milk mixture cool to about 90° F or cooler.

When the milk has cooled, stir in the yeast mixture, sugar, and eggs. Next, add the salt and then the flour a cup at a time, mixing after each addition. Add flour until the dough starts to come away from the side of the bowl. Sprinkle some flour on a clean, dry countertop, scoop out the dough, and knead, adding small amounts of flour to keep the dough from sticking to your hands or the counter. The amount of flour you use will depend on the humidity and other factors, so go by feel instead of exact quantities. The dough should be soft but not sticky. Knead for about 10 minutes, producing a supple and elastic dough.

Clean the mixing bowl and butter it. Place the dough in the bowl, turning so that all sides get buttered. Cover with plastic wrap and let the dough rise in a warm, draft-free place until doubled in size. Doubling should take about an hour. A good place for warm, draft-free rising is your microwave. Heat a mug of water, push it to one side of the microwave, and add the bowl of dough. Just be careful not to turn on the microwave while the dough is inside.

When the dough has doubled, gently deflate it and shape into a ball. Divide the dough ball into equal halves. Unless you have lots of oven space, cover one half and reserve it for baking later. From the other half, cut three small (about 1 oz.) balls to form the "cross bones" and a "skull." Form the larger piece into a round. For the bones, roll the dough into a dog-bone shape—skinny in the middle and larger at the ends. For the skull, make a simple round shape. Place the large round on a parchment-paper-lined cookie sheet. Arrange the bones in an X shape across the large round. Press down on the edges and ends. Place the skull in the center of the X, pressing down firmly. It's okay to flatten the skull because it will puff up when rising.

Cover the dough lightly with buttered plastic wrap and let it rise again until nearly doubled in size, about an hour. When the dough is nearly doubled, prepare your oven. Place a rack in the middle of the oven, with several inches of space above for the dough to rise. Heat the oven to 350° F.

Mix together the egg yolk and water. Gently brush this egg wash over the bread; keep the remaining egg wash. Place the sheet with the bread on the center rack and bake for 20 minutes. Then remove the bread from the oven and brush it again with the egg wash. Sprinkle sugar over the egg-washed bread and return it to the oven. Bake 20 minutes more or until the loaf is golden brown and sounds hollow when tapped on the bottom.

Important: resist the urge to eat the bread immediately! Let the bread cool on a wire rack for at least half an hour. Serve with butter and a cup of spiced hot chocolate. Repeat with the second loaf, which you can form and let rise while the first loaf is baking. Alternatively, you can refrigerate the second half of the dough for a few days or freeze it for several months. In that case, seal the dough in a gallon-sized Ziploc bag. Let refrigerated or frozen dough come to room temperature and then proceed with the shaping, proofing, and baking steps.

Note: if you don't like the licorice flavor of anise, you can leave out the anise seed and enjoy a buttery orange bread. You could also substitute a teaspoon of cinnamon for the anise.

Victor's New Mexican Hot Chocolate

Makes two big mugs or four 8 oz. servings

INGREDIENTS
- ¾-1 c semisweet chocolate chips
- 2 c milk (any kind, although whole milk will make a richer drink)
- 1 t vanilla extract
- ½ t ground cinnamon
- Pinch of powdered cayenne or hot New Mexico red chile powder (optional)
- Pinch of allspice
- Pinch of salt

DIRECTIONS

Place all ingredients except vanilla in a pan and warm gently, whisking, until the chocolate chips melt. Do not boil. Remove the pan from the heat. Add vanilla and whisk vigorously. Serve topped with marshmallows, whipped cream, and/or chocolate shavings, if desired. Have fun experimenting with pinches of other spices too, like cardamom, nutmeg, or cloves.

Chile Sources

Many of the recipes call for New Mexican chiles or chile powder. If you can't find any locally, consider ordering by mail. Stores and farms throughout New Mexico ship chiles fresh, frozen, powdered, and jarred. Here are just a few places to get you started:

The Santa Fe School of Cooking offers cooking classes and recipes and has an extensive online market: http://santafeschoolofcooking.com/

El Potrero Trading Post is a family-run shop located in Chimayo, a tiny village that's world-famous for its sacred chapel and its heirloom chiles. The Trading Post website provides products and prices, as well as a phone number for placing an order: http://www.potrerotradingpost.com/

The Hatch Chile Store ships New Mexico's most well-known chiles in fresh, flame-roasted, and powdered form: http://www.hatch-green-chile.com/